The District Ten police had fished the body out of the sacred current an hour earlier. It lay on the path of pale, smooth stones beside the River of Stars, eyes open, bloated face turned to the morning sky.

When I got there, the two district police officers guarding the corpse moved aside for me. I could tell by their expressions they were still digesting what they had seen, still trying to figure out what it meant.

I knew how they felt.

As an Investigator, I had seen a lot of dead people. Sometimes they were missing arms or legs. Sometimes more than that. Usually, it was hard to look at them. In this case, it was hard to look away.

I knelt beside the body and checked it for wounds, bruises, marks...something that might have told me how the guy died. I didn't see anything. Maybe he'd had too much octli, gone out for a walk, and fallen into the water.

Maybe. But I didn't think so.

"Hard to believe," the taller of the two officers said of the corpse.

"I've never seen one of them before," said the other.

I hadn't either. Not in the flesh, anyway.

I had seen them on the Mirror, fighting their wars, or explaining why they had to be fought, or signing treaties when their wars were over.

But in person?

Never.

INVESTIGATOR FOR THE EMPIRE

MICHAEL JAN FRIEDMAN

CRAZY 8 PRESS

For Perrin

Contents

Foreword

It's been twenty years since I pitched my Aztlan concept to an editor friend who worked at a major publishing house. "Aztlan. It's a 21st-century, Aztec-empire noir murder mystery," I told her. "It takes place in 2012, at the end of the Mesoamerican calendar—the end of the world by some accounts."

"That's a great idea for a book," she said. "A really original idea for a book. I want to read that book. Unfortunately, I can't buy that book. Can you imagine one of our salespeople trying to pitch it to a bookstore buyer? A 21st-century Aztec-empire noir murder mystery? Where would the guy put it in the store? His head would explode."

So I never sold the idea to that friend or any other editor for a major publishing house, even though I'd written more than 50 books for such establishments by that time.

At one point, I enlisted the skills of my friend, master illustrator Sal Velluto, to work with me on making Aztlan into a comic book series. Despite Sal's considerable talent, that approach didn't fly either.

So Aztlan sat on a shelf in the back of my mind. And 2012 loomed closer. And closer.

• • •

In the meantime, I and a half dozen other experienced writers had started Crazy 8 Press. By then, there had been some upheavals in the traditional publishing business, most notably the demise of Borders. The idea of Crazy 8 was to preserve the relationship between the reader and the writer in the face of these upheavals--because science fiction and fantasy was too important to all of us to leave it to the vagaries of market dynamics. Crazy 8 allowed us to tell the stories too offbeat for the big publishing houses to take a chance on...

Stories like the ones in my Aztlan books.

Aztlan: The Maxtla Colhua Mysteries came out in 2012 (though it feels like it was yesterday). It was comprised of two novellas, "Aztlan: The Last Sun" and "Aztlan: The Courts of Heaven."

Since then, I've written another half-dozen books under the aegis of Crazy 8 and edited a few more. But I always felt the tug of Maxtla Colhua, hard-nosed Investigator for the Empire--a fiery athlete who followed his father's path and became a detective after he blew out his knee in the ball court.

"When are you going to write another Maxtla Colhua book?" fans and friends would ask me at conventions. One wonderful couple even named their dog Maxtla. "Soon," I said. And the years flew by. And Maxtla's tug on me grew more and more insistent all the time. More urgent. More determined not to be denied. Who was I to say no to such perseverance?

So here we are—with *Aztlan: Investigator For The Empire.*

Aztec Names: A Pronunciation Key

a as in father

e as in net

i as in police

o as in note

u as in flute

au as in flautist

ai like the first e in eye

c hard before a, o, or u and soft before e or i

ch as in choose

cu like the qu in queen

h as in hello

hu like the w in way

l as in lose

m as in make

n as in nose

p as in pie

qu like the k in kite

t as in tell

tl like the ll in llama

tz like the ts in cats

x like the sh in shell

y as in you

z like the s in sun

Book One

Tlahuizcalpantecuhtli, the Lord of Dawn, was especially enthusiastic that morning. Fresh from his swim across the ocean, he filled the eastern sky with a deep, golden light.

But it wasn't Tlahuizcalpantecuhtli who had roused me. It was Calli.

"Too early," I said, turning away from her.

"Don't be an old man," she said, swatting my shoulder.

"I'm not old," I said in my defense. "Just tired." We hadn't gotten home until late the night before.

Calli whispered in my ear: "You weren't tired at the Western Markets." She kissed my neck. "You weren't tired at all."

I was just finding my strength when I heard a buzz.

"Don't answer it," Calli said, her nose buried in the hollow of my cheek. "I won't tell anyone."

I had no choice but to pick up the radio. "Colhua," I said.

"Maxtla?" It was Necalli. Never a good sign to hear from one's boss at such an hour. Especially on one's first day back from holiday.

"Nice to hear your voice," I said, making no effort to disguise my sarcasm.

"You'll think so even less when you hear what they found in District Ten." He gave me the details, especially the most important one.

"You're lying," I said.

"I'm not. Where Ayahua Street hits the River. I'll meet you there."

"Right." I put the radio down, pulled the covers aside, and swung my legs out of bed.

"Don't tell me," Calli said, propping herself up on an elbow.

"I won't. That way, maybe *one* of us will have a good day."

"They found a body?"

"Yes." I couldn't say any more. I got up, crossed the room, and found my clothes on the wooden warrior in the corner of the room.

"Maxtla," said Calli, "we just got back. You're not the only Investigator in the Empire."

She was right. I didn't have to see every body that turned up in the River of Stars. But I had to see *this* one.

"Maxtla!" Calli said, this time in a voice that demanded my attention.

I turned to look at her.

She frowned. "Either we both have a good day or neither of us does. That's how this works."

I went back to the bed, took Calli in my arms, and kissed her. I couldn't imagine what I had done in my life to deserve someone like her.

Maybe, I thought, *it's something I've yet to do*. All the more reason to find out who killed the bastard in the River.

• • •

The District Ten police had fished the body out of the sacred current an hour earlier. It lay on the path of pale, smooth stones beside the River, eyes open, bloated face turned to the morning sky.

When I got there, the two district police officers guarding the corpse moved aside for me. I could tell by their expressions they were still digesting what they had seen, still trying to figure out what it meant.

I knew how they felt.

As an Investigator, I had seen a lot of dead people. Sometimes they were missing arms or legs. Sometimes more than that. Usually, it was hard to look at them. In this case, it was hard to look *away*.

I knelt beside the body and checked it for wounds, bruises, marks...something that might have told me how the guy died. I didn't see anything. Maybe he'd had too much octli, gone out for a walk, and fallen into the water.

Maybe. But I didn't think so.

"Hard to believe," the taller of the two officers said of the corpse.

"I've never seen one of them before," said the other.

I hadn't either. Not in the flesh, anyway.

I had seen them on the Mirror, fighting their wars, or explaining why they had to be fought, or signing treaties when their wars were over. But in person? Never.

Yet there was no mistaking the bright red hair, the wide blue eyes, or the pale skin—sickly looking, it seemed to me, even for that of a corpse. Also, he was half a head taller than most people I knew.

A Euro, without a doubt. It figured that the first one I met would be dead.

"Who found him?" I asked the officers.

"A couple of old women," the shorter one said.

"Out for a walk," said the other. "We sent them home with an escort. They didn't look too good."

I thought about my Aunt Xoco, who was an old woman as well. She wouldn't have let the police take her home so easily. She would have insisted on saying prayers over the body. That way the gods would know to look for the guy in the Lands of the Dead.

Assuming Euros went to the Lands of the Dead. I wasn't sure that had ever been established.

"Move over," a voice rasped from behind me.

I looked back over my shoulder at Eloxo Necalli, bow-legged Chief Investigator for the Fourth Sector. He didn't seem pleased.

I moved aside and Necalli knelt down next to me. His eyes narrowed as they took in the sight of the Euro's face. "I thought I'd seen everything."

"The question," I said, "is what he was doing here."

Necalli nodded. "That's the question, all right."

Unless he was some kind of diplomatic envoy, the dead man would have been in the Empire illegally. But legal or not, he wouldn't have ventured out in public. He would have done his best to stay out of sight.

Yet here he was.

"You think the Emperor could have brought him here?" I asked Necalli. It was a long shot.

"No. And neither do you. If he were here to see the Emperor, he would have been in the capital."

"So what was he doing here?" It wasn't so much a question as me thinking out loud.

"That," Necalli said, "is what you're going to find out."

• • •

"Pleased to meet you, Investigator," said the guy on my Mirror screen, with barely a hint of an accent.

He was about my age, clean-shaven, fit-looking. Maybe an athlete at one time. But that was where the resemblance ended.

His face was long and pink, his eyes as blue as those of the corpse we had found. Blue as a robin's egg, I found myself thinking. His hair, which he wore long, was yellow, the color of spring corn. And he had a scar that ran along the side of his face, from the corner of his eye to his hairline.

"Same here," I said, just to be polite.

His name was Donner. That's what the Emperor's people had told me. He was an Inspector, which in England was the equivalent of an Investigator, more or less.

"You speak well," I said.

The guy's eyes crinkled as he smiled. "We monitor your Web—your *Mirror*, as you like to call it. It allows us to gain an appreciation for your language. No doubt, you do the same with our networks."

I didn't work in the Emperor's office but I imagined that he was right. Except the Euros only had to learn Nahuatl to know what was going on in the Empire. We had to learn a dozen languages to keep track of things in Europe.

"So," said Donner, "you found one of our people. And not in very good shape, I understand."

"To put it mildly," I said. "But that's not what troubles us. We're wondering why he was here at all."

It wasn't at the Emperor's request. Necalli had established that much before he set me up with this connection.

"We're troubled by that ourselves," Donner said. "But now that we have a picture of the fellow, we're hopeful that we can work out the details."

I nodded. "If I turn up anything on my end, I'll let you know."

"Brilliant. Well, Investigator, I'm afraid it's time for dinner, and my mother is visiting from Manchester. I hate to keep her waiting. If you don't mind..."

"We'll speak again," I said, and terminated the connection.

Necalli, who had been watching from a distance, joined me at my Mirror screen. "What do you think?" he asked.

"About what?"

"Do they know what's going on here? Or are they in the dark as much as we are?"

"I wouldn't depend on them to solve our problem for us," I said, "if that's what you mean. They're Euros, after all."

Necalli nodded. "So they are."

• • •

My father used to say, "It's always too early in the day to open your eyes in the Merchant City."

On some days that observation was truer than others. This day, for instance.

It was my first one back on the job, remember. After some well-deserved time off, if I had to say so myself. Had the gods been inclined to smile on me, they would have swaddled Aztlan in a golden birth-blanket of peace and harmony, leaving me and my fellow Investigators to put our feet up and search the Mirror for amusing news items—preferably the kind that described events in cities other than our own.

Instead I found myself visiting Popo Cueponi.

Cueponi was a slave dealer, one of the busiest in the Merchant City. He counted some of the highest-ranking nobles in the region among his clients.

Personally, I didn't like the idea of people owning slaves. Any people, even nobles. I don't know why. It just caught in my throat, like a fish bone.

But the Emperor didn't forbid it, so Cueponi was free to conduct his business as he liked, and pick up information I often found useful in the process. And he didn't mind my pumping him for that information.

After all, I had cleared his son of a murder charge a couple of cycles earlier. That made me one of Cueponi's favorite people in the whole world.

But when I got to his office, the fellow at the desk told me Cueponi wasn't there. "He's in prison."

Really? "Since when?"

"Since he was convicted of public drunkenness half a moon ago."

I was about to ask why no one had told me. Then I remembered: I had been away. "Thanks," I said, and headed back to the rail line.

• • •

On the outside, Aztlan's Prison House was one of the handsomest buildings in District One. Made of pale, rough-hewn sandstone with green-blue bands of copper separating its floors, it was a delight to the eye. But on the inside, it was like any other house of incarceration--stark and gray, with rows of barred, windowless cells.

The innermost compartments were set aside for the worst criminals—murderers, rapists, seditionists, and those who owed money to the nobility. The next layer of cells was for those in debt to either private citizens or the government—which was, of course, a much less egregious offense.

In the outermost layer, the Emperor kept those convicted of petty crimes—gambling, chocolate trafficking, and so on. That was where I found Popo Cueponi.

He was short and round, with a fatherly twinkle in his eye. He was also impeccably groomed, no less so in the Prison House than he had been on the outside.

Before I showed up, I had checked into his sentence. Apparently, his judge had gone easy on him. Being drunk in public usually earned the offender a couple of cycles in prison. Cueponi had gotten no more than a couple of moons.

"Maxtla!" he said when he saw me, bubbling over with delight. "I was wondering when you'd come to visit."

An Investigator in a prison house, I frowned disapprovingly at the sight of his white uniform. "Public drunkenness? Seriously?"

"I was one step from the door, Maxtla. One step, and that numbskull of a police officer hauled me in. What kind of justice is that?"

"The report said you were halfway across the street."

Cueponi rolled his eyes. "One step, halfway across the street...now we're picking apart mosquito legs."

"You were lucky the judge liked you, Uncle. You could have grown old in here."

Cueponi liked to be called Uncle. To his mind, at least, he dealt with people as if he were kin.

He shrugged. "It wouldn't be so bad, Maxtla. The food's not great, I'll grant you, but the company more than makes up for it. It's a little vacation, you know? Not the Western Markets, but what can you do?"

"You can abide by the Emperor's Law."

He smiled. "That's an option too, I suppose. Now, did you come just to make sure I'm comfortable? Or was there something else on your mind?"

"Something else." I told him about the Euro. It wasn't standard practice to share such information with a criminal, but he had to know if he was going to help.

He looked aghast. "A Euro? Here in Aztlan?"

My hopes fell. "So you haven't heard of him."

"I haven't." He scratched his chin. "But now that I think about it, there was talk not too long ago...someone coming in from out of town, a big deal for the right buyer. Maybe the Euro—"

"Is the guy from out of town." It was a possibility. "What kind of deal was it?"

"I didn't inquire. I'm a slave dealer," Cueponi said with some pride, "not a criminal, this less-than-fashionable garb notwithstanding. You need to speak with someone who accepts mysterious shipments from out of town."

I knew a few such individuals. "I'll do that."

Cueponi touched my arm. "In the meantime, Maxtla..."

In the past, I'd intervened on behalf of prisoners who had been helpful to me, seen to it that their sentences were reduced. I had no choice sometimes if I wanted to save lives.

Of course, Cueponi's sentence was light already. What could I reduce it by? A couple of days, if I were lucky?

On the other hand, he wasn't a criminal. Not really. To him, a couple of days probably seemed like an eternity.

"I'll see what I can do," I said.

• • •

I was making my way back to the Merchant City, my eyes closed so I could more easily recall the surf-laced tranquility of the Western Markets, when I got a buzz from Quetzalli, one of my fellow Investigators. "Necalli wants to see you," she said.

"He couldn't buzz me himself?" I asked.

"He's in the morgue with your friend the Euro. Apparently, there was a mark on the body, and not a random one."

"What kind of mark?"

She told me.

"On my way," I said.

I switched rail lines at the next station.

• • •

By the time I got back to the office, Necalli wasn't in the morgue anymore. He was nose to nose with his Mirror screen. If he knew I was there, he gave no sign of it.

"You wanted me?" I asked.

Necalli swiveled his monitor so I could see his screen. "Look at this."

I peered over his shoulder and saw a V-shaped cut in rubbery, grey flesh. A dead man's flesh, magnified twenty-five times.

"We almost missed it," Necalli said. "It was hidden between the Euro's second and third toes."

The V represented a bird in flight. It was the mark the Hawks left on their victims.

The Hawks worked for anyone in the Merchant City who didn't want to get his hands dirty. If you needed to persuade someone, they did the persuading. If you needed a competitor's factory sabotaged, they sabotaged it.

And they generally did it without going to the Prison House.

Sure, they were accused of this or that all the time. But they were seldom worth a judge's time, much less an Investigator's. They weren't ever the big fish. They only worked for the big fish.

Of course, the Hawks weren't the only ones who did that sort of work. There were the Coyotes, the Snakes, the Piranha

Fish. But in Aztlan, the Hawks were the most prominent.

"I'll look into it," I said.

"I could assign someone else," said Necalli.

"No need," I told him.

Even though the leader of the Hawks was family.

• • •

My father had had a half-sister, a woman several cycles his senior named Tozi, who had lived in the Merchant City. She'd had two sons. The older one, Acuahe, was a studious boy who never caused any trouble. The younger one, Ximo, was just the opposite.

As a child, I met Ximo only once, when my father took me to meet Tozi. Being almost exactly the same age—eight, I think—Ximo and I got along pretty well. He had a ball, an old one, but it still had some bounce. We pretended we were playing for Aztlan in the ball court.

That one day, Ximo didn't seem like a bad kid to me. Not at all.

But as he got older, he spent more of his time on the streets, running errands for characters on the fringe of society. Mostly the kind of characters who ran illicit gambling dens, but also those who traded in stolen goods.

After all, what judge would throw a youngster in the Prison House? So Ximo got away with a lot.

But in the Merchant City, it wasn't just the judge you had to look out for. It was the packs. In this case, the one called the Hawks.

The packs did the same things Ximo was doing, and each of

them had its own acknowledged territory. Normally, they would have overlooked a child running a few errands. But for some reason, the Hawks weren't inclined to be so magnanimous.

Maybe they wanted to make an example of Ximo. Maybe they just didn't like him. It's hard to say, especially so many cycles later.

In any case, they got hold of him and beat him. Badly.

Most kids would have stayed as far away from the Hawks as possible. Not Ximo. When he was old enough, he told them he wanted to join them.

The Hawks liked the idea that he could take his pain and turn it into something they could use. So they branded him and made him one of them.

For the most part, it was a good deal for the Hawks. Customers trusted Ximo's experience, his confidence. He brought the pack new business.

Only the leaders of the Hawks had reason to regret letting him join. One by one, they met with accidents, none of which could be pinned on Ximo with a certainty. In time, he replaced those who had directed his beating. *He* became the leader.

When his mother found out what he had turned into, she disowned him. I don't know how much Ximo cared about that, but it wasn't enough to make him leave the Hawks. A cycle later, Tozi died in a fire.

I remembered my mother being sad when she heard. She had liked my father's half-sister, even more than my father had.

By then, Tozi's older son, Acuahe, had become a priest in Tlacoco. As a member of the clergy, he was, of course, forbidden to attend his mother's funeral. But Ximo came.

My father had already died in the line of duty by then. But if he were alive, he would have been faced with a dilemma. On one hand, Ximo was his half-sister's son. On the other hand he was pack-branded, turned out by his own mother.

My father was a man who prized family above all else. But had he been at Tozi's funeral, he would likely have avoided his nephew—as if Ximo had died along with his mother.

I only learned about my father's feelings later, somehow. But then, at the time I had my share of distractions. I was a promising young player in the ball court, making a name for myself putting a rubber ball through a stone hoop.

Ximo was making a name for himself as well, finally winding up in the Prison House for running an unsanctioned gambling den.

He was still there when I blew out my knee and became an Investigator. At that point, I began looking at him with the Emperor's eyes, not those of a blood relation. In time, he got out of the Prison House and began running things as he had before, but with a little more discretion.

I followed what he was doing. It was my job. And I had a feeling he followed me as well. But officially, our paths had never crossed again.

Until now.

● ● ●

I'd expected Ximo to snarl like a mountain lion when he was brought into the Interrogation Center in his woven manacles. He didn't do that. He looked calm, composed, as if we were the street criminals and he was the one in charge.

Of course, he had been dragged down there before, hadn't he? Not lately but more than once, and procedures hadn't really changed in the last several cycles. He knew what to expect.

The only new part of the experience was me.

As the arresting officers led Ximo past my desk, he shot a glance my way. It had some contempt in it, some *Can't you see I'm better than you?* And some amusement too. Definitely amusement.

I let the officers take him downstairs to an interrogation room. Then I joined them, and gestured for them to leave me alone with Ximo. Best for the two of us to talk alone. They hesitated, but only for a moment.

After all, I'd played in the ball court. They knew I could take care of myself.

I sat down and eyed Ximo across the pitted wooden table. He looked a little older, a little harder than his file picture. Some pack leaders got soft and fat. If anything, he looked leaner than before.

Still, I saw his mother in his face, especially around the eyes. Not as she was when she died but when she was younger, happier.

Not that I was going to say so. Not there.

Unexpectedly, Ximo smiled. "You wanted to talk, Little Rabbit? Here I am."

We were by ourselves so I could ignore the slight. "There's been a murder." I didn't go into details. If he was culpable, he wouldn't need any. "The victim's got your mark on him. A Hawk mark."

He didn't move a muscle. "So?"

"So either you killed him or someone's trying to make it look that way. If you killed him, we've got nothing to talk about. But if you didn't..."

"You're giving me a chance to tell you who else might have done it and get myself off the hook."

"That's right."

He laughed. "Hawks don't squawk, Little Rabbit. They watch, they wait, and then, when the time is right, they pounce. But they don't squawk."

I wasn't surprised to hear him say that. It was the kind of thing pack members said when we tried to pry information out of them.

"We watch too," I said. "And when we do, people scurry. Not you, maybe. You're too tough. You're not worried about consequences. But all the upstanding businessmen who hire you to run their errands? They'll scurry like cockroaches. And they won't hesitate to hire someone else."

Ximo knew I was right. The Hawks' fortunes were about to see a downturn.

Still, he didn't rise to the bait. "Then watch," Ximo said. "Maybe you'll learn something."

"You're not worried about losing business?"

"Business will come back. Unless, of course, I open my mouth to an Investigator. Then it'll disappear for good."

Ximo wasn't going to budge. That much was clear.

"Think about it," I told him, knowing full well I was whistling in the wind.

He sat back in his chair. "Your time is up, Little Rabbit."

As if he were the one interrogating me. My teeth grated together. But I wasn't going to give him the satisfaction of seeing me get angry.

Had we been in public, I would have been obliged to act differently. I had an Investigator's reputation to uphold, after all. But we weren't in public.

So I got up and opened the door, and gestured for the officers to come back. "I'm done here," I told them.

And I didn't know any more than when I'd arrived.

• • •

When I got back upstairs, I saw the other Investigators clustered around a security screen—the one that showed us the street in front of our building. Curious, I joined them.

"What's going on?" I asked Quetzalli, a small-boned woman who was one of the toughest individuals on the force.

She pointed. "Looks like our friend the Hawk has an entourage."

I followed her gesture and saw what she meant. There were a dozen men standing outside our building—just standing there. I didn't need to check their files to know who they were, or why they had shown up.

"That one's Notoca," said Takun, another of my colleagues.

I nodded. Tepetl Notoca, Ximo's right-hand man, was probably a head shorter than I was. But that didn't make him any less powerful looking. His neck, I estimated, was nearly the size of my waist.

Takun laughed a short, ugly laugh. "Without Ximo, they're

lost. Notoca most of all. What he lacks in height he makes up in stupidity."

It didn't seem to me that Ximo would make someone like that his second-in-command. But I didn't question Takun's judgement. He might be a boor and a slob but he was also a pretty good Investigator.

"Hey, Colhua," someone said, "some guy's trying to get ahold of you."

I looked back at Suguey, one of our new Investigators. She was standing in front of my Mirror screen.

Donner? I wondered.

No one else would try to contact me through the Mirror. I thanked Suguey, crossed the room, and sat down in front of my screen.

It was Donner, all right. He looked tired. But then, for him it was well into the evening.

"Good afternoon," he said, smiling.

"If you say so."

"Bad day?"

I wasn't used to exchanging pleasantries when there was work to do. "You might say that. Any progress?"

"We've identified your corpse. His name is Daniel Michael Farr-Carmody. Born in Scotland forty-four cycles ago. A veteran of the British army."

"Criminal history?"

"Just getting to that. Apparently, he served time for assault, robbery, counterfeiting, impersonating a police officer...a whole host of offenses."

"Busy guy," I said.

"He was indeed."

"Any idea why he was here?"

Donner looked apologetic. "None as yet, I'm afraid. But I'm working on it."

I nodded. "Thanks."

"No problem. Speak to you soon, Investigator."

And that was it.

Better than nothing, I thought.

"Colhua?"

This time it was Necalli who had called me. He was standing on the threshold of his office, looking like he had sucked on an extra-sour lemon.

"We've got to let him go," I guessed. Meaning Ximo.

Necalli shrugged. "We've got no choice."

I understood. It was The Emperor's Law: We could only hold a suspect for so long.

"Fantastic," said Quetzalli, who'd heard the verdict as well. Takun swore beneath his breath, invoking the bloodier gods.

But there was nothing we could do.

At least Notoca would be happy.

• • •

The gods' temple on Nanahuatl Street, in District Twelve, was one of the oldest still standing in Aztlan. It was four hundred cycles old if it was a moon, yet it looked like it had been built that morning.

The main structure, which was three stories tall, was a truncated pyramid made of large stone blocks covered alternately with black paint or white adobe. It could be entered from any of the four directions through wide, doorless openings.

On top of the pyramid was a small house with a skylight in its ceiling, through which the gods could look down on their priests and smile. At least, that was the theory. And no priest would ever say a god did otherwise.

I took a moment to appreciate the structure in the golden light of early evening. But only a moment. Then I entered through its southern gate and found myself in its main hall, a place whose high, slanting walls were comprised of unadorned stones.

There were plenty of god images in Aztlan—in rail stations, on cereal boxes, in advertisements on the Mirror. But not here. In the temple, the gods' presence was invisible to the human eye.

Only our spirit could see them.

It was a lot like the temple in the neighborhood where I'd grown up. Bigger, older, but essentially the same.

I didn't have to look far to find a priest. Two of them were on their knees on the other side of the hall, performing the ritual cleansing of the floor in their white robes. I waited until they had spoken the last words of the purification prayer. Then I greeted them.

"May the gods find you worthy of their blessing," they said in unison.

"You as well," I said. "I'm looking for Acuahe Atotoli. Is he here?"

A cycle earlier, Acuahe had moved back to Aztlan from Tlaloco to become the head priest of the temple. Ximo might not have spoken to me about the Euro but maybe he had said something to his brother.

The priests looked disapproving. "It is almost sunset, Investigator. His holiness is preparing the rites of Xolotl."

"I apologize," I said, "but it's urgent that I speak with him. A matter of life and death."

The priests scowled at me a moment longer, as if to remind me that there were greater concerns than life and death. Then one of them said, "Wait here," and went up the long stairway alongside the wall.

The other one resumed the cleansing ritual, though he'd already spoken the prayer. Obviously, he was done talking with me. I looked around, but only with my eyes. My spirit was dedicated to finding out who murdered Farr-Carmody.

Finally, the priest who had ascended the stairs came back down. "His Holiness will see you in his sanctum," he said.

He gestured and stood aside. I made my way up the staircase and found myself in the little house on top of the pyramid—a sunlit space with a wooden floor underfoot.

It seemed modest for a holy sanctum. But then, I had visited the High Priest's sanctum not so long ago. Any other was bound to pale in comparison.

Acuahe wore a white robe and thread of gold sandals. He was praying, his eyes raised to the section of sky visible through the skylight.

He didn't look all that different from the way I remembered him. Like Ximo but wider, softer. More like their father's side of the family.

I waited for him to finish his prayer. It took only a few moments. When he was done, he turned to me, his expression full of Xolotl's peace, and said, "It's been a long time, Investigator."

Investigator. As if we hadn't sprung from the same blood.

I was tempted to call him Acuahe, but instead I addressed him as he'd addressed me—formally. "Your holiness."

"To what do I owe your visit?" His voice was calm, even. The voice of one accustomed to speaking with gods.

"I came about your brother," I said.

He tried to maintain his composure but I could see the concern in his eyes. "Is he all right?"

"He's fine. That's not the problem."

Achuahe's concern deepened, though his tone remained an even one. "He has done something terrible, hasn't he?"

"I'm not sure."

"I'm afraid I don't understand."

"There's been a murder. Ximo's pack has been connected to it. But to this point, there's no proof that he was involved."

Acuahe looked relieved. "Then there's still hope. I'll pray for him. But you didn't come here just to tell me that...did you?"

"No. I came because your brother has information I need. I can't tell you what sort of information but it's important, and he's refusing to share it with me. I thought he might have said something to you."

"Me?" Acuahe laughed softly. "Sorry, but I'm the *last* person he would confide in. I don't know how many times I've advised him to give up his way of life. He just grins at me as if

I'm a fool, as if I'm the one who's gotten it wrong."

He looked up at the skylight, at the fragment of sky captured in it. "I've saved a great many people, Investigator. I've shown them a way out of their pain. But I can't save my own brother."

"It's not your fault," I said.

"No? The gods tell us otherwise." Acuahe seemed determined to feel guilty about it.

"If you say so, Your Holiness. In the meantime, if Ximo *does* mention something..."

"You'll be the first to hear of it."

The first mortal. He didn't say it but I heard it.

"Thank you," I said, and turned to go. I was halfway to the door when I heard Acuahe say, "Investigator!"

I stopped and looked back at him.

"If you see my brother again, tell him it's not too late. The gods forgive more than people might believe."

"I'll tell him," I said.

For all the good it would do.

● ● ●

There was one other person I thought might have information on Ximo Atotoli.

His name was Chicome, Michi Chicome. Anyone who followed local news on the Mirror knew who he was: The guy with the wandering eye.

People burdened with that disability saw the gods with that eye, or so it was said. Only the afflicted knew for sure.

Chicome's speciality was crime stories. He was good at them.

He had contacts everywhere, even more than I did, and I had quite a few. Some of those contacts were pack members. I was sure of it, though he had never said as much on the Mirror.

I buzzed him from the rail platform and told him I wanted to see him. He said he would be at his desk all evening in the Mirror building in District Seven, but he didn't seem overjoyed at the prospect of my visit.

I knew why.

It didn't take me long to get to District Seven. Chicome was eating his dinner when I got there. Fried rabbit, from the look of it.

He finished chewing, then said, "Colhua." In his mouth, my name sounded like an accusation.

"Chicome," I said in return. I looked around his office, which had a window with a view of the sacred river. "You got a promotion."

"It was a long time coming."

Thanks to you, I heard him add, though he had said it only with his eyes. Just his good one, really.

When Chicome was young and eager, he had been in the habit of ignoring the rules. For instance, the one that said you didn't hatch a story on the Mirror when it was the subject of an ongoing Investigation.

There had been a series of murders on the rail lines, all late at night. And Chicome had shown up at every crime scene, sometimes even before I did. In fact, he was a suspect until I realized he worked for the Mirror.

At the time, I too was new to my profession. If not, I might have tried talking to Chicome, letting him know what kind of ground he was walking on. Instead I buzzed his boss and made her squash the story.

It made him look like an irresponsible kid. Which, at the time, he was. But he had never forgiven me for it.

Not because it would take Chicome that much longer to get a promotion. He didn't care about titles, I was pretty sure, despite the jab he had thrown at me.

It was my keeping him from breaking that *story*—a big one, maybe the biggest he'd ever get a chance to write—that had started him hating the sight of me.

Now, cycles later, he wiped his mouth and put his rabbit aside. "All right," he said, "what's so urgent that you had to interrupt my dinner?"

"Something I need you to keep confidential. Not even a hint of it on the Mirror."

He didn't like the idea but I was an Investigator, so he didn't have a choice. "Fine. It's confidential."

"I'm investigating a murder. Never mind whose. The important thing is that the victim had a V carved into the skin between his toes."

He grunted knowingly. "A Hawk symbol."

"Precisely."

"You've spoken with Ximo Atotoli, I assume?"

Chicome didn't know my connection with Ximo. At least I didn't think he did. And I wasn't going to tell him about it.

"I did," I said. "He didn't tell us anything."

"He'd sooner insert his hand between his ribs and pull his heart out."

"And that would be all right if this was a back-alley gambling operation, or some other little thing. But it's not. It's murder."

"Did he do it?"

Inwardly, I cursed. "I was hoping *you'd* know."

Chicome took a breath, let it out. "Atotoli and his friends have crossed the line a lot since he got out of the Prison House, maybe more times than other packs. But murder...they'd have to *really* want the guy dead."

So it was possible, but unlikely.

"One other question," I said. "If it *was* the Hawks who killed the guy, would they leave a mark on him? Even one we weren't likely to find?"

"Maybe. They do a lot of things that don't seem prudent to you and me. But those are the things that keep the pack together. Of course, there's another possibility..."

I knew what he was going to say. I'd already thought it myself. "That it was some *other* pack, trying to make it look like the Hawks' work."

"Exactly. Except it would know there'd be repercussions. When the Hawks found out—and they would—they would go after whoever tried to frame them, and with a vengeance."

"If they knew which pack it was. Which they might not."

Chicome flipped his wrist in a gesture of dismissal. "There are only so many of them, Colhua. Ximo's smart. He would figure it out."

I needed something else confirmed. "If a rival pack *did* try to frame the Hawks, it would have to be for big stakes, right?

Something worth the risk?"

"Sounds right."

"Any idea what that could be?"

Chicome smiled a bitter smile. "In other words, have I been working on anything that could shine a light on the packs, and why they might want somebody dead?"

"Have you?"

"I would have told you already, wouldn't I? That's what any responsible citizen of the Empire would do. No matter how long and hard he might have worked on his inquiry." His eyes hardened. "No matter how much it might have enlightened his fellow citizens when it appeared on the Mirror."

I'd always thought the Mirror entertained more than it enlightened. But I kept that opinion to myself.

"Unfortunately," Chicome added, "I don't know a damned thing."

"You must have a file on these packs," I said. "I'd like to see it."

He looked at me for a moment. Then he said, "Of course. As I said, I'm a responsible citizen. Now, if you don't mind, I'll get back to work."

He threw the remains of his dinner in his wastebasket. Then he turned his back on me and began pecking at his keypad.

"Thanks," I said, and got up to leave.

"Colhua," he said without turning around, "you owe me. If this turns out to be big, I want the story."

He was right—I *did* owe him. "Agreed," I said, and left Chicome marinating in his bitter juices.

• • •

Calli, like me, had had a long day. Some big project, she said when she buzzed me. We met for a late dinner at the restaurant where we'd had our first date, a place in the Merchant City where you munched free popcorn while you were deciding what to order.

That first night, I'd had the duck with cherry sauce. I ordered it again.

Calli liked that. Romantic, she called it.

Her eyes in candlelight were the loveliest things I'd ever seen. I didn't want to dim them with a description of what I'd examined that morning, but I didn't have a choice. I was investigating the murder of a Euro, after all, and she was the only person I knew who had been to Europe.

Calli made a face when I told her what we'd fished out of the River. "That's awful."

"They all are. But as you can imagine, this one raises some questions. For instance...what was a Euro doing here in the first place?"

Her eyes narrowed. "You think *I* know? Just because I've been over there?"

"You *said* you made a lot of contacts. Did anything of them say anything about sending someone over here? Even as a joke?"

"You're kidding, right?"

"I wish I were."

"I was talking with *businessmen*, Maxtla. *Legitimate* businessmen. If they'd wanted to send someone over, they would have gone through their government and the Emperor's office—the way we did."

"You were part of a delegation. How many people altogether?"

Calli gave it some thought. "Twenty or so."

"Let's say one of those delegates wasn't as honorable as the others. Let's say he wanted to smuggle something into the Empire."

"Like what?"

"I don't know. *Something*."

"In other words, you can't tell me."

"Nothing like that. It's just a hunch."

"All right." She leaned forward. "Let's say."

"If one of them *did* want to smuggle something over...with the contacts he made on that trip, how hard would it be?"

"Hard. In Europe, governments keep an eye on commerce. Much more so than the Emperor does here."

"But not impossible?"

Calli sighed. "Not impossible."

"How would he communicate with his friends, the Euros?"

"I don't know."

"You didn't have a way to get ahold of your contacts?"

"No."

"Then how could you have started a ball court league with them?"

"Through the Emperor's office."

Something occurred to me. "How well did you know the people who worked there?"

"In the Emperor's office?"

"Yes."

Calli looked at me askance. "You think the Emperor's staff

is helping to smuggle goods into the Empire?"

"Sounds crazy, I know. But no crazier than the other messes I've seen lately." That was for certain.

"What are you thinking? That you're going to investigate the Emperor's office?"

I couldn't. I didn't have access to it. I didn't have the manpower. And even if I found something, I didn't know if the Emperor would put any faith in it.

I would just have to keep working from the ground up. *For now.*

• • •

The next morning, I got up early—earlier than the sun god—to go over the file Chicome had compiled on the packs.

At least I didn't have to worry about leaving Calli in bed this time. She had sent me back to my place the night before, explaining that she needed to be rested for the day ahead of her. A bunch of meetings, apparently. Under the circumstances, I was in no position to object.

The Western Markets were starting to feel very far away.

Halfway through Chicome's file, I got a call from Necalli. He wanted me to visit the temple on Nanahuatl Street, the one where I had spoken with Acuahe.

"What's there?" I asked. I felt a pang of apprehension. "Is Acuahe all right?"

"He's uninjured, if that's what you mean. But he's been happier. You'll see what I mean when you get there."

Necalli liked to play games. This, apparently, was one of them.

A few minutes later, I was in a rail compartment on my way to District Twelve. Aztlan was quiet at that hour, the sun god still lingering beneath the horizon, the sky a fierce, red fire in the east.

When I arrived at Acuahe's temple, I saw the place was still intact. That was something. But there were two police officers at the entrance.

"Colhua," I said, showing them my bracelet.

"Go ahead," one of them said.

There were other officers inside. No priests in evidence, just police officers. I asked why.

One of the officers pointed up. "They're in the high priest's sanctum."

"Why?" I asked.

"Didn't they tell you?"

"No."

The officer gestured for me to follow him. "You're not going to believe this."

He led me downstairs to the storage cellar beneath the temple. There wasn't much light there, just what a single overhead fixture could throw. But it was enough for me to see what I had to see.

The place was full of old benches and doors and window frames. And something else—a stack of boxes that didn't look nearly as old as everything else.

One of the boxes was open. "A priest did that," the officer explained. "When he saw what was inside, he told the head priest, who called us. Then we called you guys."

I reached inside the box and felt something wrapped in cloth. Something hard and heavy. I took it out and unwrapped it.

Lands of death, I thought.

The thing in my hand was black and oily looking, like a tightly coiled snake. It gleamed in the light from the overhead fixture.

"A fire hand," the officer said, his eyes wide.

"Yes," I replied, keeping my tone as even as possible, "I figured that out."

$$\bullet \ \bullet \ \bullet$$

Alone with me in his sanctum, standing in the pale golden light that streamed in through his skylight, Acuahe dabbed at his forehead with a hand cloth and spoke in a tight, tormented voice. "Those fire hands aren't mine, Maxtla." *Now* he called me by my first name. "I've never seen them before in my life."

"Then how did they end up in your cellar?" I asked.

He eyed me. "I know what you're thinking. That they belong to Ximo and I'm working with him, storing them for him."

"The thought crossed my mind."

Acuahe held his hands out, as if to show me they were clean of wrongdoing. "I'm a priest, Maxtla. I promote peace, not violence."

"And Ximo?"

He considered the question for a moment. "I can't say for certain. But I don't think he's got anything to do with this either."

"Why not?"

"We may not be friends but we're not enemies. And he

would have to hate me a lot to put me in this kind of jeopardy."

I believed Acuahe was telling the truth.

It was a stretch, to say the least, to think a head priest would help Euros smuggle fire hands into the Empire. And an even bigger stretch to think he would then buzz us to say they were in his cellar.

"What about your fellow priests?" I asked. "You mean...did *they* bring the boxes in? It's not even remotely possible."

"Maybe they looked the other way while someone *else* brought them in."

"No, Maxtla. I know these men. They would never offer offense to the gods, and looking the other way would be an offense."

"Yet the boxes are here," I pointed out.

Acuahe didn't have an answer to that. All he could do was say, in a pleading voice, "Please, Maxtla..." As if I could appeal to the universe on his behalf and make all the boxes full of fire hands go away.

All I could do was have them transported down to the Interrogation Center. If Acuahe wanted anything more, he would have to ask the gods.

• • •

Necalli stood there in front of his window, facing the rising sun god with his back to me, absorbing what I had reported to him. Then he turned back to me, looking as if he had eaten a bad salamander.

And said in his low, gravelly voice, "There *are* no fire hands in the Empire."

It wasn't a statement of fact—not anymore. It was an almost childlike refusal to accept the truth. And I understood it completely.

Lands of the Dead, *I* didn't want to accept the truth either.

In all my cycles as an Investigator, I had never felt the need to carry anything besides my hand stick. Even that seemed too much sometimes. But if people started carrying fire hands?

Would *we* have to carry them too?

And if we did, what kind of city would we have? What kind of Empire? It wasn't a pretty thought.

"This is big, Colhua. As big as it gets. We've got to find out where those boxes came from before it's too late."

"I'll get hold of Donner," I said. "Maybe he'll have some idea of what's going on."

After all, the fire hands had come from Europe. There was nowhere *else* they could have come from.

"Do that," Necalli said. "Do it now. I don't care what time it is over there."

• • •

For the third time in my life, I found myself speaking with a Euro. Despite the hour, Donner seemed full of energy.

"Investigator," he said, smiling, "to what do I owe the pleasure?"

It was a funny way to greet someone, especially when pleasure was the furthest thing from my mind. "We found out what our friend Farr-Carmody was doing here."

I told him what I had seen in Acuahe's cellar. He stopped smiling.

"Unfortunately," he said in a considerably more sober tone,

"that makes a good deal of sense. Fire hands are a big business here on our streets, a very profitable business for certain interests. And from their point of view, your Empire must be a huge market waiting to be exploited."

Lovely, I thought.

"So...Farr-Carmody was using a priest as his distributor?" Donner asked.

"I doubt it," I said.

"But you found the weapons in a temple, yes? Or did I misunderstand?"

"You understood perfectly. It's just that..." It occurred to me that I didn't know much about the Euros' religious ceremonies, or how much respect was given those who conducted them. "Our priests don't engage in business, Inspector, much less illegal business."

"Of course," he said. "I should have known that." But the way he said it suggested I was being naive about the priesthood.

And maybe I was. As I had learned the hard way, our priests weren't beyond reproach. Far from it.

"Look," I said, "even priests aren't perfect." Strangely, it felt as if I were betraying the Empire by saying so. "But in this case, we don't think they had anything to do with it. We believe someone planted the fire hands in order to incriminate them."

"I see," Donner said. "And do you have any idea who that might be?"

"Nothing concrete."

He nodded. "Right. Well, then, Investigator, let me see what I can dig up around here. Knowing what sort of illicit activity

Farr-Carmody was involved in should make it a mite easier."

"Thanks," I said.

I almost added *Know the gods' peace*. But I stopped myself.

After all, I wouldn't want the peace of Donner's gods. Why would he want the peace of mine?

"You're welcome," Donner said. Then he vanished from the Mirror screen.

• • •

I had barely sat back from my monitor when I saw Necalli beckoning me from the other end of the room. I joined him in his office.

He had a look on his face I'd seen before. "Zayanya?" I guessed.

"Zayanya," Necalli confirmed. "He sounded like he was drowning."

Eztli Zayanya was Aztlan's First Chief of Investigators. He would have been one of the first to hear about the fire hands in Acuahe's temple. And on hearing, he would have relayed the information to the Emperor's office.

"The Emperor wants this taken care of," Necalli said. "He wants it done quickly and quietly. If word gets out, people are going to panic."

I wouldn't blame them. I was feeling a little panicky myself.

On the way back to my desk, Takun and Quetzalli intercepted me. As usual, Takun smelled from cinnamon.

"Is it true?" Quetzalli asked.

"I saw them," I said. "Gods help me, I held one in my hands."

Takun grunted. "Any idea where they came from? In Europe, I mean."

"Not yet," I told him. "But my contact over there is working on it."

"Could have been anywhere," Takun said. "The kid around the corner. The old folks' home. The local butcher shop."

"For the gods' sakes," said Quetzalli, "it's Europe. They could have been lying there in the street."

"Let me know how I can help," Takun said. "I can't stand those weasels."

"Weasels?" I echoed.

"The packs."

"We don't know it was them," I said. "Not for certain."

"Come on," said Takun. "The mark between the Euro's toes, the fact that it was Atotoli's temple where the fire hands were found...if it's not the Hawks trafficking fire hands, it's one of their rivals. No question about it."

Still, my gut told me there was more to it. And like anyone else, Takun had been wrong before.

Just not very often.

• • •

In desperate need of a lead, we brought Ximo in again. As before, Notoca and the others waited for him outside the Interrogation Center, looking sullen and dangerous.

This time I didn't get involved with the interrogation. I barely looked up as Ximo walked past me. I let Takun take care of everything.

The result was no better. Ximo still wouldn't talk. And before long, we had to let him go again.

Someone was smuggling fire hands into the Empire. We had to find out who it was, and we had to do it before we took another breath. But I had asked everyone in a position to know the answers I was looking for.

Then I remembered Chicome's file. I hadn't finished going through it, had I? The truth was I didn't think it would help, but I opened it again and began to read.

And found something after all.

• • •

Cueponi was surprised to see me in his cell again so soon.

"Not that I'm unhappy about it," he said with a smile. "To tell you the truth, I'd be happy to see my wife, and you know what *she* looks like."

"Uncle," I said, in no mood for jokes, "I have a question for you. A month ago, there was a fire in District Eight. New pyramid. Top floor."

Cueponi's face darkened. "Yes. A terrible thing. Why do you ask about it?"

I brushed past his question. "Two slaves died in the fire. Yours?"

His eyes narrowed. "One was."

"One of my colleagues investigated that fire. She didn't find any evidence of arson. But she suspected it nonetheless."

"For good reason, Maxtla."

I was hoping he would say that. "Then you did some investigating of your own."

"Naturally. You know how I feel about those I sell."

"And what did you discover?"

Cueponi made a sound of disgust. "That it was arson, all right."

"For what purpose?"

"Revenge. One businessman on another. Yet the only casualties were his slaves."

"Who set that fire, Uncle?"

He told me, his mouth twisting with anger.

"You're sure?"

"As sure as I can be."

"But there was nothing you could do about it."

He held his hands out, palms up. "I'm only a slave dealer, Maxtla. I can't punish wrongdoers as easily as you can."

"Then why didn't you mention what you'd discovered to my colleague? *She* could have seen the wrongdoer punished."

"Knowledge is one thing. Evidence is another. And from what I've seen, judges require evidence."

"But if you'd at least mentioned it to my colleague..."

"She would have failed to obtain a conviction. And eventually, the wrongdoer would have figured it was I who gave your colleague the lead. This way..." He looked past me at something I couldn't see. "Who knows? In time, I may get the chance to arrange a punishment myself."

I put my hand on Cueponi's shoulder. "You may have just done that."

• • •

It was late afternoon when we arrived at the warehouse the Hawks used for their headquarters. This time I hadn't sent a squad of police officers. I had shown up with my fellow Investigators. Takun, Quetzalli, even Necalli...twelve of us in all.

Because I trusted their skill and experience more than I trusted those of regular police officers. Because I knew none of them would tip the Hawks that we were coming, inadvertently or otherwise.

And because I wasn't after just Ximo this time.

There were only two doors to the place. I stationed two of my colleagues by the one in back. The rest of us came calling through the front, hand sticks in our fists.

The first Hawk we ran into was standing just inside the door. I leveled him with a well-placed right, saving him the bite of my bladed hand stick. Before he could come to his senses, Takun dragged him outside.

The rest of us kept going. Fortunately, there was no one else to stop us as we climbed a flight of stairs to the storage space.

Some other time, we might have found something incriminating there—stolen goods of some kind, piled on the floor or stowed on the racks that lined the walls. But now now. Not after we had come for Ximo twice in the last couple of days.

He was sitting behind a desk in the back of the room. When we poured in like flood water through a broken dam, he shot to his feet.

I noticed he had a bladed stick in his hand as well, even though it was illegal for anyone but a police officer to own one. But we weren't after him.

At least I didn't *think* we were.

We also weren't after the twenty or so other Hawks scattered around the place. Our target was standing to one side of Ximo's desk, reaching for something inside his tunic.

Notoca...

I got to him just as he started to pull it out. I caught a glimpse of an ugly, black thing gleaming in the light from the overhead fixtures, just like the one I had held in Acuahe's cellar. It was what we had feared—that he and maybe others as well would be carrying fire hands.

That was why we had moved so quickly. That was what it had been so important to surprise the pack. Because if we didn't, they would skewer us like fish in a shallow stream.

Notoca's eyes widened as I swung. This time I used my hand stick instead of my fist. It caught him in the side of the face and laid open his cheek.

But it didn't make him drop the fire hand. He held onto that somehow, half in and half out of his tunic, even as he staggered backward from the force of my blow.

It's all right, I thought. He was reeling. One more blow and I'd put him on his back.

But I didn't get the chance. As I pulled back my stick, someone slammed me from the side. His momentum carried us both into a metal rack alongside the wall, rattling my bones.

I recovered first and elbowed him in the nose, breaking it. He pushed himself away from me and I looked for Notoca again—just in time to see him go crashing through a window.

We were on the second floor. Even if the glass didn't slice him up, he'd probably break something when he landed.

But what if he didn't? What if he got away?

Unable to take that chance, I leaped through what was left of the window and followed Notoca down to the ground below.

The gods were on my side—I landed in the alley between buildings without cracking an ankle bone. But the gods had favored Notoca as well. He was tearing away at full speed, his fire hand still in his fist.

He was strong but he wasn't fast. And though I hadn't been a professional in the ball court for some time, I still played in a men's league for pride. I caught up to him as he reached the end of the alley.

That was when Notoca turned and raised his weapon and took aim at me. But I had gotten good with my hand stick over the cycles—I pulled it back and let it fly, dealing him a glancing blow before he could pull his trigger.

Then I was on him like a jungle cat, tearing the ugly, black thing out of his hands. As it went skittering away, Notoca cracked me in the side of the head. I cracked him back.

Then I did it again. And again, until he had no more fight left in him.

I was about to retrieve the fire hand when I heard my name ring out in the alley. I turned and saw Ximo coming after me, clutching his hand stick as if he meant to use it.

"Maxtla!" he cried out again. The alley echoed with his anger. "What have you done?"

I stood over Notoca, a little shakier than I would have liked, and wiped some blood from my mouth. "What have I done?" I asked. "What *you* should have done."

His eyes narrowed as he stopped in front of me, his chest

heaving, bits of glass stuck into his clothing. Apparently, he had jumped out the window as well.

"What are you talking about?" he demanded.

I gestured to the fire hand lying on the ground beyond Notoca. "I'm talking about *that*."

For once, Ximo was at a loss. "Where did it come from?"

"Your friend Notoca. He's the one who put those fire hands in your brother's temple. Maybe you thought it was another pack who did that, but it wasn't. It was Notoca."

Ximo glanced at him. "Why would he do that?"

"He wanted to draw attention to *you*. He wanted us to think you were behind the fire hands. Because if you were our suspect, no one would think of *him*."

Ximo's eyes narrowed. "Go on."

"Notoca wasn't known as much of a brain. Ximo Atotoli was capable of running that kind of operation, smuggling fire hands into the Empire. But Notoca? He was too stupid, too limited."

Ximo looked down again at his second-in-command. Notoca was in no position to defend himself. But even if he were, what could he have said? That the fire hand lying on the ground had come from nowhere?

"Of course," I went on, "Notoca's been building his own business for a long time. Little by little, behind your back. Doing an arson job, for instance—the kind of job *you* would never do."

Not after his mother had died in a fire.

"Then," I said, "an opportunity presented itself. A Euro showed up with a proposition: Fire hands! You turned it down. So did the other packs. You were doing fine, none of you needed that kind of business. Not when the police would be on it like fire ants.

"But Notoca...*he* needed that business. All those beans he would make, all that power—and so quickly. He couldn't resist. The fire hand trade would make him bigger than you, Ximo. *Much* bigger. And despite everything you had done for the pack, Notoca would become leader of the Hawks.

"Except something went wrong. Maybe Notoca didn't like dealing with a Euro. Maybe he didn't feel he was getting enough respect from the guy. Whatever the reason, Notoca put him in the River of Stars.

"But first he put the mark of the Hawks on him. Because he knew we would come after *you*, not him. And when the Hawks—the ones who weren't already in Notoca's pouch— saw how your business was dropping as a result, they would start thinking about new leadership. In other words, *him*.

"Notoca is the one who brought this plague of fire hands down on us. But he's not going to profit from it. Not anymore."

By then, Necalli and Quetzalli were on their way down the alley to back me up. But I didn't need their help any longer. I could tell that Ximo believed me.

He put his hand stick in his pouch and went to Notoca, whose face was full of blood. Then Ximo knelt beside him, put his hand on Notoca's shoulder, and shook him until he opened his eyes.

"Ximo..." Notoca said.

There was a tension between them you could hang laundry on. After all, they hadn't just been business associates. They had been brothers. Closer than brothers.

At least, that was what Ximo had thought.

"You betrayed me," he told Notoca.

Notoca lifted his chin and dismissed Ximo with a twist of his hand. "You're soft." Blood bubbled in his mouth. "The one who leads the Hawks has to be hard. Like rock."

Ximo laughed bitterly. "You don't see what you did, do you? You just opened the door for the Euros."

"You didn't have the guts to see the future." Notoca poked himself in the chest. "I did."

"Your future," said Ximo, "will not be a pleasant one, Notoca. You can count on it."

Notoca didn't know what to say to that. He was still trying to figure it out when Necalli and Quetzalli got hold of him pulled him to his feet.

"Anyone else in there with a fire hand?" I asked them.

"No," said Quetzalli. "Lucky for us."

"What about *him*?" Necalli asked me, using his chin to indicate Ximo.

"Innocent as a lamb," I said.

Necalli grunted. "Too bad." Then he and Quetzalli took Notoca back down the alleyway.

I retrieved Notoca's fire hand and put it in my pouch for safekeeping. At that point, I was alone in the alley with Ximo.

"I'm glad I was right about Notoca," I said. "And about you."

He smiled a weary smile. "You know, I followed you when you were in the ball court. Lost a few beans on you too."

I was surprised, though I probably shouldn't have been. "Sorry about that."

"It's all right. It was worth it. How many guys can say they know the player they're betting on?"

"Not many, I suppose."

"Damned right." For a moment, we were kids again. Then the moment passed. "Don't you have somewhere to be, Little Rabbit?"

My spine stiffened. But we were alone, so I let the remark go again. "As a matter of fact," I said, "I do. But before I go..." I held out my hand. "The hand stick."

He hesitated for just a moment. Then he opened his pouch and gave it to me.

And I left.

After all, I had work to do back at the Interrogation Center. Notoca couldn't have been the only Hawk in the fire hand business. We had to figure out who the others were.

The only thing I knew for certain was that Ximo wasn't one of them.

I expected he'd turn up outside the building as Notoca had, waiting for the Hawks we would release—the ones who had remained loyal to him, the ones who had been ignorant of the fire hands deal.

The others we would send to the Prison House when we caught them. And that would be perfectly all right with Ximo, I imagined.

● ● ●

That night I had dinner with Calli in the Merchant City, though not at our favorite place. The food wasn't as good but it was quieter, farther from the beaten track. Dimmer too, though not dim enough to conceal the cuts and bruises on my face.

Calli didn't like the sight of them. But she liked them better when I told her we'd caught the guy we were looking for.

"So was he smuggling?" she asked. "Or are you prohibited from telling me?"

My first inclination was to tell her she was right. But talk would leak out here and there—from the Hawks, from their prospective customers, even from the police officers who had seen the boxes at the temple.

Calli would hear rumors soon enough, and put it all together. And she wouldn't be the only one. Still, I made her lean closer before I whispered the words into her ear: "He was smuggling, all right. Smuggling fire hands."

She sat back and gave me a look. A wide-eyed look. "Tell me that's a joke."

"I wish it was."

Her brow crunched. "Here in Aztlan?"

"Right here."

Calli looked at me a moment longer, trying to come to grips with what I had told her, trying to cram the knowledge into her world without breaking it. "But it's over, right? You caught the guy."

I managed a smile. "I caught him."

But it wasn't over. Calli knew that as well as I did, even if she didn't want to admit it to herself. A door had been opened, and it wasn't going to be easy to close it.

Book Two

The Salt Merchants' Reunion was a big deal in Aztlan.

One sparkling evening every cycle, salt sellers from all over the Empire came together below the magnificent crystalline skylight of the Grand Pyramid in District Twenty to celebrate their considerable success.

Earlier in the day, they held meetings in restaurants and offices across the Merchant City. They made and dissolved partnerships, traded key employees, and fixed the price at which they would offer their product in the coming cycle.

But by sunset, all business was sealed. Every salt seller abided by that unspoken rule. Under the starry sky, in the Grand Pyramid, they had only one purpose—to enjoy themselves.

Nor was it only salt sellers who were invited to this grand event. There were also the businesspeople who made the salt sellers' prosperity possible—the mine owners who hauled the salt out of the earth, the carriers who moved the salt around the Empire, and the Mirror executives who conveyed salt's benefits to the people.

The focal point of the party this cycle, the figure who drew more attention than any other, was the Emperor's Commissioner of Trade, Aca Papaqui—a balding man with eyeglasses and a paunch born of too many business lunches—who was scheduled to deliver the keynote address to the gathering the next day.

After all, what the Commissioner said from his podium would shape the fortunes of salt sellers from one end of the Empire to the other. And any hint he dropped while sipping his octli could be of great value to the eager and the opportunistic—which was why a handful of police were on hand to keep an eye on the Commissioner and protect him from anyone he didn't wish to let into his circle.

The police contingent charged with guarding the keynote speaker was always led by an Investigator. Most cycles it was my boss, Necalli. But this cycle Necalli couldn't make it because his nephew was getting married in Texcoco.

So he chose someone from his office to stand in for him. Someone who had served on the force long enough to wear three red beads in his bracelet. Someone who had the judgment to avoid saying or doing anything stupid at a high-profile event.

Someone who had been celebrated on the Mirror earlier in the cycle for exposing Aztlan's High Priest as a ritual murderer, so the Commissioner of Trade wouldn't take the guy's appearance as a slight.

In other words, *me*.

I had accompanied Necalli to the salt sellers' gathering a

couple of times before, much earlier in my career, so I knew what to do and what not to do—and would have known even if he hadn't made a point of reminding me: *Don't insert yourself into the conversation. Hang back a little. Watch. Listen.*

Necalli knew I wouldn't have to be told twice. I had become an Investigator to bring the guilty to justice in the name of the Emperor, not to get caught up in the complicated and often tedious web of city politics.

So I was perfectly happy to remain in the background while the Commissioner shared stories with cogs big and small in the salt-selling machine—a woman who had a weed removal business in Axocopan, a short, portly guy from Yopitzinco who peddled remedies for insect stings, an older fellow who made chocolate novelties in Oxtlipa. The farther they had traveled to attend the Reunion, the more eager they were to grasp the Commissioner's hand.

More importantly, from my perspective, they were harmless, unlikely to become the slightest cause of irritation or embarrassment to the Commissioner. Which was good. An Investigator's job had more than its share of confrontations. The last thing I wanted was to have to square up on the floor of the Grand Pyramid.

Unfortunately, the last thing was what I got—because as I was busy watching a couple of merchants approach the Commissioner from one direction, Ehe Ometochtli slid in front of the Commissioner from another.

Ometochtli, a brick of a man with cheekbones that could cut glass, was one of the more powerful bankers in the Merchant

City. In fact, he was one of the more powerful bankers in the Empire.

Banking wasn't illegal in Aztlan, as it had lately become in the southern extremities of Mexica. But it was still a shady proposition at best.

On one hand, it provided an escape hatch for the debtors in society, big as well as small, who might otherwise have wound up in the Prison House. A banker could lend a guy what he needed to get his accounts straight. He could give a guy some breathing space, some time to work out his problems.

But at the same time, he would charge interest through the nostrils.

So if you owed a thousand beans on the Festival of Tezcalipoca, you owed your banker eleven hundred by the Festival of Quetzalcoatl. Maybe even *twelve* hundred.

And if you couldn't pay *him*, you didn't just go to prison. You danced a little with his employees first. You took your lumps. And you kept your mouth shut because it was better than your neighbors knowing you'd gone to a banker.

There had been talk for a while about denying bankers admission to the Salt Sellers' Reunion and other events like it. But it had never amounted to anything—because key figures in Aztlan's city government were secretly bankers' clients, or so the speculation went.

I didn't want the Commissioner implicated in such rumors, especially with his spotless reputation. So I moved to the Commissioner's side and said, "Sorry, but they're buzzing you."

I didn't know who might buzz him or why, but it seemed like a good excuse to move him away from Ometochtli. But before I could guide the Commissioner across the floor, Ometochtli caught him by the wrist.

"Relax," he said, talking to me but looking into the Commissioner's face. "I'm not here to make my friend here uncomfortable."

But clearly, he was. I was preparing to remove his hand from the Commissioner when Ometochtli removed it himself—and faded back into the crowd.

I exchanged looks with the Commissioner. His was unsettled—not just by the banker's presumption, it seemed to me, but by more than that. *So maybe he's not so squeaky-clean after all*, I surmised.

But the Commissioner hadn't risen through the imperial ranks by being rattled for long. A moment later, he was greeting another couple of out-of-towners.

At that point, my job was to track Ometochtli for a moment—to make sure he wasn't making a return visit. Which, I was pleased to see, he wasn't.

The rest of the evening went without incident. At the end of it, the Commissioner thanked me for watching out for him. "Necalli can send you along with me anytime," he said.

Which, given my view of the proceedings, wasn't the best thing I could have heard. But it also wasn't the worst.

Not having eaten anything since midday, I was about to see if there was any food left in the Grand Pyramid's kitchen— when I heard someone yell: "Hey! Colhua!"

I turned to see who had called me, and spotted Molli Inave waddling my way. *Another banker,* I thought. *What is it with me and bankers this evening?*

Of course, Inave wasn't just *any* banker. Not to me. A big Eagles fan, he always took care of our players when their careers were over. Got them work, paid for their physician bills, made them interest-free loans.

Fortunately, I'd never needed that kind of help. But I appreciated what Inave had done for my teammates.

Before he could reach me, one of the rookie Investigators in my department—a baby-faced guy named Izcuin—moved to get between me and the banker. I waved Izcuin aside. "It's all right," I said.

He looked surprised, but he let Inave go by. The banker—who looked to have added weight to a frame already tasked with carrying too much of it—held his arms out wide as he approached me.

"My friend!" he said a little too loudly.

That was the first indication I had that he was drunk on the Reunion's octli. The second was the bloodshot look in his eyes.

I held my hand up, declining Inave's embrace. "You've had a bit to drink, I see."

Inave held up his own hand, his thumb and his forefinger not quite touching each other. "Just a bit," he said, slurring his words. "Not enough for you to arrest me, I assure you."

I frowned. "I'll take your word for it."

"Besides, you wouldn't want to take your biggest informant

off the streets, would you?"

Inave was hardly my biggest informant. In all the cycles I'd known him, he had yet to give me a shred of information I could use. Still, he seemed to like the idea that he was of help to me.

"Don't give me a reason," I said because I was still on duty, "and I won't."

Inave laughed, put a meaty hand on my shoulder, and brought his mouth—and the scent of octli—close to my ear. "What I'll give you is a tip. Remember the name, Investigator: Tomatl." He grimaced. "Wait, what did I say? I meant Tamalii." Another grimace. "No, not that...Tlaco." He smiled a satisfied smile. "Yes...Tlaco."

"Whatever you say," I told him.

"He's a bad man, this Tlaco." His eyes narrowed. "Very bad."

"So I should watch out for him?"

"No," said Inave. "He's *dead*. Why would you want to watch out for a...for a dead man? Besides, the god smiles on Tlaco's work...so how bad can he be?"

How bad indeed? I thought, having no idea what Inave was talking about. "Thanks for the tip."

"Any...time, Investigator. Any...time."

Out of the corner of his eye, Inave caught sight of a server with a tray full of snacks. Inebriated and all, he managed to grab a piece of shredded tortilla, dip it in a bowl of guacamole sunken into the center of the tray, and pop the result into his mouth.

"I do love guacamole," he said around his consumption of the tortilla.

I knew that about him. I also knew I wasn't the only Law officer on the floor. If one of the others took Inave's drunkenness more seriously, there would be nothing I could do about it.

"You should go home," I told the banker. "Is one of your—" Before I could finish the question, I spotted one of his bodyguards in the background. When it came to bankers, there were *always* bodyguards.

I beckoned the guy. When he came closer, I said, "This man needs to go home."

The bodyguard, a bald fellow with a face that had seen too many brawls, nodded. Then, gently, he took Inave's arm and led him away.

"Goodbye, Colhua!" the banker called back over his shoulder.

"Goodbye," I said, though not loud enough for Inave to hear me.

"I'm sorry," said Izcuin. "I was going to arrest him for drunkenness but he said you and he were friends."

"We are," I said, "in a way. At any rate, don't worry. You did better heading off bankers tonight than I did."

Izcuin smiled. "Thanks. See you tomorrow, Investigator." And he made his way to the door.

The rookie was already through it when I heard a commotion. I traced it to the vicinity of the exit, where Inave—who else?—was pointing his finger at another man. One, I saw, who bore a close resemblance to Love Boy, a character on a Mirror drama who wore his hair pulled back and had big, pouty lips.

Fortunately, the commotion didn't last long. The guy who looked like Love Boy held his hands up in what looked like an appeal for peace, and retreated, and Inave let him go with a gesture of disgust.

Then the evening was over for real. By then, we'd passed the twelfth hour. There was no chance the kitchen was still open.

But if I hurried, I could get to Calli's apartment before she fell asleep.

● ● ●

As luck would have it, I never got to Calli's place.

There was a delay on the rail line—a rarity since the Emperor had renovated the system—and by the time the problem was resolved, it was too late for me to knock on Calli's door. Not that she would complain. But I knew she had another round of meetings the next day, and I didn't want her falling asleep in the middle of them.

So I just made my way home, watered the plant she had gotten me for the Festival of Xochiquetzal, and went to bed.

In a dream, I saw Michi Chicome. We were riding the rail line. It was night. The stars were out in force.

"You owe me," he said.

I was sure he was talking about beans. I opened my pouch to see what I could give him, but my pouch was empty. No beans. Not even my hand stick.

"Sorry," I said. "I can't give it to you right now."

It seemed to me he was going to beat me for my failure to pay him. But he didn't touch me. He just frowned.

"All right," Chicome said. "But don't forget, I'm waiting."

I was about to assure him I was good for the debt, whatever sum it was, when I heard a buzzing. It filled the rail car.

It took me a moment to open my eyes and realize the buzzing was coming from my radio. It was still dark out, but it wasn't the first time I'd been roused in the middle of the night since I'd become an Investigator. I rolled over in bed, reached for the radio, and answered it.

"Colhua," I said.

"Sorry to wake you." It was Necalli.

"Aren't you in Texcoco?" I asked.

"I am. And I had planned to remain here undisturbed for the rest of the morning, sleeping off my nephew's celebration. But someone in Aztlan had other ideas."

In other words, there had been a murder.

But Necalli had a whole department full of Investigators he could have woken, most of whom hadn't worked into the evening the night before. How did I get so lucky?

I was about to ask when Necalli said, "Molli Inave was a friend of yours, right?"

A chill climbed my spine. "You could say that. Why?"

"His cleaning woman found him this morning. He's got both feet in the Lands of the Dead."

I swore to Mictlantechutli, the god of the underworld. "How?"

"Stabbed to death. Whoever did it was more than thorough. Six wounds in all."

I swore again. Inave hadn't been a bad guy. He didn't deserve to leave the world of the living that way.

"He's waiting for you," said Necalli, "still lying in bed, where *I* should be. I've sent a transport for you."

"I'll look for it," I said.

• • •

The transport arrived just as I finished dressing. I went downstairs, exchanged early-morning salutations with the driver, a guy who'd driven me a few times before, and got in the back.

On the way to the murder scene, I thought about Inave. As a banker, he had never been terribly successful. But then, where other bankers taught their clients a lesson from time to time, he had been inclined to baby them.

His patience had had its limits, of course. But they were much farther afield than those of others in his business.

Inave's clients were small, too. The kind a guy like Ometochtli would probably overlook. But not too small to fight back if their banker were leaning on them too hard.

I recalled the exchange I'd seen between Inave and Love Boy. They didn't look like they'd enjoyed each other's company. I needed to know more about Love Boy and what he and Inave had said to each other.

Also, a list of Inave's clients. What else?

Before I could answer the question, the transport pulled up in front of Inave's place. The driver turned to me and said,

"Good luck, Investigator."

"Thanks," I said, and got out.

Night, at that point, was giving way to the first red glow of day. I could see it wedged between the slanted walls of two pyramids.

Inave lived in a single-residence building, a new kind of pyramidal structure in Aztlan. It was about the most expensive kind of housing there was, even if it wasn't in one of the more desirable districts.

Had he been living beyond his means?

A couple of District Eight police officers were standing at the building's front door, which was set into one side of the pyramid. I showed them my bracelet.

"Anyone else here yet?" I asked.

There was no need for discretion, after all. Necalli would almost certainly have called a second Investigator.

"Not yet," one of the officers said.

I took a moment to check out the door. "Looks intact. No forced entry?"

"Not that we could tell," said the other officer.

"Thanks," I said, and started inside.

"It's a bad one," the first officer warned me.

He was right. I was glad I hadn't had breakfast yet. Inave was a mess, his face as pale as ivory, his clothes and his bed-sheets drenched dark red with blood. His nightshirt had what looked like a dozen rents in it.

Inave's eyes were still open, staring at the ceiling. I closed them, knowing he would have done the same for me.

As I began checking the body, Izcuin showed up. "Investigator," he said by way of acknowledgment.

"Necalli called *you*?" I said.

It wasn't a dig. Rookies were seldom chosen to be among the first at murder scenes.

"Yes." Izcuin grimaced at the sight of the body. "He said I'd benefit from the experience."

Apparently, someone saw special promise in Izcuin. Good for him, I thought.

"Since you're here," I said, "there was a guy at the Reunion last night. Inave had words with him. Reunion management should have a list of its guests. If he was there with Inave—"

"They'll have a record of it. I'm on it."

He walked away so as not to disturb me while he made the call. As he did so, Necalli buzzed me.

"You there?" he asked.

"I am," I told him. "It's as bad as you'd imagine."

"Lovely. Any leads?"

"One." I told him about Love Boy.

"Any kin?"

I considered the question. "Inave had a daughter." I plumbed my memory for her name. "Teicu." I'd never met her but Inave had talked about her. "I'll let her know."

"I can do that," said Necalli. It was the responsibility of the department head to contact a victim's family.

"No," I said, "I'll take care of it. It'll be better if she hears it from someone who knew her father. I just need her radio code."

"You've got it," Necalli said.

Not that he was going to get me the number himself. He would ask someone back at the Interrogation Center.

"Good luck," Necalli added, and ended the call.

As I put my radio back in my pouch, I turned to Inave again. With his eyes closed, he looked peaceful, as if he had already entered the gods' embrace.

I hoped for his sake it was the first wound that had killed him.

• • •

As I was taking blood samples, Izcuin told me the Reunion Center was calling him back.

"There was only one guy in the building," he said, "and he didn't have access to the records of last night. He said he'd buzz me later."

Not good enough, I thought.

"Call again," I said. "Have him wake his boss and tell him to get his backside down to the Reunion Center. You're an Investigator for the Empire and you need that information."

Izcuin reddened. "Got it."

He'll learn, I thought, as the rookie got back on his radio.

In the meantime, I began searching Inave's premises. After a while, Izcuin joined me.

"The guy I spoke with called his boss, who yelled at him for disrespecting an Investigator. The boss is on his way down to the building now."

"Better," I said.

He nodded.

"Meanwhile, I haven't seen a likely murder weapon. Have you?"

"Nothing obvious," Izquin said.

"So whoever killed Inave took the thing when they left."

That took a certain presence of mind. Not every murderer had it.

Yet Inave had suffered six separate wounds. And the way his clothes were shredded suggested attempts at even more. That indicated anything *but* a presence of mind.

"What if it was a kitchen knife?" Izcuin asked. "The killer could have cleaned it and put it back in Inave's drawer."

I'd seen wounds inflicted with kitchen knives. Inave's were too long and deep to have been made that way.

I had barely said as much before my radio buzzed again. I answered it: "Colhua."

It was Suguey, one of the other rookies in the department. "I've got that radio code for Inave's daughter," she said. "Her place is in District Twenty-Nine."

Teicu's neighborhood was almost as nice as her father's. "Thanks," I said.

"I'll look around some more," said Izcuin.

I called the radio code. It took three buzzes, but someone finally picked up. "Yes," said a feminine voice. "Who's this?"

"This is Investigator Colhua," I said. "Is this Teicu Inave?"

"Yes."

"I'm afraid I have bad news." And I told Teicu about her father.

For a moment, I heard nothing but silence on the line.

Then Inave's daughter whispered, "Lands of the Dead." And again, with an awakening pain in her voice: *"Lands of the Dead..."*

"I'm sorry," I said.

Another pause. When Teicu Inave spoke again, her voice was thick with grief. "You said your name is Colhua?"

"Yes."

"My father talked about an Investigator by that name. A friend, he said. Someone he helped sometimes. Is that you?"

There were no other Colhuas in the department. Not anymore. "Yes."

"I'm glad. If you're a friend, you'll do everything you can to find out who killed him."

I didn't tell her that Investigators did that anyway. Instead I said: "Maybe you can help me. I saw your father arguing with someone last night at the Reunion Center. I don't know his name but he looked like Love Boy...from the Mirror show?"

She made a sound of disgust. *"Love Boy.* One of my friends called him that once."

"Then you know him?"

"I should," said Inave's daughter. "We were going to be married."

• • •

Thanks to Teicu Inave, we didn't have to wait for Izcuin to get his call from the Reunion Center.

Love Boy's real name was Ueman Zaniya, she told us. Suguey looked up his radio code for me. But when we buzzed him, there was no answer.

"Keep trying," I told Suguey.

"I will," she said.

In the meantime, I called Inave's daughter again. In the absence of Zaniya, she was an even more important part of our investigation.

"I'm sorry," I said, "but I need to talk with you in more depth. Can I come to your place?" Interrogations were always more productive when they were conducted face to face.

She said she'd rather speak with me at the Interrogation Center. "It's a mess here. I feel like the cleaning man hasn't come in a moon."

"No problem," I said. "I'll send an auto-carriage for you."

• • •

Inave's daughter was an attractive woman. I could see that even in the flat, colorless light of the Interrogation Center. Delicate bones, long lashes, flawless skin. If Inave had had a hand in her making, I saw no sign of it.

She took a sip from the cup of cane water I'd set in front of her. Then she said, "When I was little, I worried about him. You know how it is with bankers. They have enemies. I would have nightmares about him getting killed—knocked over the head, drowned, every way you can imagine."

"It couldn't have been easy," I said.

"Being a banker's daughter? Not at all. I didn't have a lot of friends. Their parents didn't want them playing with me. I wasn't…respectable."

"You said you and Zaniya were going to be married."

"Yes. Though looking back, I see it was a mistake. I never loved him, you know. Never."

"How did you meet him?" I asked.

"He worked in my father's office. We got to know each other. He liked a lot of the things I liked."

"Did you and he ever talk about your father?"

"Sometimes."

"What did Zaniya say about him?"

"He hated my father. He told me that all the time. He hated him because my father treated him like dirt. Not at first, before we started going out. But afterward…after we told my father we were together. Then he made Ueman miserable, every chance he got."

"Because he thought Zaniya was a bad match for you?"

"Yes."

"Did Zaniya hate your father enough to kill him?"

Inave's daughter took a long time before she said, "I don't know."

In that moment, the search for Love Boy became more urgent. "He's not answering his radio," I said. "And he's not in his residence. Do you know where else we might find him?"

"At his mother's place. He went there a lot to take care of her. She has something wrong with her hip."

"Do you have her address?"

She did. I passed it on to my colleagues upstairs.

But we weren't done. If we were lucky, Teicu could do more than help us locate her old boyfriend.

"Is there anyone you know," I asked her, "besides Zaniya,

who had a reason to hurt your father?"

Inave's daughter frowned. "I didn't know much about my father's business dealings. My father tried to shield me from them. He didn't want me to live the life he lived."

"So you wouldn't know if someone threatened him?"

She shrugged. "Probably not."

"Think," I said. "It might be helpful."

She thought. But in the end, she came up empty.

• • •

I talked with Inave's daughter about other parts of her father's life—the foods he liked, the shows he watched on the Mirror, and—of course—how much he loved the Eagles. None of which seemed likely to help our investigation, but it seemed to make her feel better.

Finally, I sent her home in another auto-carriage. As I was going back into the Interrogation Center, I got a call from Quetzalli, who had gone with Suguey and Izcuin to track down Zaniya.

"We found him," Quetzalli said. "In his mother's kitchen. They were eating chicken and stinkweed soup. His mother wasn't happy to see us take him."

What mother would be? "Don't tell him why you're bringing him in," I told Quetzalli.

She would know why: I wanted to see Zaniya's reaction when I told him about Inave's death.

• • •

An hour later, I was sitting across a table from Zaniya in the same enclosure where I'd spoken with Teicu Inave. Up close, his resemblance to Love Boy on the Mirror show was even more striking.

"Do you know why you're here?" I asked.

"No," he said.

I looked him in the eye. "Molli Inave was stabbed to death in his bed last night."

Zaniya turned pale. "What...?"

I repeated what I'd said. It didn't bring the color back to his face.

"I saw how he spoke to you at the Reunion," I said. "He didn't seem thrilled with you."

Zaniya shook his head. "He liked to drink. And there were police on the floor. I didn't want him to get into trouble."

"You were looking out for him."

"Yes."

"Even though you didn't like each other."

"Who—?" he began. Then he figured it out: "Teicu told you that."

"It's not true?"

He frowned. "Inave and I weren't on good terms anymore. But I still looked out for him. Someone had to."

I decided to approach him from a different angle. "I understand you had plans to marry Teicu Inave—though they've since fallen through."

Zaniya sighed. "It was my fault. I complained too much about her father. But I stopped. We were doing better. *Starting* to do better..." His voice trailed off.

I'd heard enough. "We're going to hold you," I informed

him, "until we know more."

He looked as if I'd punched him in the gut. "I didn't kill anyone," he whimpered. "I have a soft heart. I don't even kill flies."

"If that's so," I said, "you'll be all right."

"Did Teicu know you were going to arrest me?"

"No. But she'll be told."

His eyes widened. "Just...be gentle with her, please. She's not the strongest person. She's had...her share of problems."

"Oh?" I said. *What kind?* I wondered.

Zaniya frowned. "Best ask *her* about them."

• • •

I called Necalli to let him know about Zaniya. He was in a rail carriage on his way back to Aztlan when I reached him.

"Do you think he did it?" Necalli asked.

I considered the question. "He didn't get along with Inave. They'd had an argument just a few hours before Inave was killed. On the other foot, Zaniya doesn't seem like the type to stab a guy—not even once."

"You don't sound confident that he did it."

"I'm not," I said. "Unfortunately, he's the only suspect we've got."

• • •

I had barely gotten off the radio with Necalli when I received another call. "Colhua," I said.

"This is Commissioner Papaqui's office. The Commissioner has something important to share with you. He has an opening in his schedule an hour from now if you can make it."

Why, I asked, would the Commissioner want to see *me*?

"That's a question best asked of the Commissioner," came the answer.

I was in the middle of a murder investigation. But it was the Commission of Trade, after all.

"I'll be there," I said.

"The Commissioner will be pleased."

I left the Interrogation Center and picked up the rail at the nearest station, at the intersection of Amapan and Cuaxolotl Streets. It took only a few minutes for a carriage to stop alongside the platform and open its doors.

As I slid into a seat, I was reminded of the dream I'd had the night before—the one in which I was riding the rail line with Chicome—though I'd seen the stars in my dream and it was now the height of day.

I remembered what Chicome had said to me in that middle-of-the-night carriage: *"You owe me."* And how I had opened my pouch, only to find it empty.

Clearly, I felt guilty about denying the guy his scoop cycles earlier. I didn't need a dream to tell me that.

The interesting part was the beating I'd expected. The real Chicome would never have posed that kind of threat to me. However, I'd been talking to a couple of bankers at the Reunion. If they didn't bring to mind the promise of a beating, who would?

● ● ●

The Commissioner's office was in the government pyramid on Cipactli Street in District Nine.

I knew one of the police officers on guard in the lobby. She'd worked at the Prison House for many cycles.

"What are you doing *here*?" I asked. "Did they let all the prisoners out?"

She laughed. "They told me I'd earned something a little less demanding." She included the lobby with a sweep of her arm. "It doesn't get any less demanding than *this*."

I laughed too. "I guess not."

I told the officer where I was going.

"Sixteenth floor," she said.

The penthouse. I wasn't surprised. The Commissioner reported directly to the Emperor, after all.

"Thanks," I said.

I took the elevator to the last stop. It opened on a reception area with colorful paintings of animals on the walls.

A young guy in crisp business attire was sitting on the arm of a beaver-skin chair. The first thing he looked for was my bracelet. When he saw it, he smiled.

"Looks legitimate," he said. "Though I've heard there's a black market in such things."

I felt something tighten inside me. "There *was*."

It was a sore spot with the force. A couple of cycles earlier, a guy had made a batch of counterfeit Investigators' bracelets—the kind that looked real enough to create a problem. Of course, the enterprising fellow was now serving time in the Prison House.

"But," I added, "not anymore."

Papaqui's man held a hand up. "I didn't mean to offend you."

I guessed he'd seen my feelings in my expression. "No offense taken," I lied.

"Great," he said.

Not that he cared. He just wanted to be able to say he'd vetted me, if the Commissioner asked.

The guy beckoned for me to follow him, and led me down a maplewood-paneled hallway with more animal pictures. When we got to the first room on the right, he stopped, opened the door for me, and waved me in. "Commissioner Papaqui has been expecting you," he said.

"Thanks," I told him.

As I entered the room, I saw the Commissioner sitting at a large mahogany-wood desk. He took a moment to finish what he was doing—something with a map—before he got up, came around the desk, and said soberly, "Thank you for coming, Investigator."

"Of course," I said. It was my job, after all. "You said you had something important to share with me."

The Commissioner frowned. "It might be." He took off his eyeglasses and massaged the bridge of his nose. Then he put them back on. "You saw my little...we'll say *encounter* with Ehe Ometochtli at the Reunion?"

"I did. And I'm sorry we weren't able to intervene sooner."

"It's all right. Ometochtli and I..." He looked uncomfortable—confirming, to my mind, what I'd suspected the night before.

"There's no need to go into detail," I said. "We know what bankers do."

The Commissioner nodded. "They assist in...personal matters. And clearly, such a matter has compelled me to resort to Ometochtli's services. But that's not why I asked to speak with you this morning." He took on a more business-like demeanor. "I understand you've been asked to investigate Molli Inave's murder?"

"That's right."

"Well," he said, "I may be able to shed some light on what happened to him."

He'd gotten my attention. "Please do."

"Ometochtli approached me at the Reunion because he'd heard I was thinking about switching bankers—specifically, turning my accounts over to Inave."

"Were you?" I asked.

"Inave and I had discussed the possibility. *Once*, a few weeks ago, based on a recommendation from one of my colleagues. But in person, Inave didn't inspire a great deal of confidence, so I decided against making the change. Unfortunately, Ometochtli..."

"Didn't know that. So as far as he was concerned, Inave was stealing one of his accounts."

Bankers didn't take kindly to other bankers poaching from them. Some—the more aggressive of them—arranged for the poacher to meet with misfortune. On occasion, the lethal kind. It wasn't a common occurrence, but it happened.

I recalled the expression on Ometochtli's face at the Reunion. The way he pointed his finger at the Commissioner.

Was it the behavior of someone angry enough to eliminate a competitor?

"I'm afraid so," said the Commissioner.

"Thanks," I said, "for bringing this to my attention."

"Of course. I...hope it helps." Papaqui went back to his desk and buzzed someone, and said, "Investigator Colhua is ready to leave."

A moment later, the guy who'd let me in opened the door and gestured for me to come with him again. I let him lead me back out and down the hallway in the direction of the reception area.

"Good meeting?" he asked.

It was a question better suited to the businesspeople who visited the commissioner's office than to an Investigator hunting down a murderer.

Still, I said, "It was."

"Great," the guy said.

As I made my way back to the rail line, I considered what the Commissioner had told me.

Was he simply doing his duty as a citizen of Aztlan? Or was he trying to get Ometochtli thrown into prison for embarrassing him on the floor of the Reunion—and in the process, sending a warning to others who could embarrass him?

Papaqui may have seemed mild-mannered. But that didn't mean he *was*. Men didn't rise in the confidence of the Emperor by letting other men walk all over them.

• • •

I buzzed Necalli.

"Where are we?" he asked.

"I just visited Commissioner Papaqui," I said. And I told Necalli what we'd talked about.

"Interesting. So you're on your way to the Merchant City to see Ometochtli." It wasn't a question. "I'll be back in town within the hour. Let me know how it goes."

I said I would.

Then I made a couple of other calls. Inave wasn't the only banker I knew, after all. If I was going to accuse Ometochtli of murder, I had to know what I was talking about.

• • •

Ometochtli's office was like anyone's in the banking profession—dimly lit, poorly furnished, the air rancid with tobacco smoke.

But then, a banker didn't want his clients to look forward to a second visit. That would take place only if they failed to pay on time.

When I walked in, Ometochtli was seated behind a dented metal desk. "Investigator," he said, tipped the ash from his tobacco stick into a metal tray, and leaned back in an armchair that had seen better days. "What brings you to my place of business?"

I chose the least rickety looking of the wooden chairs assembled on my side of the desk and sat down. "I want to talk. About Inave."

Ometochtli scowled. "I heard."

I wasn't surprised. News got around, especially in the Merchant City.

"Nasty way to go," Ometochtli said.

"How well did you know him?" I asked.

The banker took a drag of his tobacco stick and blew out the smoke. "As well as anyone in my profession knows anyone else."

"Where he lived, certainly."

"Sure. I saw it on the Mirror. They did a piece on those new standalone houses in District Eight."

"And you saw Inave the night of the Reunion. You knew he was drunk, and that he would be more vulnerable than usual. You had a pretty good idea of when he'd be getting home. Maybe you sent someone to walk in behind him when he opened his door. To tuck him in. To make sure nothing woke him."

Ometochtli smiled. "Why would I do that?"

"I saw you talking to Commissioner Papaqui, remember? He's one of your clients, isn't he?"

"Now," said the banker, "you know people in my line of work don't discuss our clients. It's bad for business."

"And your clients don't talk about you either. But I have my sources. They tell me the Commissioner wasn't happy with his current banker. He was considering the possibility of engaging a new one."

"Really."

"And that Inave was at the top of his list."

Ometochtli laughed. "You're an amusing guy, Investigator. You ought to have a show on the Mirror: True Crimes with Maxtla Colhua, Investigator for the Empire."

We were alone, so I didn't have to respond to the less than respectful nature of his remark. "Bankers don't like it when their clients leave. I'm guessing you're no exception."

"No exception at all," Ometochtli agreed.

"You were so incensed about it that you confronted Commissioner Papaqui on the Reunion floor. In front of half the merchants in the Empire." I leaned forward. "The question is…were you incensed enough to send somebody after Inave? Maybe just to encourage him to turn your client down? And when he refused, seeing a big payday…maybe things got out of hand. Maybe you didn't tell your man to kill Inave. Maybe he just got carried away."

Ometochtli took another drag of his tobacco stick. This time, he let the smoke out slowly, in one grey ring after another.

"It's an interesting theory," he said, "I'll give you that. Except there are lots of bankers in the Merchant City, half of them trying to steal my clients. Am I going to pay them *all* a visit? Just to keep one account?"

"It's a big account."

"Not big enough for me to go head-to-head with every banker in Aztlan. Antagonize enough of them and maybe someone sends a man after *me*."

"Except," I said, "your problem with Inave went beyond his poaching your clients."

I saw a hint of a smile. "You *are* well-informed."

The bankers I'd talked to had been even more helpful than I'd expected. But then, Ometochtli wasn't the most popular guy around. "Inave owed you money."

The smile faded. "Damned right he did."

"When someone owes you money, you make him uncomfortable—even if he's another banker."

"*Especially* if he's another banker. But I don't kill people. Dead men can't pay up."

"They can serve as examples for others."

"*Unnecessary* examples. Those who owe me money are motivated to make good, I assure you. I don't have to kill anyone to get my other clients fired up."

"Until now," I said. "Lately, you've had a couple of accounts slip town."

Again, the hint of a smile. "Have I?"

"Maybe you saw a trend. A bad one, from your point of view. And you wanted to stop it before it went too far."

Ometochtli laughed. "Look, Investigator, everybody takes losses. It's part of doing business. Do I like it? I don't. Am I inclined to do something about it? You *know* I am. But risk a *murder* sentence? I have a good business. I don't have to take those kinds of chances."

"You wouldn't be the first banker who said that one day—and killed someone the next."

"Little guys," said Ometochtli. "Guys who don't have my resources…they get taken advantage of, maybe they get desperate. Maybe they send somebody to the Lands of the Dead. But if you're as well-informed as you seem to be, you know one thing for sure—I'm not a little guy."

• • •

I left Ometochtli's place no better off than when I'd walked into it.

Not that I'd expected him to fall at my feet and confess to Inave's murder. But I'd hoped to leave with *something*—a name, a place, a reference to an incident that might advance my investigation.

I hadn't picked up any of those things. But there was still an angle on Ometochtli I could pursue. Because he wouldn't have killed Inave with his own hands. He would have gotten someone else to do it. Maybe someone outside his organization who specialized in petty acts of violence, and was willing to go to another level for the right sum.

But more likely, someone already on Ometochtli's payroll. One of his guards, for instance.

It wouldn't be the first time a wealthy citizen had given an employee some extra beans to do something outside his job description. Even something *brutal*. I could name six guys we had put in the Prison House under just those circumstances— three guards and their three employers.

But...murder?

It would have taken an especially motivated employer to commission a job like that. And a very *special* employee to accept it.

One more thing: There hadn't been a sign that anyone forced their way into Inave's place. If Ometochtli hired some-one to kill his rival, it would have to have been someone Inave knew a little. Otherwise, he wouldn't have opened the door for the guy.

So the question was: Who on Ometochtli's security team would Inave have trusted?

• • •

By the time I got back to the Interrogation Center, Necalli was sitting at his Mirror station, mulling over the notes we'd taken at Inave's place.

"Welcome back," I said. "Ometochtli sends his best."

"Don't tell me," Necalli said. "He claims he's innocent."

"Of Inave's murder, if nothing else."

"He's a cuddly one, that Ometochtli. Did he give you *anything*?"

I shared my thinking that the murderer was someone Inave knew. "Someone who worked for him, maybe, who also works—or worked—for Ometochtli."

Necalli leaned back in his chair and considered the notion. "You'll find him more quickly if you have some help."

"I was thinking the same thing," I said.

Necalli assigned Suguey and Izcuin to give me a hand. Ometochtli employed more than two dozen bodyguards, after all.

Each of us took a third of them and hunkered down at a Mirror station. We'd been at it for more than an hour when Suguey called my name.

I looked past my monitor to acknowledge her. "Something?" I said hopefully.

"I think so," she said, and beckoned me over.

I joined her at her station. So did Izcuin.

Suguey pointed to her screen and said, "Take a look."

I read the information out loud: "Culanto Xiomara. He worked for Ometochtli for three cycles. And before that—"

For Inave.

"Good work," I told Suguey.

"Happy to be of help," she said, and cast a sly look at Izcuin.

It looked like the rookies had a little competition going. That was all right. I was involved in something similar when I became an Investigator.

"Keep looking," I said. "There may be others."

An hour later, we still hadn't found any. And dog-headed Xolotl would soon be escorting the sun through the Underworld.

It had been a long day, and not an especially pleasant one. If I'd told Necalli I was going home, he wouldn't have given me an argument. But I wasn't going anywhere. Not until we'd checked out Ometochtli's other bodyguards.

I'd almost reached the end of my list when Takun came over with a piece of paper. It had a radio code scrawled on it. "For you, Colhua. Next time tell the guy to get your number right."

"Who was it?" I asked.

"He didn't say. But he had one of those voices—like a nobleman's."

I hadn't been on the radio so much since the day I took down the High Priest. Still, I called the number Takun had given me. When someone picked up, I said, "This is Investigator Colhua."

"I need to speak with you about Ueman Zaniya," said the

party on the other end. Takun was right—it sounded like a nobleman.

"Who's this?" I asked.

It was a question to which I didn't always get an answer. This time, I did: "Toltecatl Yayauhco."

I knew the name. Yayauhco was the mate of Yolotli Yayauhco, the daughter of Tupec Cualli, the First Administrator of Aztlan. Not one of Aztlan's noblemen, though Yayauhco associated with them often enough.

"You're holding Zaniya as a murder suspect," he said, "but Zaniya didn't kill anyone last night. He couldn't have." A pause. "He was with *me*."

"With *you*," I said.

"Yes. At my apartment."

"We found him at his mother's place."

"He went there early this morning. She had a problem with her hip and he was concerned."

I broached a subject I had to broach: "If you don't mind my asking—"

"We have a *relationship*, Investigator. As you can imagine, it's not something I care to advertise."

Because extramarital affairs were scandalous, and the First Administrator's term of office was up for renewal. A scandal at this time would be a problem for him, to say the least.

Not that Yayauhco's indiscretion, or how it reflected on the First Administrator, was any of *my* business. I didn't work for the Mirror. I was just an Investigator trying to find a murderer.

"You understand," I said, "that lying to an Investigator is a crime in the eyes of the Emperor?"

"I do."

"And you're sticking with your story?"

"I am," said Yayauhco.

I took down his statement.

• • •

Necalli shrugged. "We could hold him anyway," he said of Zaniya. "At least until morning, when we'll be told we have to let him go."

It was the Emperor's Law: We couldn't detain anyone for long without charging them with a crime. And we didn't have enough on Love Boy to do that.

"It's all right," I said. "I never thought he was the killer anyway."

In the meantime, Suguey and Izcuin had finished their research. Xiomara, it turned out, was the only one of Ometochtli's guards who fit our criteria.

"Thanks," I told the rookies.

I sat down and read the file on Culanto Xiomara. Apparently, Inave had employed him as a "merchant liaison"—a title bankers typically gave to their enforcers. If someone borrowed money from Inave and couldn't pay it back on time, they would receive a visit from Xiomara or someone like him.

Then he'd gone to work for Ometochtli. But after that, he'd left the banking business—gotten himself what looked like some legitimate jobs. He'd even worked for a while at the Mirror, of all places.

Then he vanished. There was no working radio code for him, no address. No easy way to get hold of him, even if it was to ask him about a murder.

Fortunately for my purposes, Xiomara had done time for public drunkenness a bunch of cycles earlier, when he was a kid, so his file contained more than just his employment record. It listed the octli houses he'd frequented in the Merchant City, more often than not a place called The Angry Armadillo.

After he served his sentence, he'd gone back there on a regular basis, drinking enough to make merry but never enough to commit an offense that would put him back in the Prison House.

I sat back from my Mirror station and stretched. It was dark out. The octli houses in the Merchant City would be wide open.

If Xiomara was at the Armadillo that evening, I would see him there.

• • •

It didn't take me long to find Xiomara in The Angry Armadillo.

He was standing at the bar, a mug of octli in front of him, conversing loudly with the barmaid. Xiomara was a big guy, with broad shoulders and thickly muscled arms. But a lot of security guards fit that description.

I watched to see if he had any friends with him that could have complicated my mission there. As far as I could tell, he was alone. Before that could change, I walked up to him and said, "Culanto Xiomara?"

He turned to me, eyes narrowing beneath a ledge of a brow. "Who wants to know?"

I showed him my bracelet. "My name is Colhua," I said. "I'm an Investi—"

Before I could get the rest out, he shoved me—hard enough to send me sprawling—and made for the back door.

I was able to grab the bar to keep myself from hitting the floor, but it took me a moment to get my feet underneath me. Once I did, I took off after Xiomara.

The streets were straight and broad in that part of the Merchant City, and empty of people. I had no trouble tracking Xiomara as he fled.

He was fast, I saw. But I was faster. Not as fast as when I'd played in the Arena, but fast enough to close the gap between us little by little.

At one point, Xiomara veered right down a perpendicular street. It didn't help him. I could still see him in the glow of the streetlights. His stride was getting ragged, a sign he was tiring.

I was going to catch up to him. It was only a matter of time.

Xiomara pushed himself hard for another minute or so. Then he slowed down. By then, his legs probably felt like lead. Octli could do that to you even when you weren't running from the Law.

A few more steps, I saw, and I'd have him.

Suddenly, Xiomara stopped and turned—and drove a punch at me meant to put my lights out. But I'd chased suspects before, so his move wasn't entirely unexpected. I ducked—leaving him nothing to hit except empty air.

Then it was my turn. Already inside his guard, I drove my fist up into his chin, snapping his head back. He staggered but he didn't fall, so I struck him again—this time putting all my weight behind the blow.

It sent him sprawling headlong into the wall behind him.

I heard a crack—presumably the sound of Xiomara's head hitting a brick—and watched him crumple to the ground.

Even then, he tried to push himself up. But it was no use. He didn't have enough fight left in him.

I took the opportunity to buzz my backups—Takun and Suguey—whom I had posted a block from The Armadillo in either direction. By the time they arrived, I had yanked Xiomara's hands behind him and wrapped my rope manacles around his wrists.

Together, we pulled him to his feet and walked him in the direction of the rail line. It was funny, I thought, how things worked out. I was about to lose one suspect that evening—but just like *that* I'd gained another.

• • •

Xiomara didn't look happy as he sat in one of our interrogation rooms, facing me across a wooden table with a rip in his shirt and an ice compress on his swollen lip. Then again, I wouldn't have been happy either.

An hour earlier, he'd been looking forward to a night of

octli-fueled revelry. Now he was facing another stay in the Prison House.

"You know why you're here," I said.

He shrugged. "I have no idea."

"Which, I guess, is why you assaulted an Investigator and tried to run away."

"I had too much octli. I wasn't thinking straight."

"Innocent men don't run from Investigators, too much octli or not. Killers, on the other hand..."

His eyes flashed. "I didn't kill anyone."

"I forgot. You're an innocent man. You just had too much to drink. And on the night Molli Inave was stabbed to death? Too much to drink that time too?"

Xiomara said it again, even more insistently: "I didn't *kill* anyone!"

"Then who did?" I asked.

He glared at me, probably wishing he could cave my head in about then, and said—unhelpfully—"I don't know."

• • •

The Emperor's Law could be very inconvenient.

By the time I arrived at the Interrogation Center the next morning, we had received word that Xiomara had to be released too—no later than that afternoon, in fact. Quetzalli and others had worked through the night to turn up anything that might incriminate the guy but had come up empty.

The lab analysis we had received didn't give them a lot of help. The only prints we had turned up in Inave's place were Inave's and those of his cleaning woman, and the blood was Inave's alone.

Still, Xiomara had run from me for a reason. I couldn't prove it had anything to do with Inave's murder but there was *something* at play there. All my instincts told me so.

Then it occurred to me—I might have another source of information when it came to Xiomara. With that in mind, I called Teicu Inave.

"It's Investigator Colhua," I told her. "I've got a question for you."

"Of course," she said. "Anything."

She sounded sluggish. Had she been drinking? If it was in the privacy of her home, it was her own business.

Even so, I made a mental note to check up on her from time to time. Her father had had a habit of imbibing too much. It wasn't crazy to wonder if she had one too. And grief could turn a habit, if that was what she had, into something worse.

"Did you know a man named Culanto Xiomara?" I asked. "He worked for your father some cycles back."

"Of course," Teicu said. "I knew all my father's enforcers. When I was little, some of them sat and watched my Mirror shows with me."

"Did Xiomara?"

"No. He couldn't sit still long enough. He was always moving, walking around."

"When he left your father, would you say it was on good terms?"

"I think so. I mean, I didn't hear any disagreements. Is Xiomara a suspect?"

"I can't say," I told her. But she knew. If I was asking about him, I had to have a reason.

"What else can you tell me about him?"

Silence for a moment. Then: "He had a friend. They were always together. The man's name was Ilhica."

"First name?"

"I don't remember. But he was big. Tall, I mean. Nose like an eagle. Wherever you saw Xiomara, Ilhica was there too. I think they went to octli houses together." A pause. "I didn't like him."

"Ilhica?"

"Right."

"Why not?"

"I just didn't. Maybe it was his shirt. Blue, you know? Made of nice linen, but who wears a blue shirt?"

Blue shirts were rare, sure. But to dislike someone for wearing them? It seemed excessive.

"What else?" I asked.

Teicu didn't give me an answer right away. Finally, she said, "Uxmal."

I didn't understand. Uxmal was a pyramid on the way to Yautepec, built in ancient days. It was visited mostly by students.

"What about it?" I asked.

"That was one of the shows I watched on the Mirror. It was called Uxmal."

"Anything else about *Xiomara*?"

She didn't answer. She just shook her head from side to side.

Love Boy had told me Teicu had problems. I was beginning

to see what he meant. And if she wasn't all there, I couldn't depend on much that she told me.

But I could track down Ilhica and see what *he* could tell me.

• • •

The Angry Armadillo wouldn't open again until that evening. Fortunately, I didn't have to wait that long. There was always activity in an octli house, whether it was someone sweeping the floor or accepting shipments of food and drink or just going over the account book.

When I got there, I saw a guy behind the bar, washing glasses—a slight man with a wisp of a chin beard. The door was unlocked so I walked in and sat down in front of him.

"We won't be open until after dark," he told me.

"I want to ask you a couple of questions," I said, and showed him my bracelet.

The guy stiffened at the sight of it. "I stay within the Law, Investigator. If someone's had too much, I cut them off."

"I don't doubt it," I said. "I'm not here about how much octli you serve."

That set him at ease. "Then what?"

"You tend bar here?"

"Sometimes."

"Do you know Culanto Xiomara?"

"I do," he said. "And I watch him like an owl."

"Then you know who he drinks with."

"Most times, no one. He just sits and talks with the barmaid."

"And other times?" I could see he was reluctant to tell me, but I wasn't going anywhere until he did.

"A guy. I don't know his name."

"Is he tall? Nose like an eagle?"

He knew who I meant. "Yes."

"When was the last time he came in?"

"Last night."

"Was Xiomara with him?"

The guy said he was.

"Do you know what they talked about?"

"I don't."

"You're certain?" In other words, he'd be held accountable if I found out he knew and hadn't said so.

"I'm certain," he said. Which meant he probably was.

"Thanks for your help," I told him.

Before I left, I got his name. Sometimes people remembered things after they'd had a while to think about them.

Or after they'd considered the consequences of not remembering.

• • •

In the rail carriage taking me back to the Interrogation Center, something occurred to me: There might be another angle on this case. And Inave himself had given it to me.

It might be nothing, the ravings of a man who'd had too much to drink. But I couldn't pass up a lead, no matter how tenuous.

I called Izcuin. "Do you remember when I was talking with Inave the other night?"

"Sure," said Izcuin.

"He said he was going to give me a tip. He tried to remember a name but he kept coming up with the wrong one."

"Right."

"Do you recall the names he mentioned?"

A pause. "I think so. He said Tomatl at one point. And some other name…"

"Tamalii."

"Right! Tamalii. But he made a face because neither Tomatl nor Tamalii was the name he was trying to recall."

"Which was…?"

Another pause. "Tlaco?"

Yes, I thought. "That's *it*."

"He said Tlaco was a bad man. But that he was dead, so you didn't have to watch out for him."

"And that the god smiled on his work."

"You think there's a lead there?" Izcuin sounded skeptical.

"You don't?" I asked—partly to get another perspective and partly to help him develop his sense of intuition.

"I don't know. I mean…Inave didn't exactly have his wits about him."

"But it was on Inave's mind the night before he was killed. And we don't have much else to go on."

"So we have to check it out," Izcuin concluded. "But—"

"How?" I said.

It was a good question.

• • •

I was still pondering it when I got back to the Interrogation Center.

Had I ever seen a smiling god? I didn't think so.

Likenesses of the Divine Ones were in lots of places: murals in the lobbies of office buildings, signs in rail stations, colorful drawings on cereal boxes. Not to mention on the Mirror.

But as I recalled, they weren't smiling in these depictions. They were sneering, or snarling, or grimacing in pain, if they wore any expression at all.

So what was Inave talking about?

Quetzalli passed me on my way to my desk. "Necalli wants to see you," she said.

"Thanks," I told her, and altered my course to end up in my boss's office.

He was bent over his Mirror screen, reading something.

"You wanted to see me?" I asked.

He beckoned me over so I could see what he'd been looking at. "Take a peek."

I sat down at his terminal. It showed me an advisory from the bankers' network—the one bankers had set up cycles ago so they could let other bankers know what clients they had signed.

It was a helpful thing in those days. When a banker saw a client had been taken, he knew it would be useless to go after that client—at least for a while—and he would put his resources into trying to grab someone else.

These days, things were different. If an announcement was made, it was a warning: Poach at your own risk.

It could also be an expression of hubris. Like anyone else, bankers liked to one-up each other. Or an advertisement. If a banker hauled in an imposing client, other clients might look his way too.

Of course, the network didn't name names. It never had. But the bankers and businesspeople who subscribed to it—we Investigators among them—knew precisely whom an announcement was talking about.

The advisory on Necalli's screen was from Ometochtli. He'd secured a new contract. A big one. In fact, the biggest I'd ever heard of.

It looked to me like Ometochtli had snared a nobleman. I would have said such a thing was impossible—nobles had other means of getting beans, usually from other noblemen. But as I'd learned lately, even nobles ran into debts they couldn't handle.

I glanced at Necalli. "Ometochtli didn't mention this kind of contract when I spoke with him."

Necalli shrugged. "It might not have been finalized yet."

True. And Ometochtli wouldn't have let anyone know a deal was imminent before he nailed it down.

I sat back from Necalli's terminal. "Impressive."

"To say the least," he said. "If it's legitimate, Ometochtli's set for life. And it had to have been in the works for a while."

"Which makes it unlikely he'd have bothered with a small potato like Inave, regardless of what offenses Inave committed against him."

"I'd say so."

"Or maybe," I suggested, "it was more important to him than *ever* that he scare off the competition."

"Ometochtli's the only banker who can handle a contract

of this size. So, really, there *is* no competition."

"What about a syndicate? A bunch of bankers getting together?"

Necalli chuckled. "Bankers getting *together*?"

I had to admit it sounded unlikely. "So Ometochtli's off the hook?"

"Unless something comes up to indicate otherwise."

We were losing suspects hand over hand. Which would have been all right if we were getting any closer to identifying the killer.

But we weren't.

• • •

The more I thought about it, the more I wondered if there was something useful in Inave's ramblings at the Reunion Center.

Unfortunately, Tlaco was a common last name as well as a common first name. There had to be tens of thousands of each in the Empire. And if this particular Tlaco was dead, as Inave had said, it made the task even harder. I couldn't go through every dead Tlaco in our records, looking for a connection to Inave or his killer.

Of course, Inave had given me a couple of tools to narrow the search: The idea that Tlaco was a bad man, at least in Inave's estimate, and the notion that the gods smiled on Tlaco's work.

What was the nature of Tlaco's work? I had no clue. Where could I find it? No notion of that either.

I asked around the Interrogation Center. After all, we Investigators covered the city pretty thoroughly. No one had any idea what I was talking about.

I needed a specialist, I thought. Someone who might know Tlaco or his work or, Lands of the Dead, where I could at least find a smiling god in a city the size of Aztlan.

I was still considering the problem when Takun came to stand beside me. I looked up at him, wondering why he'd decided to visit.

"You're looking lovely today," I told him.

Takun didn't return my greeting—not even with his usual morning insult. He just put a big wad of wax paper down on the corner of my desk. Inside it was something long.

And black.

"What's this?" I asked.

"With any luck," Takun said, "it's your murder weapon."

Carefully, I unwrapped the wax paper. With each layer I took away, I got a better look at what was inside. By the time I had one layer left, I didn't need to do any more unwrapping.

It was a knife. The kind used for camping, not preparing food. And it was full of black, crusted blood.

I looked up at Takun. "Where did it come from?"

"A woman brought it in. She owns a bakery on Coatlicue Street. She was putting out the garbage in the alley behind her shop when she found *this* in her trash can. She was scared we'd think she had something to do with it."

If there were any justice in the world, there would be fingerprints in all that dried blood. Maybe on the clean parts of the handle too. If some of them matched Inave's prints, the others could be his murderer's.

"Don't say I never gave you anything," said Takun.

"Never again," I said, and sent the knife to the lab, wax paper and all.

It was after I did so, as I was thinking I was finally getting somewhere in at least one part of my investigation, that a name came to me.

• • •

Yoli Nahuatl was an archivist at the University of Aztlan.

He had been a friend of my father when they were growing up. Like a big brother, as Nahuatl was a few cycles older. I remember, as a child, visiting Nahuatl at his place overlooking the River. He and I would gaze out the window and count the gulls wheeling on the air currents high over the water, looking for fish to scoop in their beaks.

"You're a smart boy," he used to tell me.

I didn't remember why he said it, but I could picture him saying so. Not just once, but every time we went to visit him: "You're a smart boy, Maxtla."

Of course, Nahuatl was the smart one. A person couldn't become an archivist unless he was an acknowledged expert in some aspect of our civilization. In Nahuatl's case, the history of architecture in the Empire.

He'd won awards for the books he wrote on the gods' presence in our public works. Works of all kinds—residences, offices, temples, and so on—as well as bridges, and ball courts, and the statuary found in every square and outdoor market.

It was a lot of information to command. But Nahuatl commanded it.

Shortly before my father's death, he and Nahuatl had a falling out. I asked about it, first as a boy and then as a man, but I was never given the details. All I knew was that my aunt Xoco refused to say Nahuatl's name.

Out of respect for my father, as well as my aunt, I never reached out to Nahuatl. For all I knew, Nahuatl wanted it that way as much as they did.

But I wasn't thinking about him now for personal reasons. I had a mystery to solve and only the most cryptic of clues left, and Nahuatl was better equipped than anyone to give me a hand with it.

He lived in District Twelve, in a modest, almost shabby old pyramid that probably appealed to him in a way I couldn't see. I remembered his building being a lot nicer to look at. Of course, I was a child at the time. I was impressed by things that no longer impressed me.

Putting that aside, I knocked on Nahuatl's door. After a moment, I heard footfalls on the other side. A moment after that, the door opened.

And there was Nahuatl. Heavier than I remembered. And older. Gray around the temples. Still, it was him, the figure from my childhood with the round face and the space between his front teeth, and it made me smile to see him.

Nahuatl smiled too. "Maxtla? It's been a long time."

Not "Investigator." But considering the place he had held in my family, I was comfortable with his calling me by my given name.

"A long time, all right."

"Please…" He stood aside and indicated a couple of chairs in an anteroom, on either side of a standing lamp. "Let's sit down like civilized people."

I went in and we sat. "How are you?" I asked.

"Well enough. And you? And your aunt?"

"Fine, both of us."

He frowned. "I was sad when your father died."

"It was a sad day," I said.

"And your mother…"

"Sad as well."

For a moment, we sat in silence. Then he said, "Can I get you something? A drink, maybe? You used to like mango juice."

I had forgotten. "No, thanks."

"So…"

"Why am I here? I'm pursuing a case, and I have a problem I'm hoping you can help me with."

"Of course," Nahuatl said. Did I catch a glimmer of disappointment in his eyes? I wasn't sure.

"The other day," I began, "we found a man named Inave dead in his bed. Stabbed six times." I wasn't accustomed to sharing the details of an investigation, but if Nahuatl was going to help me, he might need them. "As the gods would have it, I saw Inave the night before he was killed. He said something to me…it may be a clue to the identity of his killer or it may be nothing. But leads are scarce in this case, so…"

"Talk to me, Maxtla."

"Inave mentioned someone named Tlaco—though he was a little drunk and he was having trouble recalling the name, so

I can't be sure it wasn't something else."

Nahuatl chuckled. "That's a good start. What did he say about this Tlaco?"

"That he was a dangerous man. Also that he was dead."

"All right…"

"Also that the god smiles on Tlaco's work. But he didn't say which god. And he didn't say what kind of work."

Nahuatl frowned. "Not much to go on."

"I wish there were more. But if there were, I wouldn't have asked to see you. No one knows the city as well as you do."

He nodded. "That's my reputation, whether I've earned it or not."

"So…do you think you can help?"

"Give me some time," he said." I'll dig a little and see what I can come up with."

For the time being, it was all I could hope for. I thanked him.

"Of course," he said.

On my way out, he patted me on the back. "Let's have dinner some time. You know, catch up."

"Sounds good," I said.

To me, at least.

My aunt, I suspected, would think otherwise.

• • •

I was sitting in a rail carriage bound for my office, the lowering light of Tonatiuh in my eyes, when Necalli buzzed me.

"The lab found only one set of prints on the knife," he said. "They're Inave's."

So no sign that Zaniya had handled the knife. Or Xiomara, for that matter. Or one of Ometochtli's men.

Analysis of the blood on the weapon would take longer. But I didn't expect it to help. If the murderer had known enough to keep his prints off the thing, it was even less likely we'd find his blood.

"The gods," said Necalli, "aren't exactly showering us with their gifts."

"They're not," I agreed.

I told Necalli about Nahuatl. "It may not go anywhere, I know. But—"

"It's better than sitting here and sharpening our hand sticks. Let me know if your friend finds anything interesting."

"I will," I said, and cut the connection.

Necalli hadn't sounded optimistic about the smiling god angle. But then, why should he? Even Inave might not have known what he was talking about.

I was halfway back to the Interrogation Center when I got another call. This one was from Teicu Inave.

"Investigator?" she said. "I think I know who killed my father."

• • •

Inave's daughter didn't want to elaborate on her statement over the radio. She said she didn't trust the privacy of our connection.

I suggested that she meet me at the Interrogation Center again, but she didn't like that idea. I guessed her opinion of it had changed after she'd been there.

"At my place," she insisted this time.

It took me only half an hour to get there by rail. When Teicu opened the door, I saw the red rims around her eyes. She looked like she had been crying.

"Investigator," she said, a catch in her voice.

"Are you all right?" I asked.

"I'm a mess." And she was. Her clothes looked like she had slept in them. She beckoned me inside.

Unlike Teicu herself, her place was spotless, tastefully decorated, and in perfect order. I guessed that her cleaning person had shown up since we last spoke.

"Please sit down," Teicu said.

I sat. "You said—"

"That I knew who my father's murderer was. And I do. His name is..." She sobbed, and sobbed again, and tears traced their way down her cheeks. "Mishtli Chapolin."

"Chapolin," I echoed. I'd heard the name before, though I couldn't remember where. "And how do you know he killed your father?"

"Mishtli *hated* my father. He said it over and over again. He hated the way my father treated him."

I'd heard that sentiment from her before, and in much the same words. "How did Chapolin and your father know each other?"

"We were going out," said Inave's daughter.

"You and Chapolin? When was this?"

"Just after I broke off my relationship with Ueman."

Zaniya had said he and Teicu were starting to do better, as if the relationship hadn't been broken off at all. But then, he'd been fooling around on the side, according to Yayauhco, so it was hard to know what kind of relationship Zaniya was talking about.

"When did that happen?" I asked, trying to establish a timeline.

Teicu sniffed. "About a moon ago."

Last time I saw her, I'd asked if she knew of anyone who would want to hurt her father. She'd said she didn't. Yet now she was accusing Chapolin of Inave's murder.

So what had changed?

"And why," I asked, "did your father treat Chapolin so poorly?"

This time I let *her* say it: "My father didn't think Chapolin would make a good mate for me."

"I see," I said. "And you think Chapolin hated your father enough to murder him?"

"I do." The tears fell again. "Gods help me, I *do*."

In Zaniya's case she had only speculated. This time she seemed *sure*.

"Thanks for telling me," I said.

"Of course," Teicu breathed. "I just want to see justice done."

Maybe, I thought. Or maybe she'd just discovered a way to punish guys who didn't like her the way she liked *them*.

Which didn't mean there wasn't a kernel of truth in what she'd told me. Zaniya had confirmed that Inave mistreated him. Had Inave abused Chapolin too?

Maybe the banker abused *all* his daughter's boyfriends. It was possible. Some fathers were like that.

But had he abused Chapolin to the point where he went to

Inave's place and stabbed the banker six times—then wrapped the murder weapon in wax paper and dumped it in a trash can?

That was the question.

And until I had the answer, I had to run down every lead I could.

• • •

I knew I'd heard the name Chapolin before.

A Mirror search showed that his father had been a tax collector, and a powerful one, before he died. Then his fortune had gone to his wife and her three sons from a previous marriage.

Mishtli Chapolin was the youngest son. There wasn't much to read about him. Just that he'd gotten a job in his father's office a couple of cycles earlier.

No surprise there. Sons often followed their father's trails. God of flowers, that's what *I* had done.

The older sons were a different story. They had no jobs. Nor had they ever had them. From what I could see, neither of them wanted to work at *anything*.

But then, why should they? Their family had enough beans to last them several lifetimes.

The middle son, Nama, was the most intriguing. He'd been arrested on at least two occasions for assault—once in an octli house a cycle earlier and more recently in a private ball court. A police investigation in the second instance revealed a pattern of lesser incidents, fueled by anger at what he saw as insults.

I shared the information with Necalli. "Interesting," he said as he delved a little deeper into Nama's file. "In neither case was he charged with anything."

"I know," I said.

It wouldn't have been the first time a wealthy parent paid her son's victims to drop their charges. There was nothing illegal, after all, about settling assault cases outside the courts.

Privilege, I thought.

It had served Nama Chapolin well. Gotten him off the hook when he'd let his tendency toward violence get the better of him.

But it wouldn't keep him from becoming a person of interest in my investigation.

• • •

Mishtli Chapolin was easy for the Merchant City police to find. In fact, his office was right around the corner from Ehe Ometochtli's.

He was smiling when he showed up at the Interrogation Center, escorted by a couple of officers in red vests. I noted Mishtli's appearance—piercing eyes and a blue-black feather dangling from his ear.

"Investigator," he said cheerfully, as if he were on a tour of the place.

"We'll go downstairs," I said.

When we arrived at my favorite table, the officers left us. Mishtli took the place in at a glance. "You like it down here?"

"Well enough. Have a seat."

We sat down.

"You need some windows," Mishtli observed. "To let the light in."

"We're in a basement," I pointed out.

He shrugged. But then, he came from a place in society where all things were possible. Including, I supposed, windows in basement offices.

"Let's talk about Teicu Inave," I said.

He looked intrigued. "If you like."

"She said you and she were dating."

Mishtli laughed. "Is that why you called me down here?"

"*Are* you?" I asked.

"Teicu and I saw each other a couple of times. That's about it."

There was an undercurrent of disdain in his voice that rubbed me the wrong way. More so, maybe, because it was Inave's daughter he was talking about.

"She made it sound like it was more than that."

"Teicu's been been known to say all kinds of things." He pointed to his head. "You know she has problems, right? She loses touch with reality, on and off. She has ever since she was a teen-ager." He smiled to himself. "She likes to make love in odd places. *Public* places. In alleyways. And building lobbies where there's no doorman on duty."

"I get the idea," I said. Zaniya had said Teicu had problems too, but he'd been gentleman enough not to go into detail.

I recalled the way Teicu looked when I showed up at her door. How disheveled she'd been. Was she even more unbalanced than I'd imagined?

"She's seen physicians," Mishtli said. "Plenty of them. She mentioned a couple to me. I can give you their names."

Dutifully, I took them down. After all, I might need to know more about Teicu and her illness down the road.

A question came to me that I didn't have to ask. It had more to do with my relationship with Inave than the case I was working on.

I asked it anyway: "Teicu had a history of mental instability...and yet you decided to carry on a relationship with her?"

Mishtli shrugged. "She's good-looking—you can see that. And exciting. I never intended to get into anything permanent with her."

It was the attitude of someone who had never been held accountable for anything.

Someone who had been educated in the best schools beans could buy, but had never been taught to value the feelings of others.

Privilege, I thought again.

I had an urge to grab Mishtli by his tunic front and let him know people weren't his playthings. But I was an Investigator for the Empire, so I said, "That's all for now. If I need to speak with you again, I'll buzz you."

"Then I can go? he asked.

"You can go," I confirmed.

I led the way back up to the lobby. Mishtli had been brought in by himself but since then someone had shown up to wait for him.

An attractive young woman in a tight dress, who threw her arms around Mishtli as soon as he got close enough. "You all right?" she asked.

"Never better," Mishtli told her. "Ready for dinner?"

She smiled suggestively. "Sure. And afterwards, we can have some *dessert*."

Mishtli looked back at me and grinned, as if to say: *Why would I kill somebody when I live like* this?

• • •

I had dinner plans as well. Mine were with Aunt Xoco.

As I rode the rail to her place, a gourd of octli in one hand and a bag of limes in the other, I felt a pang of guilt. After all, I had betrayed my aunt's trust.

She'd made it clear over time that she wanted no part of Nahuatl. That he wasn't to be spoken of, much less spoken *to*.

And yet I had called him. Gone to his place. Visited with him.

I hadn't done it on a whim. I'd had good reason. Still, I'd committed a breach. And it would be worse if I tried to keep it a secret.

As I watched the sun drop toward the horizon, I thought about the best way to broach the subject of Nahuatl. For one reason or another, none of the approaches that occurred to me seemed advisable.

When I arrived at my aunt's door, I still hadn't hit on a strategy. I knocked anyway.

As soon as Aunt Xoco opened the door, she said, "You're late, Maxtla. Sit down before everything gets cold."

I walked into my aunt's eating room, where I'd shared so many holiday dinners with her, first as a child and then as an adult, and sat as I'd been instructed. A moment later, there were three steaming platters of food on the table, joining the smaller plates of maize cakes and bundled vegetables she'd put out before I arrived.

"I hope you're hungry," my aunt said.

I looked at her. "Do I ever show up *not* hungry?"

As she sat down opposite me, she hummed to herself. Not loudly but happily, I thought. Even the jangling of her silver bracelet, handed down in our family from generation to generation, sounded a little happier than usual.

I didn't know *why*. And if this time was like others, I might *never* know. Aunt Xoco was like that.

But I could tell she was happy, and I hated the prospect of putting a dent in that happiness. So, like the coward I was, I waited with the news about Nahuatl.

In the meantime, Aunt Xoco removed the cover from one of the platters—the orange, blue, and white one with the image of Patecatl, her birth god—and said, "I tried something new."

"Oh?" I said.

The exposed platter was full of little orange duck legs. Aunt Xoco pointed to my empty plate. "Take."

I picked up the platter and placed a bunch of the duck legs on my plate. Then I put the platter back in the center of the table.

"Well done," said my aunt.

"I've had practice," I told her.

The duck legs were delicious. Sweet and spicy by turns, with a hint of nutmeg that lingered after everything else was gone.

"What do you think?" Aunt Xoco asked.

"They're wonderful," I told her.

Her eyes narrowed. "You're not just being kind?"

"No," I said, "I mean it. I'm adding it to my list of my favorite Aunt Xoco dishes."

A smile of satisfaction spread across her face. "Gods be praised."

"The gods," I said, "only wish they could cook the way *you* do."

My aunt's eyes opened wide. "No one prospers by offending the gods, Maxtla." But her horror seemed tempered with a guilty pleasure at the comparison.

"And what's *in* this heavenly offering?" I asked.

Aunt Xoco shrugged. "What do you think?"

It was a game we'd begun to play lately—my guessing what she had put into a particular preparation. "Chili," I said.

Grudgingly, she said, "Yes."

I licked my lips. "Honey?"

Again, grudgingly: "Yes."

"Achiote."

"Yes. And...?"

I had reached the end of my culinary expertise, as she knew I would. "You've got me."

My aunt smiled. "Too bad for you."

I didn't let my failure spoil my appreciation of the beaver and the venison that flanked the duck legs. Otherwise, we would *both* have been disappointed in ourselves. By the time it was dark outside, I had finished two helpings of each, and I still hadn't decided how I would tell my aunt about Nahuatl.

I watched her stand at her counter and wrap the uneaten

portions of beaver and venison in wax paper, which she would send home with me. It was her favorite thing to do, even more than the preparation of the food in the first place.

I couldn't see Aunt Xoco's face because her back was to me, but I could feel her contentment. How could I salt her maize soil when she was so happy? Then again, how could I leave without letting her know what I'd done?

Finally, I just said it: "I saw Nahuatl."

I could see my aunt's shoulders tense up. "On the street?" she asked.

"No." I had made a wound. No sense in stitching it when there was still dirt in it. "I went to his pyramid. I'm working on a case and I thought he could help me."

Aunt Xoco didn't turn around. She just kept wrapping the leftovers.

"I know," I said, "that you don't talk to him anymore. You never said why. My parents either."

"How is he?" my aunt asked, refocusing the conversation.

"He looked good," I said. "A little older but the same guy. I think he misses us."

A pause. For a moment, I thought Aunt Xoco might say she missed Nahuatl too. Then she said, "The venison was tough, wasn't it? I have to tell the meat monger I'm disappointed." A hard right though my comment had gone left.

"The venison was delicious," I told her. "No need to scold the meat monger. And Nahuatl suggested that we have dinner some time."

My words hung in the air for a heartbeat. Then another.

"You know," my aunt said, "I don't think I'm feeling well. I hope you don't mind cleaning up."

And she did something she'd never done before in all the time I'd known her: She left me sitting there alone at her table.

• • •

I was on my way home, thinking about the way I had disappointed Aunt Xoco, when I got a call on my radio. "Colhua," I said.

"My name's Ilhica," said the voice on the other end. "I understand you've been looking for me."

Ilhica, I thought. *Xiomara's friend*. Maybe the gods had decided to take pity on me after all.

"I want to ask you some questions," I said. "The kind that are best asked face to face."

"That's the way I like it too," came the response. "There's a restaurant in the Merchant City called The Jaguar."

I didn't know it. And I didn't like the idea of walking into a place Ilhica knew better than I did.

I told him to meet me in the Interrogation Center instead.

"There are things I need to tell you," he said, "that are best told outside the Interrogation Center. When you hear them, you'll know what I mean."

I thought about insisting. But Ilhica wasn't a suspect, and neither was Xiomara at that point. So, while Ilhica couldn't outright lie to me in an interrogation, he didn't have to say much either.

And I wanted him to say a lot. "Somewhere else in the Merchant City, then."

"How about The Serpent Skirt? On Xochipilli Street?"

That place I knew. It was friendly, law-abiding—a favorite venue for retirement parties, including a couple I'd attended for police officers. The last place that would lend itself to some treachery.

And Ilhica's comment about preferring to talk outside the Interrogation Center had piqued my curiosity.

"All right," I said. And I set a time for us to meet.

• • •

The Serpent Skirt was louder and more crowded than I remembered. However, it had private booths upstairs where patrons could carry on a conversation.

Ilhica was waiting for me in one of them, wearing one of the blue linen shirts Inave's daughter didn't like. This one had an image of Huehuecoyotl, the god of music and dance, embroidered on the shoulder in red and green threads.

There were plates of food on the table in front of Ilhica: rolled slices of broiled venison, crayfish deep-fried in pigweed batter, and spiced corn cakes, along with a pitcher of cane water and a couple of mugs.

"My treat," he said. Before I could comment, he tapped the image of Huehuecoyotl on his shoulder and said, "I'm a musician."

Musicians were paid well in Aztlan. Especially those who performed at the parties of the right noblemen.

My first inclination was to decline Ilhica's offering. On the other foot, I'd been taught since infancy that it was an affront to Mixcoatl to let food go to waste, so I took a couple of pieces of crayfish and a corn cake, and put them on my plate.

They were tastier than I'd expected. Enough so that I made a mental note to return to The Serpent Skirt with Calli.

Ilhica didn't take anything.

"Not hungry?" I asked.

He shrugged. "I ate already." Yet there was clearly more food there than I could consume. "Maybe," he added, "you know a place that can use the leftovers."

"In fact," I said, "I do." The temple a few blocks from my pyramid delivered meals to the elderly. "But why not take them somewhere yourself?"

"You were in the ball court," said Ilhica. "You had certain superstitions? Well, musicians have them too—those of us who are serious, anyway. We play better when we're generous to others, and even more so when we encourage others to be generous."

I hadn't heard that one. I said so.

"You need to spend more time with musicians," Ilhica said. "So...I understand you've been asking about me."

"I have," I said.

"Because of my friendship with Xiomara."

I didn't comment. Xiomara was under investigation, after all.

"You suspect him of something because you don't know him," Ilhica said. "He's not what you think he is."

"What is he?" I asked.

Ilhica tilted his head, as if sizing me up. "What I'm about to tell you...it has to stay between us."

"I can't give you any assurance of that. It's my job to expose crimes. If Xiomara's guilty of one, I'll pursue it."

Ilhica frowned—but he didn't leave. Despite what I'd said, he must have seen a benefit in staying to talk with me.

"All right," he said finally. "You know Tlazolteotl House?"

I did. "It helps those who've left the Empire."

It was a polite way of describing such people, if a misleading one. In fact, they continued to live within the borders of Mexica. However, they had given up their citizenship, along with their jobs and everything their work paid for.

It was difficult to understand why. In most cases, the change in them took place without warning. They just left everything that had been important to them, even their families in some instances.

They still walked the streets, still felt the rays of the sun. But they couldn't afford a place to live any longer, so they slept where they could and ate what they could find.

Tlazolteotl House, which sat on the edge of the Merchant City, tried to help such people. It gave them food when they were hungry and a roof when they needed one. It wasn't clear where the funding for the place came from, but it was rumored to be the project of some noble family.

"Some who benefit from Tlazolteotl House are debtors," said Ilhica. "In fact, their despair of paying off their debts is often what drove them over the edge. But, technically, debtors are criminals."

It wasn't news to me.

Then Ilhica said, "Three nights a week, Xiomara and I work at Tlazolteotl House unloading boxes of food."

I looked for signs he was joking. I didn't see any.

"We don't get paid," he added, "so there's no record of it."

Even harder to believe. I hadn't imagined Xiomara was the charitable type.

"Which is good," said Ilhica, "because Xiomara did time in the Prison House, and he's got to watch who he gets involved with. The people who come to Tlazolteotl, the ones in debt...I don't have to tell you, right? Associating with them can get Xiomara another sentence.

"But that doesn't stop him." Ilhica leaned closer to me. "Because when Xiomara was little, his father was one of those people. One day the guy just walked out the door—no explanation—and wasn't heard from again.

"So Xiomara...he knows something about those who've left the Empire, and he knows even more about their families. And despite what you may think of him, that's why he works at Tlazolteotl three nights a week.

"Unfortunately, he has to look over his shoulder those nights. For guys like you, who maybe can't see past their oaths to why Xiomara's doing what he's doing."

I understood now why Ilhica hadn't wanted to meet in the Interrogation Center. He didn't want to take a chance that someone would overhear what he was saying, and feel compelled to arrest Xiomara for it.

"When my friend saw your bracelet at the Angry Armadillo, he panicked. He thought you were coming after him about Tlazolteotl House. Not because he killed someone, for the gods' sakes, but because he was helping people like his father." Ilhica leaned back. "And that's the truth."

In the next booth, someone laughed. There was a clatter of dishes being placed on a table, a scrape of soles on the wooden floor as a couple of patrons headed for the stairs.

I wasn't sure what I'd expected to hear from Ilhica that evening—but what he'd told me wasn't it. Of course, his story wouldn't be difficult to check out.

"You believe me?" Ilhica asked me.

"I'll look into it," I said.

"You can't ask the people at Tlazolteotl House," Ilhica noted.

Because then I would be forced to pursue the case, no matter how trivial it might be—and in the end, all I'd be doing was depriving Tlazolteotl of two strong backs. But there were other ways to test Ilhica's story.

I had friends in that part of the Merchant City after all, and they had friends, and someone would be able to tell me if Xiomara was working at Tlazolteotl or not.

"I'm not planning on it," I told Ilhica.

"Good," he said. "Nice talking with you."

Then he laid some beans on the table, got up, and left me sitting there. I watched him go down the stairs. Then I went to the front end of the floor, where there was a window, and looked down at the lamplit street, and waited for Ilhica to appear.

I didn't have a particular reason for doing so. Just an Investigator's compulsion to gather every morsel I could, because I never knew which of them would mean something.

A moment later, I saw Ilhica emerge from the restaurant and turn right on Xochipilli Street. There was a rail station in that direction that would take him east, toward some of the more affluent districts.

So as many beans as he was giving to charity, he wasn't giving *all* of them.

I recalled something Ilhica had said, apart from his revelations about Xiomara: *"You need to spend more time with musicians."*

I would take the advice.

If there was a hole in my knowledge of Aztlan, it fell on me to fill it. That was something I'd learned from my father, even if he had never lived long enough to know it.

In the meantime, I would search the Mirror for men named Xiomara who had dropped out of society around twenty cycles ago. If Ilhica had told me the truth about his friend's father, I'd be able to confirm it soon enough.

On my way back to my table, I asked the waiter for wax paper bags for the food

Ilhica and I had left uneaten. After all, there were elderly in need, and Ilhica had earned the gods' favor at his next performance.

• • •

The next morning, I was putting breakfast together in my eating room when my radio buzzed. I took it off the table, put it to my ear, and said, "Colhua."

"Maxtla?"

It was my aunt's voice.

She didn't sound angry. A good sign, I thought, hopeful there would be others. "Good morning," I said.

"Call Nahuatl," Aunt Xoco told me. "Tell him I'm setting a

place for him tomorrow evening at six."

Call Nahuatl. I replayed the words in my head, one by one. They were, after all, the last ones I'd expected to hear from her.

All the more reason to respond before her invitation could be withdrawn. "I'll call him," I promised.

"I'm serving snake," said my aunt. "Poached."

"I'll pass that on," I said, though I doubted it would make a difference to Nahuatl. He would care more about who was sitting *at* the table than what was sitting *on* it.

• • •

I didn't go straight to the Interrogation Center that morning. I went to the Prison House to see Popo Cueponi.

It was worth a try. He knew the Merchant City as well as anyone, even if he wasn't in the habit of hanging out with bankers.

"Any idea who might have wanted to see Inave dead?" I asked him.

He thought for a moment. "I'd say another banker. One he beat for an account, maybe—though I think it happened more often that other bankers beat *him*. But you don't need me to tell you that."

He was right. I didn't.

"If you hear anything," I said, "let me know."

"It would be my great pleasure. By the way…how did that other matter turn out?"

The Euro, I thought. "It was resolved."

In fact, the murderer was sitting in the Prison House along with Cueponi, albeit in a different layer of cells. But I didn't tell him that. "I'm glad to hear it," he said. "Oh, and thanks for speaking with my judge. I'm getting out a couple of days early."

I nodded. "Good for you, Uncle. Just take care you don't end up back here."

"The *utmost* care," he assured me.

• • •

Some cases moved like rivers in spring flood, thundering to a conclusion. Inave's wasn't one of them.

I'd had plenty of suspects: Zaniya. Xiomara. Ometochtli. Mishtli Chapolin. But none of them had panned out.

And the trail was getting cold. I knew from experience that my chances of finding the murderer diminished with time.

Somewhere out there in my city, Inave's killer was walking the streets, breathing the air Inave couldn't, basking in the sun Inave missed in the Lands of the Dead. It bothered me that it was so.

Bothered me all day, as I saw in front of my Mirror station and looked for some clue I'd missed. Some connection. Some detail in someone's past.

Over, and over, and over again.

• • •

Even before Tonatiuh's journey came to an end, I was exhausted.

Normally, I would have looked forward to dinner at Aunt Xoco's place. However, this dinner promised to be as exhausting as the rest of my day.

I did my best to get to my aunt's apartment early. That way, if she wanted to cancel her invitation to Nahuatl, there would still be time.

Fortunately, she made no mention of canceling. But she

didn't say anything else to me either—not even when I told her how nice she looked. She just let me in and went about her business in the kitchen.

I hoped she would say something to Nahuatl, at least. Otherwise, it would be an even longer evening than I'd anticipated.

At exactly six, I heard a knock on my aunt's door. Aunt Xoco took a breath, let it out, and smoothed the front of her shift. Then she went to the door and opened it.

And I saw Nahuatl, standing there in what looked like a new tunic, with a colorfully painted gourd in his hands. He smiled at my aunt.

Whatever her emotions might have been at that moment, one couldn't tell from her expression. "You're right on time," she said.

If there was a more neutral comment she could have made, I couldn't imagine what it might have been.

Nahuatl held out the gourd. "I brought some octli."

My aunt accepted it. "You didn't have to."

Nahuatl shrugged. "I wanted to."

Octli in hand, Aunt Xoco led the way into the eating room and said, "Please, sit down."

"Thanks," said Nahuatl.

In the old days, there would have been some banter before we went into the eating room. Some story about the trip our guest had made to get there. We would be skipping that, it seemed, and going right to the table.

One step at a time, I told myself.

I wanted to ask Nahuatl if he'd made any progress on the

task I'd given him, but it would have been rude of me. This was a meal, after all. Besides, I knew I wouldn't have to prompt him. If Nahuatl had something to tell me, he would find a moment before the evening was over.

In the meantime, Aunt Xoco wasted no time uncovering the meal she had prepared: a fat, pale water snake, as fragrant as any I could remember her serving.

I looked across it at Nahuatl, who had perhaps forgotten how savory my aunt's water snake could be. He looked like a man who'd seen a god and didn't know what to say by way of a greeting.

If Aunt Xoco noticed, she didn't say. She just uncorked the octli and poured us each a glass.

Then she doled out the snake, first to Nahuatl, our guest, then to me, and finally to herself. It was as delicious as it smelled. That much I could have predicted. It was the rest of the evening I was unsure about.

● ● ●

We ate in silent for a few minutes. Then Nahuatl said to my aunt, "It's good to see you, Xoco."

"You as well," my aunt replied—but only cordially, without her usual warmth.

"Nahuatl lives in the same pyramid I remembered," I said, hoping the comment would lead to something resembling a conversation.

"I do," said Nahuatl. "I wish I could tell you it's as nice as it used to be. The truth is its owners have allowed it to go down-hill a bit. Still, it meets my needs."

Aunt Xoco didn't pursue the subject. Instead she said, her eyes on her plate, "And you're an archivist."

"I was…last time we spoke," said Nahuatl. "Just not a first-rank archivist as I am now. You know how it is. You get your work featured in a history program on the Mirror and you move up in the world."

Aunt Xoco nodded, still looking at her plate. "I'm glad to hear it."

We talked about this and that: The Eagles' losses in their last three matches. The discovery of buried pyramids farther north than ever before. The birth of triplets to the First Administrator of Malinalco.

But not the past, much less the past we shared. In fact, the one time I recalled an event from my childhood—the day Nahuatl took me to an ancient-music festival and accidentally fell into a reflecting pool—my aunt quickly and sternly changed the subject.

Neither Nahuatl nor I commented. But it was clear from that moment on that the past was forbidden ground.

Fortunately, there were other things to talk about. Me, for instance. I was tired of telling the story of how I'd taken down the High Priest, but it beat a resounding silence.

Finally, Aunt Xoco pointed to the snake and asked us, "More?"

Nahuatl chuckled and held a hand up. "If only I had some-where to put it. This is the best snake I've had in…well, I guess since the last time I was here. You haven't lost your touch, Xoco."

"You're too kind," said my aunt.

"In your case," said Nahuatll, "there's no such thing."

For a moment, Aunt Xoco stared at our guest. It wasn't a hard stare, either. Quite the contrary.

Then she got up and started clearing the dishes. Nahuatl got up too, and rolled up his sleeves.

Aunt Xoco looked at him. "What are you doing?"

He smiled. "I'm helping with the dishes."

I remembered his doing that when I was a child. And I remembered what my father, who had notoriously disliked doing dishes, always said: *"Better you than me, my friend."*

"Nonsense," said my aunt. "You're a guest." And she moved to the sink, heading him off.

Nahuatl looked at me and shrugged. As if to say, *I might as well fight the storm.*

But we didn't sit at the table while Aunt Xoco washed the dishes. We stood there with her and talked some more, touching on the subjects people touched on when they were trying to pass the time.

At last, Aunt Xoco put aside her dish cloth and said, "All right, then." The way she said it told us the evening was at an end.

Nahuatl put his hands together. "The meal was a gift from the gods. Not that I'm the least bit surprised. And—" He included me with a glance. "—the company was even better."

"It was my pleasure," my aunt said.

No mention of getting together again. Not even a wish that we remain in touch.

"Well," Nahuatl said, "I guess I'll be going."

"I should go as well," I said.

"Know the gods' favor," Aunt Xoco told us.

In the end, the evening was, as my mother would have said, "better than some things but worse than others."

It wasn't the way it used to be. But we had made progress.

At least I hoped so.

● ● ●

"That was nice," Nahuatl said as he and I made our way to the rail station.

"It was," I agreed.

It was a clear night. The stars were out in force, shivering in the wind.

Nahuatl turned to me. "Do you remember your father's broom?"

I smiled. "The one he used on the festival of Ochpanitztli?" I hadn't thought about it in a long time.

"He used to make me laugh," Nahuatl said, "the way he swept the house. Like a maniac, attacking every corner, poking under every piece of furniture."

"I laughed too," I said.

Nahuatl chuckled to himself. Then he turned to me again and asked, "What did you think of the octli?"

"It was good," I said. "*Very* good."

"I got it at Cozcatl's. Their best blend, they said."

"I believe it."

A pause. Then: "Your aunt didn't drink any."

I'd noticed. "She's not a big octli drinker these days." It was a lie, though it was told for a good cause.

"I understand," said Nahuatl.

We walked up the steps to the platform. At the top, Nahuatl asked, "Which side are you on?"

I pointed to the near platform. "This one."

"I'm on the other side."

"Know the gods' peace," I said.

"You as well," said my father's friend. Then he made his way to the far side of the platform.

Nahuatl was as kind as ever, I thought, as I watched him go. And as eager to be a part of our family.

But clearly, there was a rift between him and my aunt. I wished I knew why.

• • •

I was getting into bed when I heard my radio buzz.

It was Nahuatl. "Sorry, Maxtla. Is this a bad time?"

I told him it was fine.

"I know it's late," he said, "but I didn't want you to think I'd forgotten the assignment you gave me."

"I didn't," I assured him. "Any luck?"

I heard him sigh. "Smiling gods, it seems, are harder to find than I would have thought. But rest assured, I'm still looking."

I felt my heart sink. But what I told Nahuatl was, "I appreciate the help."

"Of course," he said. Then: "Dinner was wonderful."

"It was," I said.

A long pause. So long that I had to ask Nahuatl if he was still on the line.

"Sorry," he said. Another sigh. "I guess you're wondering what I did to get myself kicked out of your family's lives."

I hadn't expected him to bring that up. "If you don't want to tell me—"

Before I could finish, Nahuatl said, "I asked your aunt to marry me."

At first, I thought I had misheard him. Then, as I realized I'd heard him perfectly, it started to make sense. I had always thought of Nahuatl as my father's brother. And for my father's brother to ask my father's sister to marry him…

Not that Nahuatl was my *real* uncle. He was my father's friend. There was nothing to stop him from courting my aunt.

It was just…his having done so felt so…*unexpected*.

And if it felt that way to *me,* so many cycles later, how must it have felt to Aunt Xoco—a woman who preferred to live on her own, then no less than now?

"So that's it," I said.

"That's it, Maxtla. I asked and your aunt answered. She didn't love me, she said. Not *that* way."

I could see her saying so. Hard-eyed, looking away. It hurt me, and I wasn't the one confessing my love for her.

"I would have been content," Nahuatl said, "to remain your father's friend, and your aunt's as well. I could have gone on that way. But things had changed. Your aunt couldn't look at me the same way."

In a whisper, he called on the goddess Xochiquetzatl. "It's the biggest regret of my life. By a long stretch. If I had known how things would turn out…how your aunt would feel…

believe me, I would never have asked."

But that would have been bad as well, wouldn't it? To love someone and never tell her...how could he have kept something like that inside?

"Unfortunately," said Nahuatl, "what's done is done. I'll keep looking for your smiling god, Maxtla."

And, a little too abruptly, he ended the connection.

• • •

I was woken by a buzzing. The sky, I saw, was only beginning to lighten in the east.

Necalli, I thought. He was the only one who called so early. I reached for my radio and said, "Colhua."

"Maxtla?"

It was Nahuatl.

"Good news," he said. "I think I've found what you were looking for."

I looked at my chronometer. It was barely six in the morning—which meant I hadn't spoken with Nahuatl all that long ago.

"Were you working all night?" I asked.

"Not *all* night," he assured me.

• • •

"Remember," said Nahuatl, as we rode the rail line out to District Twenty-Five, "it's not a perfect world, Maxtla."

"Because," I said, echoing what he'd told me twice already since we boarded the rail carriage together, "the god's not exactly smiling."

"That's right. But," he said—also for the third time—"it's

almost a smile. Very nearly so. And nothing else in Aztlan even comes close."

Nahuatl wasn't used to just coming *close*. But then, the challenge I'd put in front of him wasn't an insignificant one. He'd worked on it longer, he said, than he'd worked on his first treatise.

An exaggeration, sure. But *still*.

A moment later, the carriage came to a stop and its doors opened. We walked out onto a platform like any other on the city rail line.

Nahuatl pointed to something. "You see? Over there?"

It was a statue, all right. Standing on a concrete pedestal maybe a hundred hands away, across a sea of purple-blossomed jacaranda trees. *Yacatecuhtli,* I thought. I could tell it was him by his large nose, and the bundle of sticks in his hand, and the game bird hanging from his belt.

Yacatecuhtli was the god of travelers, so it made sense that he would be watching over a rail station. But was he smiling?

I walked over to a protective railing to get a better look at him, shaded my eyes from the sunlight—and saw clearly what Nahuatl wanted me to see. Then I smiled along with the god. "You did it," I told Nahuatl.

He chuckled. "You think so? I mean—"

"It's a smile," I said.

Nahuatl had prepared me for something less. But it was as much a smile as any I'd ever seen.

Of course, it remained to be determined why the statue was on Inave's mind. And if it was a key to his murder, as I'd hoped, or just the ranting of a man who'd had too much octli.

Nahuatl breathed a sigh of relief. "I didn't want to disappoint you, Maxtla."

I turned to him. "And you didn't."

My father's friend nodded. Then he looked across the jacaranda grove at Yacatecuhtli, and said, "There's still a lot to figure out."

"There is," I agreed.

Inave had said the god smiled on Tlaco's work. But all I could see between us and the statue were the jacarandas.

Were *they* the fruits of Tlaco's labor? And if they were, how were they going to help me find Inave's murderer?

I felt a breeze on my face, bringing the sweet scent of the jacaranda blossoms to me. "I'm going to go down there," I said, "and take a look around."

Nahuatl pointed to the jacarandas. "Down *there*? It looks like there's a fence around them."

There was. But it wasn't so high that I couldn't climb over it. "Not a problem," I said.

My father's friend smiled. "You always were an agile kid."

"I'll try not to be too long," I told him.

"Take your time," said Nahuatl. He went and sat down in the shadow of the station roof. "I'll be here in the shade if you need me."

Catching up on his sleep, I thought.

• • •

I made my way down the stairs to street level. Then I eyed the fence separating the jacarandas from the walk, got a running start, and leaped as high as I could—high enough to grab the horizontal pole at the top of the fence.

With an effort, I pulled myself up and over, turned in mid-air, and came down on both feet. The scent of the jacaranda blossoms was stronger there, more insistent. I walked into the midst of the trees, and saw the dried-up remains of the previous bloom strewn on the ground.

I saw something else as well—concrete troughs sunk into the earth. The kind designed to hold orchids and honeysuckle and pineapple sage. Now they were full of weeds, but at some point they'd had flowers in them.

I looked up at the canopy of jacaranda branches, thick enough to keep out all but a few glints of sunlight. Thick enough to keep the flowers in shadow and kill them off, until the trees were all that was left.

Bad planning, I thought. If the plantings in that place were Tlaco's work, he'd done a lousy job.

Unless at some point there hadn't been so many jacarandas. Or any at all, for that matter. I touched one of the tree branches, felt its rough, flaky bark. It wasn't a young tree, so it had been there a while.

But not long enough, maybe, to be part of the original design.

I looked around. Rail stations were built on public land. So it couldn't be a matter of a private owner deciding he'd prefer purple blossoms twice a cycle to troughs of ornamental flowers.

Someone had planted the jacarandas for a different reason. And planted them close together so they would fill the place up. So, the Investigator in me said, they would hide something.

But what? The flower troughs? What else was there to hide? What did the jacarandas keep me from noticing?

The rail station…?

It was true that I couldn't see it any longer. The canopy was too thick. But if I'd remained with Nahuatl, I could have seen it without any problem. So *not* the rail station.

Or…not that *part* of the rail station.

I was standing on a level with the station's concrete base. Thanks to the jacarandas, I couldn't see it. Nor would anyone else, even if they happened on an angle that would otherwise have given them a glimpse of it.

It was a reach. But I was there already. How hard would it be to check out the base of the station?

I sidled and ducked and otherwise negotiated a path through the jacaranda branches until I reached the concrete structure. I wasn't sure what I was looking for, or if I'd understand the significance of it if I found it.

But I looked.

The concrete surface that stretched up from the ground was shaded by the trees, but up close I could make it out. At first, I didn't notice anything out of the ordinary.

Then I did.

The concrete in one part of the structure was different from the concrete in other parts. Smoother, with fewer pebbles mixed into it. As if the platform in that spot had been repaired.

Big deal, I thought. Platforms had to be repaired sometimes, didn't they? Hadn't I seen repair crews around the city from time to time?

Still, I looked around some more.

There were no other patches on that surface. But when I turned the corner and inspected the wall perpendicular to it, I found another patch after all—and this was bigger than the first one. *Much* bigger. Maybe twenty hands high and ten wide.

That seemed like a lot to me. I went the rest of the way around the base. There was nothing else—no other patches, certainly.

But there was another structure toward the end of the jacaranda grove—a support for the rail line as it left the station, in the mold of the thousands of supports one could find around Aztlan.

It was even harder to reach than the base of the rail station. I had to wrestle with a hundred branches, pushing them up or to the side until I could get past them. But I was driven by a sense that maybe—just *maybe*—I was onto something.

When I reached the support, it was drowned in shadow and hard to see. At least at first. But after a while, my eyes adjusted.

Even then, I didn't catch sight of anything. No patches where the concrete's different, I thought.

Then I realized…there weren't any smooth spots because the whole *thing* was a smooth spot. The support hadn't just been *repaired* with a finer grade of concrete. Unless I was mistaken, it had been *replaced*.

And *that* was something I'd never heard of. In fact, the rail system prided itself on never having to take a station offline for more than a day.

I thought about Inave. *Tlaco's work*, he'd said. Was this *it*? And if it was, what did it mean?

I didn't know.

But I was going to find out.

• • •

Naturally, the Mirror was the first place I looked for information on the rail station. Apparently, it had been built nearly thirty cycles earlier, to address a population surge in the suddenly chic District Twenty-Five.

I found a few articles on the project. One said it was getting started, another said it was almost done, and a third celebrated its completion. None of them mentioned a section of the line having been repaired or replaced.

But I'd seen what I'd seen. The Mirror reporter who'd written the story either wasn't aware of the fact or didn't think it was worth mentioning.

And maybe it wasn't.

But, as I'd complained before, leads in the matter of Inave's murder were hard to come by. I couldn't afford to discard any of them.

My next recourse was to speak with those who had been involved in the construction of the station. It would have had an architect, after all. And a builder. And people who worked with them, and for them.

I spent the afternoon checking them out. One by one.

Unfortunately, the architect—a man of advanced age—had gone to the Lands of the Dead eight cycles earlier. A cycle later, the builder had joined him, the victim of a boating accident off the shore of the Western Markets.

The builder's two associates had died as well, one from a long illness and one from a stroke. In fact, everyone I could find who'd been associated with the project had passed from the precincts of the living.

I'd have been suspicious if they were younger, or if some of them hadn't died from natural causes. But it had been thirty cycles since the project was finished. It wasn't hard to believe those responsible for it had since joined the gods.

I tracked down other possibilities. Brothers. Sisters. Wives. Husbands.

A few of them, it turned out, were still alive. I was able to get them on my radio. But they weren't any help. If they had known anything about the District Twenty-Five project, they had long since forgotten.

Or had decided not to say. It was hard to tell which.

Where else could I look?

Once in a while, our files included information on relationships outside of marriage—but that was only when those relationships produced children, who might someday enjoy rights of inheritance and therefore had to be tracked.

It wasn't the kind of knowledge that would be available to the public. But we on the force would be privy to it.

A long shot, sure. But sometimes long shots panned out.

• • •

The next morning, I met Izcuin and we took the northeast rail out to its end. We emerged from the station in a quiet neighborhood, the kind that had once been an estate of a rich family but had since been subdivided.

It was an odd way to live, apart from the city center's grandeur and scale. But it wasn't unpleasant, especially in small doses.

The house we were looking for was at the end of Xocotzin Street. The place was made of red brick, like its neighbors, but it was larger and statelier looking.

I knocked on the door. There was no answer. Not even after a couple of minutes. "Maybe he's out," Izcuin suggested.

I didn't think so. Not from what I'd learned.

I was about to knock again when I heard footsteps inside the house. Izcuin smiled. "I guess he's in after all."

But it wasn't the fellow we were looking for who came to the door. It was a woman in a yellow nurse's tunic. Standing in a bar of sunlight, she looked from me to Izcuin and back again. "Can I help you?" she asked.

"We'd like to speak with Acalan Cuetzpallee."

"He's not receiving visitors," the nurse said evenly.

"It's important," I told her. I showed her my Investigator's bracelet.

"I saw it," she said. "But a citizen's health is paramount—as I'm sure you know. Unless, of course, there's an imminent danger to another citizen."

There wasn't.

But there was the matter of bringing a killer to justice. And Acalan Cuetzpallee held a key we might not find anywhere else.

I was about to ask if there was a better time to see him when a voice from inside the house—a thin, wavering voice—said, "It's all right, Azti."

I peered past the nurse and saw a scarecrow of a man in a blue cotton robe. He approached the door with the help of a cane. As he entered the bar of light, I saw how gaunt he was. How sunken his eyes were in their sockets.

"We're Investigators," I explained to him, relieving him of the need to ask. "We're working on a murder case."

He didn't seem surprised to hear it. "Please," he said, "come in."

The nurse stood aside and we entered the house. The walls, I saw were covered with old pictures of buildings under construction. I recognized one of them as the Grand Pyramid, though in the picture it was only half-finished.

"My father's work," Cuetzpallee said, noting my interest. "Uappatzin Oxomo was the premier architect of his day—and the inspiration for my becoming an architect as well—though, of course, my talent paled beside his. But then, you know all that, don't you?"

I said that we had done our research. I didn't go into detail—that I'd discovered Oxomo had a son born outside his marriage, or that the son—like all such sons—had to take his mother's name.

In this case, Cuetzpallee.

"Come," he said.

We followed him down a short hallway into what looked like a meeting room. It contained a lacquered black table surrounded by four lacquered chairs. Here too there were pictures of partially built pyramids on the walls.

"Please," Cuetzpallee said, indicating the chairs on one side of the table. He pulled one out on the opposite side and, with an effort, sat down.

Suddenly, he started coughing. After a moment, he produced a white cloth, and held it to his mouth until the coughing stopped. When he took the cloth away, there was blood on it.

"I'm sorry," Cuetzpallee said. "I'm not well."

"I'm sorry to hear it," I said.

He nodded. No doubt, he'd heard such sentiments before.

Izcuin and I sat down too. "You weren't surprised to see us," I observed.

"I wasn't. When I saw Molli Inave was found dead…I had a feeling I'd see *someone*. Either the police or…" He shrugged his bony shoulders.

"Did you know Inave?" I asked.

"Not well. I was introduced to him one day when my father was working on the rail station in District Twenty-Five. Which, I imagine, is what you came to see me about."

"It is," I confirmed. "Inave referred to the station the night he died. Not directly—he made mention of a smiling god. Also, the name Tlaco."

Cuetzpallee chuckled. "My father's nickname."

Which Inave could have known him by. Another piece of the puzzle.

"My mother gave it to him," Cuetzpallee explained. "It was the name of the clothing store where they met: Tlaco's Fine Garments. The place was closed a number of cycles ago. There's an octli shop there now."

"Inave," I said, "referred to Tlaco as a dangerous man. Your father is in the Lands of the Dead. Do you have any idea how he could be dangerous to anyone?"

Cuetzpallee smiled a thin smile. "Actually," he said, "I do."

• • •

The Mirror maintained several different facilities in Aztlan. I'd visited some of them—the place where Chicome worked, for example, and a couple of the studios where features were made, and one of the garages that housed the auto-carriages that took reporters to the scenes of news events.

I'd even looked in on the Mirror's Director of Programming in the Merchant City, back when I was a rookie Investigator. But I'd never been to the Mirror's main headquarters in District Eight, so I'd never seen the two-story high waiting room outside its leader's office.

It was every bit as impressive as I'd heard. The wall on either side as I walked in was dominated by a faceted figure made of polished, black obsidian with threads of red running through it.

The figure to my left was a jaguar-man, fierce, terrible, teeth bared as he leaned into his hunt. In one hand he held a bow, in the other a sheaf of fiery arrows.

The figure to my right leaned as well, but as if it were reaching for something. Its features were calm, composed, a cloak of feathers trailing from its shoulders. And it wore a smooth, flat breastplate that reflected my face back at me.

The two faces of Tezcatlipoca, god of the smoking mirror: One seeking blood, the other seeking wisdom. The one on the right was meant as a warning to us, to remind us of how close we were to the savagery of our past. The one on the left was a model for us, an encouragement to learn more about our world and ourselves.

The one who managed the Mirror, it was said, had to keep both Tezcatlipocas in mind.

"Investigator?" The woman who had spoken was sitting in a curved, bloodwood enclosure that concealed all but her head and shoulders. She smiled. "Administrator Nenetl is expecting you." She pointed to the door behind her.

"Thanks," I said.

I circumnavigated her enclosure, opened the door, and entered the office of the woman in charge of Aztlan's Mirror network: The attractive, charming, and widely respected Xipil Nenetl.

I would have recognized her anywhere, with her almond-shaped eyes and her expressive lips. But then, hardly a moon went by when she wasn't sitting with an interviewer and discussing a matter of public interest, or lending her considerable presence to a live event—each time making viewers like Aunt Xoco wonder how she managed to look so young.

At the moment, Nenetl was seated at her desk—which was made of the same bloodwood as her receptionist's enclosure—and tapping something into the keyboard of her Mirror station. Not a state-of-the-art machine, surprisingly, but a model a couple of cycles older than the one I had at home.

As I closed the door behind me, Nenetl's gaze rose to meet mine—but just for a moment. "Pardon me," she said. "I'll be with you in a heartbeat."

"Take your time," I said.

Not that I'd expected her to wait for my permission. I watched as she continued tapping, her brow creased ever so slightly. She went on longer than the heartbeat she'd mentioned—for a full couple of minutes, in fact.

Finally, Nenetl looked up again—and smiled.

Not in a perfunctory way, as her receptionist had done. But then, Nenetl's smile was that of a former Mirror personality, calculated to inspire the kind of trust normally reserved for family and close friends.

Before Nenetl made her way to the top, she had been a reporter like Chicome. First in Oxtlipa, then in Texcoco, and finally in Aztlan. The frequency with which she had moved was an indication of her popularity—which she had earned with her screen appeal as well as the quality of her work, but no more so than many other smart, driven, often good-looking men and women.

Then, some thirty-five cycles ago, she produced a three-part feature on the Empire's salmon farming industry, which was injecting its fish—touted for the longest time as a wholesome source of nutrition—with bleach and other chemicals, and paying off the Emperor's inspectors to keep the practice a secret.

Overnight, the story made her the brightest star on the Mirror.

A couple of months later, the leader of Aztlan's Mirror system stepped down. The choice of a replacement was no choice at all. It had to be Nenetl.

And it had remained Nenetl since that time. First

Administrators had come and gone. Even the Emperor had gone to the Lands of the Dead and been replaced by his nephew. But Nenetl had remained a fixture in Aztlan.

Which was why I had expected her office to be a thing of grandeur—especially after what I'd seen in the waiting area. It wasn't that at all.

The wall framing the door through which I'd entered was covered with a dozen oversized Mirror screens, each one showing a different program: A report on the storm that had hit the Western Markets, a feature on tourism in the Bay of Ice, an educational show for children, the replay of the Eagles' victory the night before.

It was impressive, but only in in a businesslike way. And there were no other adornments in the room. Not even a window, though the south-facing view would certainly have been breathtaking.

I understood why. The glare would have made it difficult for Nenetl to see the screens. And nothing would be more important to the leader of the Mirror than seeing what her people were putting out over the network.

Nenetl's desk, and the two lizard-leather chairs in front of it, were the room's only concessions to luxury. There wasn't even a carved totem on the woman's working surface, or a souvenir, or an image of a loved one—just the three-cycles-old Mirror station.

"Investigator," she said, her voice as well preserved as the rest of her—clear and resonant, like a festival bell. "Please… won't you have a seat?"

"Thank you," I said. I sat down in one of the lizard-leather chairs. "It's good to see you again."

I wondered if she would remember our service in the High Priest's Honor Guard at the last Renewal. I shouldn't have. "And you as well," she said without hesitation. "A terrible thing, that business with Itzcoatl."

"Terrible indeed," I said.

Nenetl leaned forward ever so slightly. "You know, it's not often I receive a visit from the police. If they speak with anyone, it's one of my reporters."

"In this case," I said, "it had to be you."

"I'm intrigued."

I knew she would be. But I didn't throw my dice right away. Instead I said, "People say you've got the best job in the Empire."

"People who say so," said Nenetl, "don't understand how hard I work. How much I'm called on to do in the course of a day."

"You decide what makes it onto the Mirror," I said, "and what doesn't. It's a great deal of power for one person. A lot of temptation, no doubt, to abuse that power."

If my host was put off by the comment, it didn't show in her face. "There is," she conceded. "It's something of which I remind myself every day—which is why, in all the time I've been in charge of the Mirror, we're never had a scandal. Not one."

"You've run the cleanest operation in the Empire."

"We pride ourselves on that achievement."

"Or," I suggested, "maybe the things you've done just haven't come to light."

That brought another crease to Nenetl's forehead. "If you've come across a problem with our business, Investigator, I would love to hear about it."

Good, I thought. Because that was why I'd come. "Thirty cycles ago, shortly after you became leader of the Mirror here in Aztlan, District Twenty-Five was beginning to become popular. Especially with young people, who saw it as an affordable alternative to the more expensive parts of Aztlan. But District Twenty-Five had never been considered in the original design of the city's rail system. Rail service ended in District Twenty-Four.

"So our First Administrator at the time, Nappa Cochimetl, hired an architect to draw up plans for a new rail spur. The architect's name, which may sound familiar to you, was Oxomo."

I looked for recognition in Nenetl's eyes, in her bearing. If she knew who I was talking about, she didn't let it show.

"He was a good man, by all accounts," I continued, "and a good architect. He designed a stretch of railway that would meet all the challenges in the area, and would do so at a reasonable cost to the city.

"The builder selected by the First Administrator may sound familiar as well. A guy by the name of Nochehuatl. He ran what had long been a reputable construction company. But underneath its glowing reputation, it was losing beans hand over hand—which was why it had to borrow from a banker named Molli Inave to stay in business. Not once, but three times.

"Increasingly desperate, Nochehuatl cut corners on his construction of the rail spur. He may not have believed they would make a difference in the end, but they did. Almost immediately, cracks began to appear in the rail line's supports. A trial run had to be aborted because the rail under the carriage was starting to bow. Had it done so with passengers aboard, the carriage might have run off the rail entirely.

"First Administrator Cochimetl was livid. He fired the builder and brought on a new one, who tore down a lot of what the first one had put up and replaced it. In the meantime, Nochehuatl became despondent. Before, he'd at least had his reputation; now, he knew, he wouldn't even have that.

"In the end, he took his own life. But no one ever heard about it. He was a prominent citizen, a well-known donor to charitable causes, yet his death was reported as a boating accident on the Mirror.

"Why, I wonder? The same reason, apparently, that the failure of Nochehuatl's construction failure went unreported—because that was the way the First Administrator wanted it. It had been his decision to hire Nochehuatl in the first place. If word of the rail problem got out, it would have cost him his position—and he dearly loved his position. So he paid off everyone who had knowledge of the trial run, everyone who could say what had happened—from Oxomo to the guy who drove Cochimetl's auto-carriage."

I looked Nenetl in the eye. "Everyone—including *you*. Except the First Administrator didn't pay you in beans. He paid you in something you stood to profit from even more—opportunities. Leads to stories you never would have gotten otherwise. Stories that cemented your standing as a dedicated servant of the people, who would go to any length to bring them the news they needed.

"Except for one *particular* piece of news. But what was that one piece, you may have asked yourself, in the scheme of things? Did the citizens of the Empire *really* need to know about a failed rail spur?

"It's a good question, you have to admit. If you agree that the Mirror was created to give Mexica's citizens a chance to decide what's important and what isn't—as it says in the Mirror's charter—then maybe they *did* need to know. But they would never find out about the rail spur…because you killed the story."

Nenetl didn't move a muscle. She just sat there and listened.

"You must have believed," I said, "that was the end of the matter. Even when First Administrator Cochimetl died, those he had paid off couldn't say anything. Lands of the Dead, they'd made themselves complicit by taking beans in exchange for their silence. If they incriminated *you*, they'd be incriminating *themselves*. So you knew you wouldn't be exposed—until a moon or so ago, when Molli Inave paid you a visit."

Nenetl didn't react to the mention of Inave any more than she had reacted to anything else. I respected her ability to remain composed in the face of what she'd heard. But I wasn't finished.

"Inave knew what you'd done. He'd been keeping Nochehutal afloat, after all, so he was an insider, one of those who'd been privy to the problems with the rail.

"Now it was *Inave* who needed to be kept afloat. He'd

gotten greedy, lent his beans to clients he should have known could never pay. At one point he'd had to borrow from another banker, then tried to steal one of that banker's most prestigious clients.

"He was at the end of his rope, willing even to risk a sentence in the Prison House. So he threatened to expose your cover-up unless you paid him off.

"Of course, there's never an end to extortion. You'd know that from all the stories you covered for the Mirror. It starts with one payment and then there's another, and another. So paying off Inave would only have delayed the inevitable.

"And you couldn't risk the Emperor finding out what had happened. Confronted with a scandal of such proportions, he would have had no choice but to strip you of your office. You couldn't allow that. Like the First Administrator cycles earlier, you'd come to love your job and all that went with it.

"So you chose the only real option you had—the one that presented you with a permanent solution. You killed the man who would have exposed you."

Nenetl's brow furrowed. "You're saying *I* killed Inave?"

"That's what I'm saying," I told her.

I could see the emotions flitting across my host's face. But she never quite lost control. It took a moment but she said, in a remarkably calm voice, "You should have a show on the Mirror, Investigator—Unsolved Murders with Maxtla Colhua."

I recalled the comment Ometecuhtli had made to me. "You're not the first one to tell me so."

"Unfortunately for the sake of your theory, I'm no more

responsible for Inave's death than you are—something you'll find out eventually, though it may be at some cost to your reputation and that of your department. As for the cover-up you say you've discovered in District Twenty-Five…go ahead and expose it, if you think you've got sufficient proof. Because you'll need it."

Nenetl had barely finished saying so when her chronometer beeped. She glanced at it, then picked up a remote-control device attached to the arm of her chair and used it to change the image on one of the screens behind me—the one that was covering the storm in the Western Markets.

Before, it had displayed the flooding in one of the region's biggest towns. Now I saw a woman—a reporter—standing on a pier, where the wind was whipping froth from line after line of oncoming waves.

There was no sound, but Nenetl seemed to be able to read the woman's lips. She was so intent on doing so, on measuring every aspect of the coverage—not just the woman, maybe, but the framing of the scene, and the lighting, and who knew what else—it was as if I were no longer in the room.

Lands of the Dead, as if I had never shown up in the first place.

What was I, after all? Just an Investigator, regardless of what kind of problem I'd brought to Nenetl. She was still the leader of the Mirror in Aztlan. Someone of that stature might be able to get around the obstacle I'd placed in front of her.

After a minute or so, my host turned to me again. If I'd shaken her confidence, it seemed shaken no longer. She looked energized, reminded of who she was and what kind of power she wielded.

"You know," she said, "that I report directly to the Emperor—who, it's only fair to tell you, is fond of the Mirror and the job I've done here in Aztlan, and has said so on several occasions. Anything short of an airtight case against me—and I mean *airtight*—just might draw his ire. Something you may wish to take into account, Investigator."

"Thanks," I said, "for the heads up."

At that point, it was time for me to go.

It was all right. I'd done what I'd set out to do.

• • •

I lay awake that night.

Halfway through it, I heard the door to my residence open. I had locked it, but someone seemed to have had the tools to open it anyway.

I pulled the covers up over my face. Covers I had picked specifically for their ability to let light through if one held them close enough to one's eye.

After a while, I heard the intruder's footfalls on the wood of the bedroom floor—soft, careful, so as not to wake his intended victim. Then I saw him too, or at least the dim impression of him the covers allowed.

Saw him come closer, and closer still.

And lift his hand, as if he intended to strike me. With a knife, insofar as I could tell.

I waited until I couldn't wait any longer. At the last possible moment, I rolled out of the way—so that the knife sliced through the bed cover and buried itself in the bed, but not in *me*. Then I whipped the covers aside, revealing myself to the killer...

And the killer to me.

There, in a bar of silver moonlight, stood the guy who worked for the trade commissioner—the one who had commented on my Investigator's bracelet—a long knife in his gloved hand. The kind of weapon the woman from the bake shop had found in her trash.

Seeing it was me in Cuetzpallee's bed and not the aged, infirm man he had intended to dispose of, the guy froze. I could only imagine the thoughts going through his head in that moment—the pieces that came together for him, fitting one into the other, completing the picture there in Cuetzpallee's bedroom.

One thing was certain—the guy knew he had little to lose at that point, because he came after me again with his knife. This time I wasn't encumbered by a bed cover. I used my hand stick to deflect his attack.

Then I drove my fist into the guy's mouth.

He groaned and pulled back. But the knife was still in his hand, so I couldn't rest on my ocelot skin. Cuetzpallee's bedclothes kept me from getting a lot of traction, but it was enough for me to launch myself at the guy.

I could feel my hand stick bite where it hit him in the chest. But it must not have bitten deep, because he shrugged it off and took another swipe at me.

Fortunately, I caught his wrist on my forearm before the

knife could reach me. Then we wound up in a heap on the floor, each one struggling to get to the other.

The guy was quick, and stronger than he looked. If we had gone on wrestling much longer, he might have planted his knife somewhere inconvenient. But it wasn't my first day on the job, so I hadn't gone to Cuetzpallee's on my own.

As my adversary pulled free with his knife hand, I saw another hand—a big one with an Investigator's bracelet—grab him by the wrist, and twist. With a cry of pain, the guy contorted and dropped his knife.

Then Takun, still holding the assassin's wrist, planted his knee in the guy's back—and held him there until Quetzalli could add her weight to Takun's, and pull the murderer's hands together, and bind his wrists with her manacles.

As Takun yanked the guy away from the bed, Quetzalli turned to me and asked, "You all right?"

"I will be," I said, "as soon as I get some sleep."

Takun grunted. "I didn't sleep tonight either." He grinned a lopsided grin at me. "Not a lot, anyway."

I got to my feet, took my attacker off Takun's hands, and dragged him to the nearest wall. Then I pulled him up to a sitting position.

Wheezing, blood dripping from his nose, he didn't look like he was in a mood to talk. So I started talking for both of us.

"I have a feeling," I said, "that you're going to like the Prison House. At least I hope so, because you're going to be a resident there a good long time."

The guy glared at me and sniffed back some of the blood

falling from his nose. "I can help you," he said in a decidedly denasal voice.

"Really," I said.

"I didn't do this on my own," the guy went on.

Quetzalli held out an identification card she'd taken from him. "His name is Huay Chaneque."

The guy glanced at her. "I have no offenses on my record." He turned back to me. "I work for Papaqui. You know that. Papaqui was the one who made me do it."

"How so?" I asked.

"I need you to help me in return. With my sentence."

"That depends," I said, "on what you tell me."

I could see the guy thinking about it. He didn't have a lot of options. He had to know that. "All right," he said. "All right. Inave...he was squeezing people...something about the rail line, cycles ago. Papaqui was one of the people."

Another piece fell into place. "Tell me more," I said.

• • •

Commissioner Papaqui didn't expect me to enter his office unannounced. But then, as luck would have it, his well-dressed receptionist wasn't on duty that day.

Papaqui was sitting behind his mahogany desk, a look of surprise on his face. As before, he took off his glasses. "Investigator," he said, massaging the bridge of his nose. "I wasn't expecting—"

"Your man Chaneque to walk into a trap?" I said.

He blinked. "A trap? I'm sorry, I don't—"

"Chaneque told us everything," I said. "How you were one

of the deputy commissioners who had responsibility for the rail line project all those cycles ago. How you avoided the blemish of scandal on your record when Nenetl covered up the story. How, without that blemish to hinder you, you were able to gain the Emperor's confidence, and rise through the ranks of public service, and eventually grab one of the highest offices in Aztlan.

"Then Inave reared his head. Despite the harm he might be doing to himself, he was going to expose everyone—Nenetl, *you*—if you didn't push a hill of beans his way. Of course, there was no guarantee he'd be satisfied with just one hill. Once he asked, who was to say he wouldn't ask again?

"Or that he wouldn't just blurt out the truth in the wrong company? The way he drank, that was a possibility, wasn't it? And you couldn't afford the Emperor's getting a whiff of the story. Not when your job depended on it.

"So you worked out a way to keep Inave quiet. You already had an employee with a rare combination of talents—a former enforcer with the know-how and experience to protect you from anyone who came after you—as well as the poise to serve as your receptionist.

"A more obvious bodyguard might have raised some questions. But Chaneque? As charming as he was, who would have suspected he'd been engaged in violent confrontations as a teenager? Or that he'd be willing to take his violence to the next level...for the right price?

"Of course, Inave had bodyguards too. However, as his fortunes went down the gopher hole, so did his ability to pay them. Little by little, he had to cut their hours, forcing most of them to look for work elsewhere.

"Yet he was still protected. He lived in a good neighborhood, and long before that he'd taken the precaution of reinforcing his doors and windows. In the belly of such a fortress, he was safe from anyone who wanted to come after him.

"But like any fortress, it could be entered through its front door—provided the owner was amenable to the idea. You knew that. And you made arrangements to take advantage of the fact.

"As soon as Inave started putting the squeeze on you, you sent Chaneque to Inave's place with payments. Not as big as the ones Inave wanted, but enough to make him think you were operating in good faith. Meanwhile, Chaneque was becoming a familiar face at Inave's door. Familiar enough that when he came over late at night with a knife hidden in his tunic, Inave—whose judgment was still impaired by the Reunion's octli—didn't hesitate to let him in.

"Chaneque was more thorough than he had to be. But then, he was trying to put it in our heads that the murderer was an amateur. Then he took the murder weapon with him and disposed of it—in a trash can, of all places. Again, to make it seem he didn't know what he was doing.

"Not that we were going to be able to trace him anyway. Not when he'd worn gloves to keep his prints off the knife handle."

"Have you been drinking?" Papaqui asked me. "Because—"

"But," I continued, "Inave gave me a clue before he died. He mentioned a smiling god. And someone named Tlaco. And that led us to the rail station in District Twenty-Five, and then to Acalan Cuetzpallee—the illegitimate son of the project architect.

"He was dying. His one regret was that he had never revealed the rail station scandal. His father had insisted that he keep the matter to himself, that no one would ever be hurt by it.

"Then he read about Inave's death, and he saw that his father had been wrong. But there were powerful people involved in the scandal. How could he go up against them? I gave him a way.

"Soon after, he called Oxomo's widow, with whom he'd spoken from time to time after her husband's death. Cuetzpallee warned her that he was going to expose the scandal to an Investigator—and that she should cover her complicity as best she could.

"Oxomo's widow called Nenetl and told her what Cuetzpallee had said. So even before I walked into Nenetl's office, she had an inkling of what I'd be talking to her about.

"I didn't think Nenetl had killed Inave. Not for a moment. But according to Cuetzpallee, she knew about the rail station, and she knew who *else* knew—and, being a good reporter, she would know as well who had taken Inave's life.

"If I lit a fire under her, I thought, she might call that person to share what I'd told her. And she did. She called *you*.

"To that point, you weren't a suspect, Commissioner. Cuetzpallee mentioned other possibilities, but not you. And, of course, I had a list of my own suspects, at least in my head—but you weren't on it.

"Until Cuetzpallee forced your hand. He had to be silenced

before he could testify to a judge. Maybe down the line, you would try to shut me up as well. But in the moment, Cuetzpallee was the priority.

"So you sent Chaneque out again, to take care of another loose end. But it wasn't Cuetzpallee he found. It was a bunch of Investigators, who were able to grab him and his knife, and give him a picture of what awaited him in the Prison House.

"That was when Chaneque decided it was smarter to put his interests ahead of yours. And here we are."

Papaqui shook his head. "That's insane. I didn't send Chaneque anywhere. If he committed a crime, he did it on his own."

"His word against yours," I said. "And who's going to believe Chaneque's word over that of the Emperor's hand-picked Commissioner of Trade?"

Papaqui didn't say it out loud, but I could see the answer in his eyes: *Nobody.*

"On the other foot," I said, "they might believe the head of the Mirror."

"The head of...?" The commissioner blinked again, and put his glasses back on. "You're delusional."

"Am I? You'll recall that Nenetl buzzed you after I left her office. Almost immediately after. In the course of that conversation, you told her not to worry. You would take of Cuetzpallee the way you took care of Inave. You also talked about...let's see...Nenetl's retirement, which she'd been planning for a few moons already, and didn't want to complicate with a scandal. You mentioned the Emperor too, if I recall—how he'd never suspect either one of you."

A bead of sweat ran down the side of Papaqui's face.

"Crazy," I said, "isn't it? It's as if I listened to your conversation—because I *did*. Not at the time you had it, because I was still leaving the Mirror's offices. But later, when Necalli played it back for me.

"I know—Nenetl runs the Mirror. Normally she would say who has access to radio communications and who doesn't. But here's a little-known fact: In the course of a murder investigation, a Chief of Investigators—in other words, Eloxo Necalli—is able to obtain access as well, and to do so without the knowledge of those taking part in the conversation. Even if one of them is the head of the Mirror."

Papaqui's mouth fell open.

"You look surprised," I said. "You're in good company. Nenetl was surprised too. Which is why she caved in after all.

"Necalli is sitting in her office now, taking down her statement. About how she called you *innocently* to share what I'd said to her—never dreaming that the Commissioner of Trade would send an assassin to Cuetzpallee's place to do to him what he'd done to Molli Inave."

Papaqui drew in a trembling breath. He looked like he wanted to say something but couldn't get the words out.

Then his head fell and he began sobbing. Like a baby. It wasn't easy to watch.

I opened my pouch and took out my rope manacles. "Sorry to spring this on you, Commissioner. I know it's a lot to digest. But then, you didn't give Inave a lot of warning either...did you?"

• • •

I didn't need help to take Papaqui to the city's detention center, where he would remain—no doubt, under a mountain of regrets— until a judge could see him.

I had done my part to see justice done for Inave. But I had another score to settle, so as soon as I finished filling out the paperwork for Papaqui, I took out my radio and punched in a number.

"Chicome," came the response.

"It's Colhua," I said.

I could feel the chill on the other end of the line. "What do you need now, Investigator?"

"Nothing," I said.

"Nothing...?"

"Not a thing. I had a case with some gaping holes in it, but I've managed to fill them."

"Then what...?" A pause. Followed by a chuckle—a bitter one. "For a second there, I allowed myself the foolish hope that you were calling to pay me back."

"I can't do that," I said. "My investigation is still ongoing. You know how that works as well as I do."

"Right. So—"

"On the other hand, this particular investigation...and it's a big one, with some interesting twists and turns...will be over before too long. At which point the public will need to know about it."

"Really," said Chicome.

I imagined him bringing the radio a little closer to his ear.

"I think so. But here's the problem—whoever breaks this

story won't be working at the Mirror much longer. It's got some…sensitive details, we'll say."

"Sensitive," he repeated, no doubt wondering what that meant.

"So on the plus side, that person's work will be remembered for a long time to come. Held out as an example, maybe, of what the Mirror is supposed to do. On the negative side—"

"He'll be out of a job."

"I'm pretty sure. But he might be somebody for whom a story this big is more important than a few beans and a byline. You know anybody like that?"

Another pause. A longer one this time. And no chuckling. "I might," Chicome said finally. "I just might."

• • •

I didn't like to watch the Mirror in the evening. Especially when I knew what story it would be leading with.

Calli, on the other hand, said watching the Mirror helped her catch up with the world. It made her feel like she had been part of it, even if she'd been buried in her office all day.

So we had a difference of opinion.

It was all right. We were adults. We had a great deal of affection for each other. That night, as on all nights, we reached a compromise.

We watched the Mirror.

"Tonight," said the woman delivering the news that evening, "I have a sad story to report. The story of an eminently successful executive and a tentpole of the community stepping down from her position. The executive in question, I regret to say, is the one in charge of the Mirror—Xipil Nenetl."

Over one of the woman's shoulders, a rectangular image appeared. It held the face of Xipil Nenetl. A drawn and tired-looking face. The kind of face the mighty wear when they've fallen from the heights of their power.

"Nenetl's resignation comes as a surprise to all who knew, admired, and worked for her. Asked for her reasons, she said she had done all she could for the Mirror over the course of her long and satisfying career, and that it was someone else's turn to pick up the hand stick."

Or she knew that with the trade commissioner's arrest fueling a series of questions, what she had done cycles earlier would inevitably come out into the open—and she wanted to resign her office before the Emperor asked her to leave.

"This is huge," Calli said. She turned to me, eyes narrowed accusingly. "Did you know about this?" And then, because I wasn't good at keeping a straight face: "You *did* know about this."

I shrugged.

"And you didn't tell me?"

"Do you tell *me* everything?" I asked.

"Of course not." She studied me some more. "And there's more to it…isn't there?"

I didn't say a word.

Not that she wouldn't find out when everyone else did. But Calli liked to know things *before* everyone else did. It was one of the qualities that made her successful at what she did.

She leaned closer until her lips were almost touching mine. "I mean…just a *hint*…?"

"Investigators don't hint," I told her.

She kissed me. Softly. "Never?" she whispered.

It was then that something occurred to me. "This isn't right," I said.

Calli sat back and looked at me. "What?"

I reached past her for one of the two ceramic bowls on the low, wooden table in front of me, picked it up, and showed it to her. The bowl had only a few smears of green fruit meat left in it. "Lands of the Dead, we're out of guacamole. What kind of host am I?"

Bowl in hand, I got up and headed for the kitchen. Behind me, Calli snapped, "Maxtla!"

"I'll be right back," I threw back over my shoulder.

"Maxtla!" she snapped again.

There was an edge in Calli's voice I hadn't heard before. A sharp one. Had I taken the joke too far? Did I have to calm the waters before things got out of hand?

I was in the kitchen by then, but I was ready to go back and apologize. Then it was too late, because Calli had followed me, holding something behind her back.

Before I could ask what it was, she produced the *other* bowl that had been sitting on the table. "Here," she said. "We're out of tortillas as well."

I laughed. I couldn't help it.

Calli draped her arms around my neck. "This is why you love me. Go ahead and say it."

I said it.

Calli refilled the tortilla bowl and took it back to the other room with her. I stayed in the kitchen to make more guacamole.

As I was mashing the avocado meat in the bowl, I found myself thinking about Inave. About how partial he had been to a bowl of good guacamole.

In the end, he'd been a useful informant after all. Even if what he'd told me didn't help me until after he was dead. Still, I thought, he would have been pleased.

The guy had been a banker, not exactly an example of virtue for school children to follow.

But he'd been my friend, in some ways. And a decent father. And he'd treated his clients better than he should have.

That should count for something, I thought. *Not just in the eyes of the gods. In the eyes of men too.*

When they spoke of Inave in cycles to come, I hoped they would be kind.

• • •

Chicome's story hit the Empire like a hand stick in the face.

Everybody in Aztlan was talking about it. On the streets, in building lobbies, in restaurants...even in temple. So it wasn't a surprise when Necalli sent me a message that he wanted to see me.

He was looking out his window when I entered his office. "I just read something on the Mirror," he said.

"Did you."

"About Xipil Nenetl, and the rail line story."

"Oh," I said, "that. I saw it too."

"Lots of juicy details. Written by that guy Chicome."

"I noticed."

"You wouldn't think somebody would jeopardize his job

writing something like that about his employer. And yet...he did."

"I guess getting the story out was more important to him than his job."

"I guess so," Necalli said. "Funny...for cycles, the truth lies hidden. Then it comes out—the *moment* First Chief Zayanya clears us to talk about it." He turned to look at me. "I mean the exact *moment*."

"Quite a coincidence," I conceded.

"A big one," said Necalli.

• • •

As I'd expected, Chicome got fired.

It was announced on the Mirror. With a certain amount of satisfaction, I thought. As if Nenetl had written the notice herself.

Maybe she had—as her last act before she resigned.

I called Chicome to offer my condolences. He didn't call me back. I figured he'd decided he'd made the wrong choice after all, and was blaming me for it.

The next day I saw another notice on the Mirror: Chicome had been hired back. And promoted—*big* time. In fact, he was the new Number Two on the Mirror, reporting to the woman who was taking Nenetl's place.

I smiled to myself. Partly for Chicome, because a guy who makes a sacrifice for the right reasons should be rewarded.

And partly for me—because I wouldn't have to see him in my dreams anymore, demanding what I owed him.

Book Three

It was hard to get anything past my Aunt Xoco. Or, for that matter, to avoid her message that it hadn't gotten past her.

If the octli I brought to her dinner table on the occasion of some festival was a bit too strong—or too *weak*—she would invariably tell me so. Not always in words, but in expressions I had come to understand better than words.

If her mouth opened, it meant she was overjoyed—always for my good fortune rather than her own. If her eyes narrowed, even a little, it meant she disapproved of something. And if her lips pressed together, it meant she was withholding comment—no small effort when it came to someone like my aunt.

For several cycles, even before I left the ball court, she had been prodding me to take a mate. It was time, she told me, for a guy my age to do so. *Past* time, in her estimate.

Which was why she tried to set me up with women she thought would be good matches for me. Attractive women, she said, with good heads, from good families.

But I never saw them the way Aunt Xoco did. So each time, I wriggled off the hook.

When I found someone, I told her, it would be my own doing. Or that of Xochiquetzal, the goddess of love, if she preferred to look at it that way. Either way, my aunt didn't need to interfere.

Not that it kept her from making remarks. Or slipping in subtle inquiries at the dinner table. Or speaking with other women about their daughters.

So when I started mentioning Calli, in response to some offhand question about where I was going and what I was planning on doing there, I wasn't surprised to see the further questions hatching in Aunt Xoco's eyes.

Who is this Calli? Where did you meet her? What are your intentions regarding her?

She didn't give voice to her curiosity, but it was present nonetheless. Like a salamander larva trying to wriggle out of its shell, on the verge of emerging into the light but not quite there yet.

For weeks, my aunt pressed her lips together when Calli's name came up. Pressed them harder, I thought, than she'd ever pressed them before. But there would come a time, I knew, when she would stop pressing them.

That time was after I took Calli to the Western Markets. Not right after, of course, because I was working the fire hands case and then Inave's murder, but the first evening I was free, when I sat down for a feast of Aunt Xoco's grilled venison.

For a few minutes, we talked about small things—the

injuries suffered recently by my old team, the Eagles, and the section of railway undergoing renovation in District Nine, and of course how much I loved the venison.

Then my aunt looked me in the eye and said she wanted to meet "this young woman" I had been speaking of.

It wasn't a suggestion.

• • •

It also wasn't a subject I looked forward to broaching with Calli. She and Aunt Xoco had been cut from different rubber trees, after all.

Calli was a businesswoman, as cultured as anyone I had ever met. My aunt prided herself on being neither of those things.

To Aunt Xoco, society was built on simple, honest traditions—the ones she observed in temple, or along the River on the Emperor's Days, or in her kitchen. She didn't disdain what went on in the Merchant City—not in the least. One of the women she'd tried to match me with was in the furniture business, after all.

But in the end, my aunt placed family on a higher shelf than profits. And family meant little ones. It was that—the part about little ones—that I thought would make Calli most uncomfortable in meeting my aunt.

Our future was something Calli and I hadn't talked about. Marriage, children…as much as we enjoyed each other's company, those topics hadn't come up. Not yet.

But Aunt Xoco would *bring* them up. Of that, I had no doubt.

"You don't have to do this," I told Calli over my radio, after my aunt made her demand. "I can make an excuse for you. Working long hours on some important project…"

"Nonsense," Calli said. "I can't wait to meet your aunt."

If she'd meant to be ironic, I had missed it. "Really?"

"Of course. You think things are any different where I come from?"

Calli came from wealth. I'd known that from the moment I met her. While I'd never met any of her kin, I had always assumed they were as worldly as she was.

"Every family has an Aunt Xoco," Calli said. "She's looking out for you, Maxtla. It's sweet."

I let out a breath I didn't know I'd been holding. "I'm glad you think so."

I waited for a response, but all I heard was silence. "Are you still there?" I asked.

"Of course. I'm just thinking."

There it is, I thought. *The second thought. The question of whether she wants to get involved with Aunt Xoco after all.*

And by extension, with me.

"About?" I asked, wincing a little as I anticipated the answer.

"About where to meet your aunt. I want to take her to a place she'll enjoy."

"*You* want to take her?" It was customary for a man to introduce a prospective mate to his family.

"Why not?" Calli asked. "She and I will get to know each other better if you're not there gumming up the works."

It made sense. I just hoped Aunt Xoco would see it that way.

"Does she like gopher?" Calli asked.

"The way *she* makes it," I said, "yes."

I imagined Calli frowning. "That could be a problem. Is there something she likes that she *doesn't* make?"

I thought for a moment. "Beaver. She tries but she says it doesn't come out right."

"Excellent. I've got just the place. The Beaver Dam. The stuffed beaver there is to die for."

"It can't be too fancy. Aunt Xoco likes simple preparations. Traditional recipes."

Calli laughed. "You're worried. Don't be. We'll have fun."

"Who's worried?" I asked, worrying.

• • •

As luck would have it, I had a game the night Calli was to meet Aunt Xoco. Which was fine with me.

I preferred losing skin to the walls of a ball court to sitting at home wondering if Calli and my aunt were getting along.

Besides, I'd missed a game while I was following the trail of Inave's killer. I looked forward to going back into the tlachtli and getting some blood pumping.

Unfortunately, my team—the Scale Beetles—was down a couple of players. One, Ocelopan, was out with a sprained ankle and the other had to go to a baby-naming ceremony. If we couldn't replace them, we would forfeit the match—something we hadn't done in all the time I'd been on the team, which was one of the reasons we were so often at the top of the standings.

Worse, I would have to wait another thirteen days to play a game.

Ocelopan, who ordinarily manned the attacker position as I did, was the team manager. In the past, he'd been able to find stand-ins when we needed them. But not in this case.

"I don't know what it is," he told me two days before the match. "Everyone I know has said he can't make it. Investigators have to run down criminals, right? There must be someone in your office who can hold his own."

I could think of only one guy—Izcuin. He didn't strike me as the athletic sort, but he'd played in leagues as a kid, or so he said.

"Ask him," said Ocelopan.

I asked.

"I'd love to," said Izcuin.

"Great," I said, knowing we would at least avoid the forfeit.

• • •

The night of the match, I met Izcuin at the entrance to the building that housed the ball court, thanked him again for coming, and took him down into the locker room.

Huemac, our center, greeted my colleague with his customary refinement. "Who's this, Maxtla?" he barked. "I didn't know you had a sister."

I'd prepared Izcuin for Huemac's bluster, and he was a good-natured sort anyway, so he took the jab with a smile. "Maxtla says you guys are good," he said. "I hope I don't drag you down."

Huemac slid a glance at Ecatzin, who was busy applying beetle's-blood paint to his forehead. "Well," he said, indicating Ecatzin with a jerk of his thumb, "you can't be any worse than *this* has-been."

Ecatzin just laughed to himself.

But for Izcuin's benefit, I said, "Ecatzin played in the Sun League."

"As Maxtla did," Ecatzin noted.

Huemac dismissed us with a flip of his hand. "These old men...they can't wait to remind us they were famous once."

"Once," said Atl, one of our defenders, "is better than not at all."

"I could play in the Sun League *tomorrow*," Huemac told Izcuin. "I just don't want to make Maxtla look bad. His feelings get hurt so easily."

"Don't listen to Huemac," I told Izcuin. "I taught the guy everything he knows."

"Fortunately," Huemac said, "I've been able to forget most of it."

And so it went, until a friend of Atl's arrived to play defender and round out our roster, and we entered the ball court to play the Grey Wolves.

Atl's friend wasn't as useful as he might have been. Atl had to play twice as hard to make up for the guy's blunders—and because he couldn't make up for all of them, we fell behind two goals to none.

Izcuin, on the other hand, was better than anyone expected. What he lacked in athleticism, he made up in court sense. Whenever the Wolves got something going, Izcuin was in a position to break it up.

After a while, Ecatzin took the game over. Some nights he was just all right. On others he was a blur, reminding us how good he had been in the Sun League.

This was one of the nights he was a blur. He scored two goals and assisted on a third, which I put through the stone hoop with seconds left in the match.

We were winners when we got back to our locker room, riding high as a result. And though Ecatzin got his share of accolades, it was Izcuin who received the biggest praise.

"You kept us in that game!" said Huemac, pointing a crooked finger in Izcuin's face. "Don't think I didn't notice!"

Ecatzin patted Izcuin on the shoulder. "I hope you're not taking on anything demanding for the next couple of moons. We expect regular attendance of our players."

Izcuin grinned at the vote of confidence. "I'll make sure I'm around."

"And bring a skin of octli for each of us," Huemac said. He shot a look at me. "You told him about the octli...right?"

• • •

On the way to the rail line, I assured Izcuin that there was no need to bring octli.

"I could," the rookie said.

"Huemac would only ask for something else the next time. Something illegal, more than likely." In fact, he'd asked Atl for *chocolate* when Atl joined the team. But I'd advised Atl as I was advising Izcuin: "So don't."

The rail lines, east and west, were separated by a tunnel that went under the tracks. My train was at the far end of the tunnel.

"Anyway," said Izcuin, "they seem like a good bunch."

"When they win," I said.

Just then, my buzzer went off. I answered it: "Colhua."

"Maxtla?"

It was Calli. I recognized her voice, though it was little more than a whisper.

She was keeping something from Aunt Xoco, I thought. *That their evening didn't go well. That Aunt Xoco made her crazy. That she's never going to see me again.*

Then Calli spoke again, quicker, harsher: "Maxtla!"

This time, the anxiety in her voice was unmistakable. Something had happened, all right. Something worse than a disagreement with Aunt Xoco.

"Are you all right?" I asked. "Is Aunt Xoco all right?"

"Maxtla, someone's *following* us!"

I felt my throat tighten. "Where are y—?" I started to ask. Then I remembered: The Beaver Dam. It would take me an hour to get to District Nineteen—too long for me to be of any help.

But we had officers all over the city. I had to call Necalli, get someone over there…I just didn't want to lose the connection with Calli.

"Give me your radio," I told Izcuin.

He didn't hesitate. He took his radio out of his pouch and handed it over.

"Hang on!" I told Calli. "I'm going to get someone to you. What street are you on?"

"Teteo, near the River. Please," said Calli, "hurry!"

Hurry, I thought. The word was a knife in my gut.

Still, I forced myself to remain calm as I punched in Necalli's number. A moment later, he answered: "Izcuin?"

"No," I said, "it's Colhua. My Aunt Xoco, my girlfriend…

they're on Teteo, near the River. They say someone's *following* them."

Had it been Calli alone who thought so, Necalli might have questioned her judgment. But not Aunt Xoco, my father's sister.

"They need whoever—" I started.

"I've got District Nineteen," Necalli said, interrupting me. And a moment later, "Two officers, on their way."

Thank the gods, I thought.

"I'll call you back," Necalli told me.

As he said so, Izcuin's rail carriage pulled into the station. Izcuin didn't get in. His place was on the other side of the city from District Nineteen, but he wasn't going to leave my side until he knew Calli and Aunt Xoco were all right.

Just as I wouldn't have left *his*.

• • •

Long before I could get to Teteo Street, Necalli called to tell me the officers had reached Calli and Aunt Xoco, and they hadn't been harmed. I breathed a little prayer of gratitude—first to my aunt's birth-god, and then to Calli's.

"I'll have them brought here to the Interrogation Center," said Necalli.

He also told me there was more to their story.

When I got to the Interrogation Center, Calli and Aunt Xoco were sitting in Necalli's office, sipping cinnamon tea. Calli was holding my aunt's hand.

If Aunt Xoco was shaken by what had happened, she wasn't showing it—not any more than my father would have.

But when our eyes met, I saw the concern in hers. Having

been briefed by Necalli, I knew the reason for it.

I knelt in front of the two women I cared most about in the world, put my hands on their hands, and looked from one to the other. "Are you all right?" I asked.

Calli shrugged. "Under the circumstances."

Aunt Xoco looked at me. "They told you about the sound we heard?"

I nodded.

"Was it what I think it was?" my aunt asked.

"I don't know," I said.

And I didn't. I hadn't been there, after all. And, like Aunt Xoco, I only knew what a fire hand sounded like from the features I'd seen on the Mirror.

"Did you get a look at the guy?" I asked.

"Not a good one," said Calli.

I turned to Aunt Xoco.

"Nothing that will help you," she said.

Necalli smiled at Calli and then at my aunt. "You two stay here. He looked at Izcuin, who was standing by the window. "Get them whatever they need, right?"

"The second they need it," Izcuin assured us.

Necalli took me by the arm and led me out of his office, into the array of monitors set up for his Investigators. At this hour, there was no one using them.

"It's possible," said Necalli, "it was just a robber. Two women, walking the streets alone..."

"In District Nineteen?" I asked. "Is there a safer part of the city?"

My boss frowned. "I know."

"And what they heard…"

"A fire hand—or something else? We still don't know. Either way, I'm going to assign an officer to each of them, your girlfriend as well as your aunt. An Investigator, if I can. I'd assign a whole squad, but…"

"I understand," I said.

Calli and Aunt Xoco weren't nobles. Common people weren't supposed to be eligible for police protection—especially when they hadn't actually been attacked by anyone.

Though if it *was* a fire hand they'd heard…how much help was an officer going to be anyway?

"By the way," said Necalli, "I think you've got some time coming."

My week at the Western Markets had used up whatever vacation time I'd accumulated. Necalli knew it, too.

"Of course," he said, "I could be wrong. But by the time Zayanya's office figures it out…"

"Thanks," I said.

"Don't thank *me*. Thank your father. His friends would cut my heart out if I let something happen to his sister."

• • •

Aunt Xoco's bodyguard turned out to be Takun. She didn't know him but she accepted him without comment. Then again, she had been part of the police community long enough to see others receive such unofficial protection.

Calli wasn't as willing. "I've got people to see," she told me. "Meetings to attend. Deals to make. I can't do any of that with a police officer tagging along."

"Even if your life depends on it?" I asked.

She sighed. "Look. I believe someone was following us. I caught a glimpse of him, just as your aunt did. But the rest of it—"

"The fire hand?" I said.

"That part," said Calli, "I'm not so sure about. You know I've heard them, right? On that mission?"

She had been to Europe on a trade mission for the Emperor. Her last night there, her hosts had arranged a sharpshooting demonstration. Ten men and women had competed to see who could display the most accuracy with a fire hand.

Calli had described the sounds to me. Like the cracks of a whip, she'd said, but louder. So she knew how a fire hand sounded.

"You're not sure?" I echoed.

"That it was a fire hand. In fact, I barely heard anything. It was your aunt—" She stopped herself.

"It's all right," I said. "You can say it."

"Maxtla, I *like* Aunt Xoco. I just—" Again, Calli stopped in mid-sentence.

"You think she heard something that wasn't there."

"I don't know. I mean, there have been rumors, just as you said there would be. Stories about fire hands here in the Empire. If Aunt Xoco heard the rumors, and then heard a sound…"

It wasn't an unreasonable conclusion. But even if Calli was right, it didn't change anything.

"There's still a stalker," I said. "You saw him. You *both* did.

If he goes after you again—"

"I won't go anywhere alone," Calli said. "And I'll be home well before dark. I promise."

I didn't like the idea of her going around Aztlan without protection. Especially when she was used to braving the seedier parts of the city without a second thought.

But it was her life. I couldn't tell her what to do with it.

• • •

After talking with Calli, I was less certain that the stalker had a fire hand. But I also couldn't rule it out. It was the possibility that my aunt was right after all that led me back to my cousin Ximo.

After Notoca was arrested, his accomplices in his fire hands gambit had gone into hiding, or so I'd heard from my street sources. So Ximo wouldn't have a direct line to any fire hands business.

Still, it was worth checking with him—especially in that Aunt Xoco was *his* aunt as well.

His mother and Aunt Xoco had only been half-sisters, true. And like my father, Aunt Xoco had lost touch with Ximo's mother over time. However, the sisters had shared a bedroom for a while growing up, eaten at the same table, played the same games. There was a bond there Ximo would know about and honor.

I went to visit him at his headquarters. Instantly, I was surrounded by Hawks—no less than I'd expected.

A moment later, Ximo appeared at the top of the stairs. "You're becoming a regular here," he observed.

But he didn't tell me to go away. Instead, he waved away the other Hawks. Reluctantly, they dispersed.

"Come up," Ximo said.

I went up the stairs and followed him to the desk where I'd seen him the last time. It was only the two of us there, as far as I could tell. But then, Ximo was the Hawks' leader. If he wanted to talk to an Investigator, it was his business.

"Aunt Xoco," he said.

So he'd heard. I wasn't surprised. ""If you have any idea who might have been following her…"

"Unfortunately," Ximo said, "I don't. But if we see anything, you'll be the first to know."

"*See* anything?" I asked.

He smiled a hard smile. "You think you're the only one with eyes on Aunt Xoco?"

So it wasn't just the police who would be looking out for her. I nodded. "Thanks."

"No need," said Ximo. "She's my family too."

• • •

If Notoca hadn't been in a cell, he would have been the first one I suspected of stalking Calli and my aunt.

However, the judge had seen Notoca's crime the way I had—not just as murder, which would have been bad enough, but as a threat to our way of life in the Empire. Which was why he had sentenced Notoca to thirty cycles in prison.

A big chunk of the guy's life, no question. But what he had done called for nothing less.

As an Investigator, I had access to every part of the Prison

House—including the *cuauhcalli*, the innermost block of cells, where we kept those who'd committed the most serious crimes in the Empire. Murder, of course, was one of them.

It wasn't the cheeriest place in the building. But it was where I would find Notoca.

It was lunchtime when I entered his cell. On seeing who had come to visit him, he cursed under his breath.

"Notoca," I said.

Again, he cursed.

It seemed to me I'd started a fire in him, one that was eating him from the inside. As if it were my fault, and not his, that he'd killed that Euro and dumped his corpse in the River of Stars.

To that point, Notoca hadn't given up the details of how he'd gotten the fire hands—who had delivered them, or how, or when, or where. So I wasn't surprised when he put aside the remains of his food, turned to the wall beside him, and said, "I'm not a *warbler*."

Warbler was one of the names gangs had for guys who incriminated their former associates.

"I know," I said. "Which is why, normally, I wouldn't ask for your help. But last night, someone followed a person who's important to me. Any idea who the someone might have been?"

Notoca cast a sideways glance at me, but he didn't comment. I wasn't his favorite person, after all.

"You know," I said, "that you can help yourself. Cut your sentence down a little."

"Why?" Notoca sneered. "So I can get out a little sooner? Have a little *less* time before Ximo breaks my ankles?"

"It might help you with Ximo too. This person is important to him as well."

Notoca looked at me. *Who can it be?* he seemed to be wondering. *Someone who's precious to both a gang leader and the Emperor's Investigator?*

For a moment, I thought the possibility of pleasing Ximo might be enticement enough for him to help me. But in the end, Notoca just sat there.

So either he didn't know who'd followed Calli and Aunt Xoco, or he knew and wasn't saying. Either way I was going to leave empty-handed.

"Suit yourself," I said, and turned to go.

"Investigator," he said, stopping me.

I turned back to him.

"Someday," Notoca continued, "I'll get out of here. And I'll remember who put me in the Prison House."

"I'll worry about it then," I said, and left him sitting there in his cell.

• • •

I didn't expect Donner would be of any help in finding our stalker.

It would have been hard for him to identify the provenance of a single fire hand even if he had found it on his doorstep—much less across a wide ocean. And we didn't have a weapon in hand, so I couldn't offer him a description.

Still, Donner was our expert on fire hands. If the stalker had discharged one—and I still had to entertain the possibility that he had—it made sense to give the Inspector a call.

As before, he appeared on my Monitor screen mere seconds after I reached out to him. But this time was different from the others.

Donner was wearing a droopy red cap with a white puff at the end of it. The puff sat on his collarbone like a fat, white guinea pig.

His eyes, I saw, were bloodshot. Had he been imbibing? At *work*?

It seemed unlikely. But then, Europe was a different world.

Donner grinned a lopsided grin. "Looks like you've caught me in the midst of our holiday celebration."

Someone I couldn't see called out in a raw voice, and Donner laughed and swiveled in his chair, and called back in response.

Finally, he turned to me again. "Sorry, Investigator. It's the way it is this time of year. Is there something I can do for you?"

"I hope so," I said.

I told him what had happened to Calli and Aunt Xoco. As I spoke, Donner's demeanor changed. By the end of my account, he looked utterly sober.

"We haven't found a shell," I said, "but the sound alone…"

"Would seem to indicate you haven't yet found all the guns in the Empire."

"I'm just taking a shot here," I said, "but if there's anything on your end…"

Donner shook his head. "Nothing I'm aware of. Of course, my net only spreads so wide."

Pretty much what I had expected he would say.

"Sorry, mate. I wish I could have been of more help."

"It's all right," I said. "Enjoy your holiday."

"Thanks," Donner said. "Cheers, Investigator."

And my screen went blank.

• • •

I went over to Calli's that night for dinner. If I couldn't get her to accept a bodyguard, I figured I'd keep an eye on her myself.

She saw my intention from the moment I walked in with a bag full of chicken mixiotes.

"You know," she told me, accepting the bag, "you don't have to watch over me, Maxtla."

"Who's watching?" I said, following her into her eating room. "I'm just visiting a woman I've become fond of."

"You know how many times you've come over for dinner during the week?"

I didn't.

"This time," she said, "is the first. But you're not watching over me, right?"

I sighed. "And if I am? Is that so terrible?"

"Of course not. It's nice to have you here. *Always*. It's just—" She frowned and turned her attention to the barbecued chicken pieces, which she was laying out on a plate.

"What?" I asked.

"I'm just not sure about the whole stalker thing."

"You mean about the fire hand."

She turned to me. "Not just that. I'm not sure there was a stalker at all."

I was surprised. "You said—"

"I know. I said I saw him. But the more I think about, the more I wonder…did I just *think* I saw him? Aunt Xoco was so sure of it…"

And people could be influenced to see things that weren't there. I knew that too well from my investigations.

Yet my aunt had sounded positive—not just about the stalker, but about the fire hand. And she had never been one to let her imagination get the best of her.

"Look," I said, "police err on the side of caution. That's how we're trained. If it turns out there's nothing to be afraid of, great. But if there *is* something, we're there to deal with it."

Calli nodded. "I suppose. And if it turned out I was wrong, and something happened to Aunt Xoco…."

I took Calli in my arms. "It's not your decision. Don't worry about it."

She kissed me, her lips warm on mine. "I'll try not to."

As it turned out, we didn't eat the mixiotes until later than night. *Much* later.

• • •

The next morning, I called Aunt Xoco.

I didn't want to ask her if she felt safe. She would be insulted. After all, she prided herself on being my father's sister.

So instead I asked, "How's Takun doing?"

"Fine, Maxtla. He's a good eater, you know."

I imagined my aunt stuffing Takun with delicacies. But that wasn't why he was there. "I don't mean as a house guest, Aunt Xoco. I mean as your bodyguard."

"Don't worry, he watches me like a white-tailed hawk. Your

father would have liked him."

Somehow, it bothered me that she thought so. My father had always been sensitive to the needs of others, and Takun... well, *wasn't*.

Nonetheless, I said, "That's good to hear. So where are you taking Takun today, Aunt Xoco? To the market? The park?"

"I have a physician's appointment today."

"Oh?" I said.

A pause. Then: "It's nothing. See you later, Maxtla." And my aunt ended the conversation.

I stood there with my radio in hand, staring out the window of Calli's apartment. Aunt Xoco had never rushed me off the phone that way before.

Was it possible she had come to prefer Takun's company to mine? Or did she have another reason?

Something about the physician she had mentioned?

I was concerned. Aunt Xoco wasn't a young woman, after all.

Cycles earlier, in a moment of uncharacteristic level-headedness, she had agreed to put me on her medical list of trusted relatives. In fact, I *was* her list of trusted relatives.

Which meant I had permission to look up her medical appointments on the Mirror.

By then, Calli had gone to work, so I could sit at her screen without explaining why I needed it. Which was good. I didn't want her thinking I made a habit of invading my aunt's medical records.

It took only a moment to bring them up. Aunt Xoco had been pretty healthy all her life, so I didn't see anything out of the ordinary. And that morning's appointment wasn't out of the ordinary either—just a routine checkup.

It was the *other* appointment that drew my attention. It had been made for the following week. With a hearing doctor, whose name sounded familiar to me.

I buzzed his office. After a moment, I heard a man's voice: "Physician's office."

"This is Maxtla Colhua," I said. "My aunt's name is Xoco—"

"*Colhua*. It's about *time* you called me. I've been trying to get ahold of you for three moons now."

I hadn't received any calls from him. I said so.

"Hold on a moment. Let me get your aunt's records."

He was gone for a couple of minutes. When he got back on the line, he said, "Is this your radio code?" and read off a series of numbers that were unfamiliar to me.

"It's not," I said.

"Well, that explains why I couldn't get in touch with you."

I suggested that he or someone in his office had written down the wrong number.

"Actually," he said, "your aunt was the one who wrote it down. Not that it matters. I've got you now."

Then he told me what he was calling about. "She never mentioned this to you?"

"She didn't," I confirmed. "But rest assured, I'll mention it to *her*."

• • •

I waited until Aunt Xoco would be finished with her checkup. Then I called her.

"Is everything all right?" she asked.

I understood her concern. We had just spoken a couple of hours ago, after all.

I went straight to the heart of the matter. "I spoke with your hearing physician."

Silence for a moment. "*Him*?"

"He said he wanted to fit you with a hearing aid. But you refused it."

"He just wanted to pull a few more beans out of my pouch, Maxtla."

"He said you need it."

"It's so ugly. And so unnecessary. I hear you fine." She said something to Takun. I could hear him reply. "You see?" said my aunt. "Takun says I hear fine too."

"Takun has no say in this," I told her. "You ignored your physician's advice. And then, it seems, you gave him the wrong number to get ahold of me."

"I didn't like him, Maxtla. He looked like that boy you grew up with. The one who liked to tease cats?"

The boy's name was Xahcalli. But I wasn't going to let my aunt change the subject.

"He's a reputable physician, Aunt Xoco. Remember when you said your ear hurt a few cycles ago, and I asked people who they used? And his name came up more than any other?"

"Still," she said.

"No," I said. "I know you. It wasn't the physician. It was the hearing aid."

"It makes me look old, Maxtla. Do you think any of my

friends wears an aid? Not one. And their hearing is a lot worse than mine. And I heard that sound last night, didn't I? Well, didn't I?"

That was the question, even if I didn't say so out loud. "Aunt Xoco, if your physician says—"

I heard a gasp on the other end of the line. "Maxtla! Don't tell me you don't believe me! I heard what I heard!"

"I'm not saying I don't believe you," I told my aunt.

At least, her nephew wasn't saying that. The Investigator in me had his doubts.

• • •

That afternoon, I visited Teteo Street. It was, as I'd remembered, one of the nicer thoroughfares in District Nineteen.

Not *the* nicest. After all, I'd warned Calli about Aunt Xoco's allergy to anything fancy. Still, it was a street that boasted wrought iron streetlights in the forms of winding serpents, and ceramic pots full of flowering plants, and flecks of mica glittering in the concrete under one's feet.

It was hard to imagine the prospect of violence there, or terror, or the crack of a fire hand going off. Especially during the day, when there were no shadows in which to hide.

Still, Teteo Street had seen—and heard—all those things the night before, if Aunt Xoco's account could be believed. And I couldn't dismiss it, even if I had reason to do so. Which was why I was there, looking for evidence.

It wasn't hard to find the restaurant where Calli had taken my aunt for stuffed beaver. The place was closed at that hour but there were people inside, mopping the floor and polishing the woodwork, and they'd already put out some tables and chairs for those who preferred to eat outdoors.

I knocked.

A man rolled his eyes, said something to the rest of the staff, and opened the door. "We'll be serving lunch in a couple of hours," he told me.

"I'm not looking for lunch," I said. "Though I've heard your stuffed beaver is among the best in Aztlan."

I pulled up my sleeve and showed him my bracelet.

"Ah," said the man. He gestured for me to enter. "Please."

I went inside and took a seat at a table. My host, who identified himself as the owner of the place, sat down opposite me. "You're here," he said, "because of what happened last night."

"I am," I said. "What can you tell me about it?"

"Only that the women ate here and enjoyed their meals, judging from the comments I overheard. I'm not sure what their relationship was, but there were times when they seemed a little uncomfortable with each other."

"Uncomfortable?" I said.

"Yes. The older woman especially. She fell silent now and then. When that happened, the younger woman had to carry the conversation by herself."

As interested as I was in how dinner had gone, that wasn't why I was there. I had come to get an understanding of what happened *afterward*.

"They told me they were being followed," I said. "Did you see any indication of that when they left?"

"None. Nor would I think to look for any. This isn't the kind of neighborhood where people are followed out of a restaurant."

"Did anyone else leave your place about the time they did?"

His eyes narrowed. "You think—"

I wasn't there to share theories with him. "Did they?"

He thought for a moment, or at least seemed to. "I don't believe so."

"Did you hear any odd sounds?"

He thought again. Finally, he said, "Nothing out of the ordinary."

I thanked him and left the restaurant.

• • •

Before I put Teteo Street behind me, I looked around. Despite Calli's skepticism, and Aunt Xoco's hearing problem, and what I'd just heard from the restaurant owner, I wasn't ready to set my aunt's account aside.

If someone had discharged a fire hand, there might be evidence of it. A bullet casing, maybe. A chink in the stone of a wall the bullet struck.

I spent some time searching the place. I checked the walls and the walk. Looked and felt under the restaurant's outdoor tables and chairs. Peered into every cranny I could find.

And found nothing.

Just for good measure, I went down to the corner and turned onto Citlalolli, the cross street. There was another restaurant there. It had the same scattering of tables and chairs—no doubt to compete with the first place.

I hunkered down, as I had on Teteo Street, and looked in

the shadows under the first table. There was nothing there. Then I ran my fingers along the table's legs, one at a time. It was as I felt the third leg, just under the table top, that I felt something.

A projection. A metal projection, it seemed to me.

I turned the table over to get a better look—and there it was, embedded in the wood of the leg: *A metal casing.*

I smiled to myself. My aunt hadn't been seeing things after all. Or hearing them, for that matter. Someone had discharged a fire hand the night before.

Of course, I didn't want that to become common knowledge, so I took my hand stick out of my pouch and used it to hack the casing out of the table leg. Then I put the casing in my pouch, along with my hand stick, and turned the table over again.

I have to call Necalli, I thought, and took out my radio.

But before I could punch in his code, my radio buzzed. I answered it: "Colhua."

"It's Necalli." There was an urgency in his voice that sent a chill up my spine. "The stalker showed up again. Your aunt is fine—but Takun was hurt."

Gods... "How bad?"

"We don't know yet. Call your aunt."

Takun, I thought, my throat constricting. Then I tamped down my feelings, because Aunt Xoco would need me to be calm, and called her.

"Maxtla!" she answered, her voice full of pain.

I clenched my teeth. Then I said, "It's all right, Aunt Xoco."

"They hurt poor Takun."

"Necalli told me. Where are you?"

"At the House of Healing. With some officers. They say Chief Necalli is on his way."

"So am I," I said.

• • •

On my way to the House of Healing, I called Calli.

She answered, "Maxtla?"

"Aunt Xoco was right," I said. "There's a stalker. He put Takun in the House of Healing."

I heard a whispered prayer.

"Where are you?" I asked.

"At a client's office. In the Merchant City."

"Stay there. I'm sending over a couple of officers. Don't leave until they get there."

I half-expected Calli to refuse the escort. Thank the gods, she didn't.

• • •

The House of Healing was only a few rail stops away. It felt like a lot more.

As I walked into the lobby, I saw my aunt sitting there. She looked the way she'd looked when we heard about my father.

No tears. At least not on the outside. But on the inside, a flood of them.

I sat down next to her and took her hand. "I'm so sorry, Aunt Xoco."

She drew a ragged breath. Then she said, "It's not your fault, Maxtla."

Except it was.

I was responsible for the stalker. I didn't know how, but I was.

"I have to go upstairs," I told my aunt. That was where Takun was, after all. And where Necalli would be.

"I understand," she said.

"I'll get an auto-carriage for you."

"Necalli called one already. But I won't leave until I know about Takun."

I knew better than to argue with her. "Fair enough. I'll let you know what I find out."

"I'll be here," said my aunt.

• • •

By the time I was ushered up to the visitors' alcove on Takun's floor, Necalli was standing there talking to a physician. As I approached them, I looked for news in their expressions.

For a moment, I thought I saw something dark and tragic there, and my heart fell. Then Necalli turned to me and said, "They don't think there's any permanent damage."

I expelled a breath I didn't know I'd been holding.

"Your colleague's injury was deep," the physician added. "All the way down to the skull. But he should make a full recovery."

I was confused. "They shot him in the head…?"

"His assailant didn't use a fire hand," Necalli explained. "He used a hand stick."

I absorbed the information. "Then…"

"What?" said Necalli.

I took him aside, reached into my pouch, and took out the bullet casing. "I found this," I said, "around the corner from where my aunt and Calli ate dinner last night."

Necalli frowned. Deeply. "So your aunt was right. The stalker had a fire hand."

"Which raises a question. If it was the same guy…"

"Why didn't he use the fire hand on Takun?"

Neither of us had an answer. At least not yet.

"I have to call my aunt," I said. "She's—"

"I know," said Necalli. "Go ahead."

I buzzed Aunt Xoco and told her Takun was in better shape than we had feared. I heard her expel a breath. "The gods are kind, Maxtla."

Sometimes, I thought. "You can go home now."

"Yes," my aunt said.

There would be another escort waiting for her at the entrance to her building. Not Takun, but a police officer Necalli knew and respected.

Though the knowledge didn't fill me with as much confidence as it should have. There was no one tougher than Takun. If he couldn't stop an attacker, what hope did anyone else have?

• • •

That night, I got a call from Ximo.

"I owe Aunt Xoco an apology," he said.

It wasn't something a guy like him said every day. "It's all right," I told him.

"It's *not* all right. We should have been more alert. Our eyes were on Aunt Xoco, not your friend, but we should have seen the guy coming. We should have seen where he *went*."

"Don't beat yourself up. Takun didn't see the guy either."

A pause. "How is he, this Takun?"

"He'll be fine," I said.

"Good. From what I understand, Aunt Xoco took a liking to him."

"That she did."

"We'll do better next time, Little Rabbit. Count on it."

I smiled to myself. Ximo was smart enough to say that only where no one else could hear it.

"Know the gods' favor," I told him.

"You too," he said.

• • •

It wasn't until the next day that any of us was allowed to visit Takun. Normally, it would have been Necalli. In this case, Takun asked for *me*.

Necalli understood. It was my aunt Takun had been watching, after all. Takun wanted to make sure she was all right, that she was getting the protection she needed.

And he wanted to apologize for letting her down.

Not that I blamed Takun for what had happened. First, Aunt Xoco hadn't been injured, not even after Takun went down—a mystery, though I wasn't complaining. Second, anyone in our line of work knew we could be only so vigilant. If an attacker was determined enough, they would get to you eventually.

Just as they had gotten to Takun.

"You've got five minutes," his physician told me outside the door to Takun's room. "Absolutely no more. And he's on pain medication, so he may not be all there."

"I hear you," I said. Still, I had questions, and Takun was

the one who had the answers.

I opened his door and entered his room. He was sleeping in a bed against the far wall, hooked up to a tube on one side and a monitor on the other.

He looked terrible. His eyes were puffy and dark, though the rest of his face was pale as a lizard's belly.

The worst part, of course, would be the wound his attacker had inflicted on him. Fortunately, I couldn't see it because of the bandage on his head. But I knew what a hand stick could do in close quarters.

"Takun?" I said, softly so as not to startle him.

He opened his eyes. Partway, at least. "Colhua," he said, his voice thin and weak. And then: "Your aunt...?"

"She's fine. Thanks to you."

He sighed. "They told me last night...but I didn't trust them. I wanted to hear it from *you*."

"We've only got a few minutes," I said.

Takun grunted. "The damned physician."

"Exactly. So..."

"Go ahead," he said.

I asked about his attacker. Unfortunately, Takun hadn't glimpsed enough of the guy to be of help. "But," he said, "I got *this*..." And he pointed to a drawer in the night table beside him.

I opened the drawer. There was a bracelet inside—a blue rubber bracelet. I turned it over in my hands. It had a stylized symbol incised into it and painted a bright yellow: An elk with an eight-point rack.

"It was in my hand," Takun rasped, "when they found me. Maybe it…" He swallowed. "Maybe it fell off the guy. Maybe…"

I put my hand on hi shoulder. "Take it easy."

He ignored my advice. "Maybe I grabbed it…I don't know…"

"Takun…" I said.

"They asked me about it…when I woke up. I told them…to put it in the drawer." He looked at me. "It could…"

"I could mean something," I said, finishing the thought for him. "It could. Good work."

"Yeah," said Takun. "I really…really used my *head*…" And he made a sound in his throat that I took for a laugh.

I laughed a little too. Until I saw Takun grimace.

"It hurts," I said.

He seemed to sink deeper into his pillow. "Yeah."

"I feel bad," I said. "It should have been *me* that guy attacked."

"You know," Takun breathed, "I've been thinking…the same thing…"

I smiled. "It's good to see you haven't lost your sense of humor."

"Just some scalp. You…owe me, Colhua."

"I figured you'd say that." Taking out of my pocket the little paper bag I'd brought with me, I pressed it into his hand.

He looked at it, held it to his nose, sniffed—and took on a contented look, pain and all. "Cinnamon gum."

"I asked your doctors if it was all right," I said. "They told me it might make you uglier. I told them that was impossible."

Takun eyed me through his swollen, dark eyes. "You're a good guy," he whispered, his concentration weakening. "I can't remember now…why I thought so little of you…"

Takun's physician appeared at the door and pointed to the chronometer on his wrist. I nodded to him.

"I've got to go," I told Takun.

"Thanks for the gum…" he said.

I patted his shoulder. "Don't chew too hard, all right? It'll loosen your stitches. And get better quick. It's hard to make fun of you when you're lying there like that."

Takun didn't answer. He just closed his eyes and drifted off to sleep again. But he didn't drop the bag of gum.

Outside my colleague's room, his physician said, "I hope you got what you needed."

"I hope so too," I told him.

• • •

Behind the House of Healing, I sat with Necalli in front of an otherwise lonely reflecting pool and went over what we knew.

"Someone attacked Takun," I said. "Probably the stalker, though we don't know for sure. He used a hand stick, after all."

"And not a fire hand," said Necalli.

"But why go after Takun? Whoever it was, he didn't take anything. Not even Takun's hand stick, which he could have sold as a trophy."

"He also didn't go after your aunt. So that wasn't his objective either."

"Then what was it? His way of telling us we can't protect Aunt Xoco or Calli—even with police escorts? Why would he want to make that kind of point?"

"Why would that be important to him," Necalli said.

I reached into my pouch and took out the rubber bracelet Takun had given me. "Before the guy got away, Takun got hold of this."

I handed it to Necalli. He looked at it, turned it over in his hands, looked some more. In the morning sunlight, the yellow drawing of the elk on the bracelet seemed to burn even brighter.

"What is it?" he asked.

"I have an idea," I said.

After all, I'd seen something like it before. And I believed I remembered where.

• • •

Paynal Mizquitl had played with me on the Eagles for just one season. He had done well enough to remain on the roster—and probably would have—if a talented rookie hadn't joined the club in the offseason, edging him out.

Getting cut broke Paynal's heart. Understandably so. The night he found out, I and a couple of his other teammates took him to an octli house in the Merchant City. It wasn't the end, we told him. He was good. He would hook up with another team. And he did.

But at the end of the next season, he was cut again. And again, he had to find another place to play.

Paynal hung around the Sun League for four more cycles, clawing his way onto this roster or that one. But he never had a season quite like the one he'd had with the Eagles. In the end, he went back home and opened a sweat lodge, or so I'd heard.

Paynal had worn a bracelet much like the one Takun had

given me. It didn't have an elk on it, but it was the same blue rubber band with the same primitive style of artwork.

I got Paynal's radio code from the Mirror. As I'd hoped, he was happy to hear from me.

"I saw you on the Mirror, Maxtla. The High Priest! It took stones to arrest someone like that."

"All in a day's work," I said. Then I told him one of my colleagues had been injured in an attempted arrest—of a man with a bracelet like his. "Fortunately, the Investigator grabbed it before the man could get away."

"What does it look like?" Paynal asked me.

I described it. "Sound familiar?"

"It does. It's the symbol of the Ozomahtli family. They live west of here, deep in the mountains."

Deep in the mountains was one way of putting it. Tlacamayeh tecuani—*wild bears*—was another. Bears were solitary animals, after all, preferring to hunt on their own rather than form a much larger community.

And there was a third way: "Isolationists."

"Exactly," said Paynal.

I considered the possibility. "It seems unlikely that one of them would set foot in Aztlan."

"It does. But it happens, Maxtla. More often than you might think."

• • •

"Isolationists…?" said Necalli.

"That's what my friend said," I told him.

He made a face there in his office. "Those buzzards shun

cities the way cockroaches shun the light. Aztlan's the last place they'd want to visit."

"And yet," I said, "one of them has. And according to my friend, he's not alone. He said there are dozens of tlacamayeh tecuani here at any given time. They just don't advertise the fact."

Necalli didn't seem eager to embrace the possibility. "What if it's just his bracelet that's paying us a visit?"

"You mean to throw us off the track? I thought of that. My friend said it would never happen. Isolationists don't take off these things for anything. They get married in them. They're buried in them."

Necalli looked out the window. The sky outside was dark and shifty. "Storm's coming," he said.

I knew my boss. He wasn't talking just about the weather.

• • •

Once, the people known to us as Isolationists had lived in the cities, like most everyone else in the Empire. Then, a hundred cycles ago, give or take, one family rejected city life, taking to the forested mountains in the West. And another followed, and another.

Maybe the Isolationists remembered the names of these families, but no one else did—because they only gained significance after there were hundreds of such clans in the mountains, refusing to observe the Emperor's laws or pay his taxes or so much as acknowledge they were citizens of the Empire.

They eked out a living from the land, as our ancestors did. Or so the story went. In reality, they did a good deal of business with the Emperor's cities, supplying them with lumber, rubber, and metals like copper and silver.

But only through the over-the-road carriers they picked to represent them. Never directly. Never where they had to so much as speak with city people.

It was an odd arrangement but one that worked, and had for many cycles.

Nobody complained about it. Not even the Emperor, who was being cheated out of his taxes.

Then again, the tlacamayeh tecuani didn't ask anything from the Empire, and they didn't bother anyone. They kept to themselves.

Until *now*.

• • •

"I have to look in on my aunt," I said. "She plays my father's sister but she's got to be shaken up by what happened to Takun."

Necalli nodded. "Go."

I went.

Unfortunately, I hadn't gotten two blocks from the Interrogation Center when the sky finally opened up. One moment, the streets were dry. The next they were teeming, rain pelting them in twists of big, heavy drops.

We didn't get a lot of precipitation in Aztlan. But when we did, it was often like this—a downpour.

The rail station was only a block away. But it was a block over a walkway sizzling with the hiss of falling water.

I squeezed into a crowd that had gathered under the awning at the front door of a pyramid. Everyone was looking up at the sky, hoping the torrent would stop. I could hear them mumbling a prayer to Tlaloc, asking the god for restraint in what he gave us this day.

I prayed too. But I could see the blue-gray bellies of the storm clouds, and how ponderously they moved across the sky, so I wasn't optimistic that Tlaloc would relent any time soon.

I glanced at the rail station again. Twenty strides was all it would take, I estimated, and I'd be under the roof of the station. And for the gods' sake, it was only *rain*.

"Pardon me," I said.

My neighbors under the awning turned to me, realizing what I had in mind. The older folks among them looked at me like I was crazy.

I smiled. "I'm an Investigator," I said by way of explanation.

Once they knew that, they understood why I might brave the rain. I was pursuing the Emperor's business, and such business often couldn't wait. Without hesitation, they made a path for me, moving to one side or the other. "Thanks," I said.

Then I put my head down and ran.

Unfortunately, the rain chose that moment to come down even harder. I could barely see the ground in front of me, it was exploding so violently under the downpour.

I thought about turning around—except I was already halfway to the station. It made sense to just keep going. But if I'd envisioned arriving at my goal only a little damp, I'd vastly miscalculated. My clothes were as sopping wet as if I'd gone swimming in them.

Then I heard something—what sounded like sandals slapping

the walkway behind me. Some other idiot who had underestimated the god's enthusiasm, I thought. We could share a laugh after we reached the station.

Suddenly, I felt something in the back of my head—something hard and searing-hot, as if someone had branded me there.

The next thing I knew, I was lying on the ground, the rain pelting my face, the back of my head a red, raging fire. I tried to push against the ground with my elbow, to roll over. But I couldn't. There was a weight on my chest.

I forced my eyes open despite the rain—and saw a face looming over me, almost close enough to touch mine. A big face with small, black eyes. It didn't look familiar.

Something pressed itself into my cheekbone. I didn't have to see it to know it was the barrel of a fire hand. Or to know that the face above me belonged to the stalker.

He was young, not more than twenty cycles, his mouth twisted in what looked like anger. Then, over the hiss of Tlaloc's bounty, I heard the last words I'd expected to escape his mouth: "I'm sorry."

He meant it. I could tell from the red rims of his eyes. But he didn't stop pressing the fire hand against my cheek.

"For what?" I asked, turning my face to keep my mouth from filling with water.

"Your women," he said. "Your friend. He shouldn't have come after me that way."

His speech was slow. Slurred. I didn't smell octli on his breath. A mental deficit, then.

Which made the fire hand in his fist that much more of a concern.

"Why are you telling me this?" I asked.

He showed me his wrist. It was bare. "My bracelet—I need it back! I need it *now*!" He howled the last word with an almost childlike desperation.

"I don't have it with me," I told him. "But I can get it for you."

His eyes screwed up as he took in what I'd said and tried to decide how to respond. I made it easy for him. I grabbed the wrist of the hand that held the weapon. Then, with my free hand, I belted the guy in the mouth.

He screamed, fell back, spat blood. Freer now, I took another shot at him—but I could reach only as far as his chest.

Still, I made it hurt. Enough, I hoped, for him to forget he had the fire hand.

He didn't forget. But instead of firing it, he used it to smash me in the face.

Everything went dark—but only for a moment. Then I got my bearings again—in time to see my assailant go running off, a vague grey figure behind the curtain of rain.

With an effort, I dragged myself off the ground. But by the time I was upright, the stalker was nowhere to be seen. It was as if he'd been swallowed by the storm.

I lurched the rest of the way to the rail station and the protection it afforded from the downpour. Then I felt the back of my head. It stung like crazy. And my hand came away with blood on it.

I swore to myself. Then I reached into my pouch and called

Necalli. He was surprised to hear from me so soon.

And even more so when I told him who I'd run into.

• • •

"Better me than my family," I said.

The physician attending to the wound in the back of my head—a younger one than the guy who'd worked on Takun—looked at Necalli. "Is he always this dense?"

"Always," said Necalli.

"You've sustained a significant head injury," the physician said, more slowly this time. Apparently, he thought it would sink in better that way. "You escaped a concussion somehow, but you need to rest. Several days, just in case."

I gave him the same answer as before: "Not happening."

The physician looked at Necalli, who shrugged and said, "Dense, all right."

"Then take it as easy as you can," said the physician.

I nodded. "Sure."

As soon as he was gone, I turned to my boss. "The guy had a fire hand. I *saw* it."

It wasn't a theory anymore. It was a fact.

"We'll assign a task force," Necalli said, "to watch you, your aunt, and your girlfriend. They'll blend into the background, no vests. The next time this guy goes after one of you, we grab him."

"And what if he uses the fire hand?" I asked.

Necalli didn't have an answer for that one.

"We can't wait for him to make a mistake," I said. "We've got to take the initiative. Find out where he got the weapon, and why in the gods' names he's after me and my family."

Necalli didn't argue the point. But he also didn't have a plan.

"Someone needs to go out there," I said, "to the Western Mountains. Poke around."

Necalli's brow puckered. "Meaning *you*?"

"Who else?"

"Someone from Zempoala maybe, who knows the region."

"An Investigator," I said.

"That's right."

"Because those Isolationists love to talk to the Law."

"But they'll talk to *you*?" said Necalli. "A stranger with a city accent?"

"My friend can set me up with a guide," I told him. "I'll keep my mouth shut and nod a lot."

"You're crazy. If anything happened, there would be no one there to back you up."

"What's the alternative? To sit here and wait for whoever hurt Takun—and me—to take a hand stick to my aunt next time? Or to Calli? Or to put a bullet in one of them?"

Necalli bit his lip.

"Look," I said, "I'll be careful. You know I will. I just need to get to the bottom of this."

My boss swore under his breath, to not one god but three. But in the end, he gave in. "You'll buzz me twice a day. At least."

"As if you were my mother," I assured him.

Necalli heaved a sigh. "I don't know who's crazier, Colhua… you for wanting or go, or me for letting you."

• • •

I called Paynal and told him I was coming to visit. And I told him what I had in mind, or most of it.

"I can't do it without you," I said.

Unlike Necalli, he didn't try to talk me out of it. He just said, "I'll do whatever I can."

"Thanks," I said.

• • •

"I won't be gone long," I told Calli.

I said it again a couple of hours later, this time to Aunt Xoco: "I won't be gone long."

The truth was I didn't know how long I'd be out of town. I only knew the stalker's bracelet was the only lead we had.

Neither Calli nor Aunt Xoco was especially enthusiastic about the idea.

Aunt Xoco knew what it took to carry out an investigation in Aztlan. She didn't know what it took in other cities, much less outside them.

For that matter, neither did I.

But I couldn't just wait for the stalker to attack again. If I had a chance to learn something about him—something that might help us catch him—I had to grab it with both hands.

• • •

I was on my way to the rail station, my pack slung over my shoulder, when I got a call on my radio.

I took it out of my pouch and said, "Colhua."

It was a police officer in District Five. "We've got a body," he said. "It fits the description of your stalker." And he gave me the location.

A moment later, I got another call. This one was from Necalli. "Where are you? I'm sending an auto-carriage."

It must have been on its way to my place already because it showed up in no time. A good thing, because it was a long ride to District Five. Long enough for me to consider the implications if the dead man was in fact our stalker.

First, that someone had known where to find him. Second, that they'd been able to kill him despite the fire hand in his possession.

And third, that their reason for killing him may have had nothing to do with his stalking us.

At the very least, we had another crime to solve. Murder was murder, regardless of how helpful the murderer had been to me and my family. He had to be punished—assuming we could ever learn enough about the deceased to identify the individual who had ended him.

• • •

The auto-carriage took me to one of the worst-kept pyramids in a district known for its badly kept pyramids.

I found Quetzalli in a small, two-room apartment on the third level, dusting the place for fingerprints. "Back here," she said, and gestured for me to follow her.

The corpse was lying face up in a corner of the second room, his mouth open, staring at the ceiling as if he found something endlessly fascinating there.

It was the guy I'd seen in the rain, all right. Except he wasn't sitting on my chest, pressing the barrel of a fire hand to my cheek. He was taking stock of his prospects in the Lands of the Dead.

The side of his face was caked with dark, dried blood. More of it had pooled on the floor underneath him. The source was a head wound—an oozing fissure just above the guy's ear.

I didn't have to ask what kind of blade was responsible for it.

"Neighbors complained to the landlord about sounds of a fight," Quetzalli said. "When she showed up, there was only this guy. Whoever else had been here was gone."

I looked at the door. It was undamaged. Like Inave, the stalker had let in his assailant without an argument.

"What about his fire hand?" I asked.

"We're still looking," Quetzalli said. But she didn't sound optimistic.

So even if the stalker was no longer a threat, the same couldn't be said of his weapon. Or whoever had taken his life.

I was about to leave when I realized I had the dead man's bracelet in my pouch. I remembered the look in his eyes when he demanded that I give it back. How frantic he had been. How desperate.

Having described the bracelet to Paynal already, I didn't have any further use for it. I took it out and slipped it onto the stalker's cold, stiff wrist.

Then I helped Quetzalli look for prints.

• • •

An hour later, I crammed into Necalli's office along with a half-dozen other Investigators, including Quetzalli, Izcuin, and Suguey. Takun would have been there too if he weren't still recuperating.

At least temporarily, my trip had been postponed.

"All right," said Necalli. "There's *who* and there's *why*."

"*Who* is easier," I said. "The door was intact, so the victim let his attacker in. And the guy was killed with a hand stick."

"And outside of the police," Quetzalli noted, "only Isolationists carry hand sticks."

"So he was killed by his own people?" said Necalli.

"Looks that way," said Suguey.

"All right," said Necalli. "Now the hard part—*why*."

It was the hard part, all right. We looked at each other.

"We don't know all their customs," said Izcuin. "Could have been a lot of things. Revenge, maybe, for something he did back home."

"Maybe it was just his being here," said Quetzalli. "He was attracting attention and Isolationists hate attention."

"So they *killed* him?" said Necalli. "And left his corpse for us to find?"

"So we would know," said Quetzalli, "that he wasn't a threat anymore."

"They didn't know how much damage he did," Suguey pointed out. "If it wasn't a lot...maybe they thought we'd let the matter drop."

"Except they committed a murder in our city," said Necalli. "We don't drop things like that. Especially when there's something as dangerous as a fire hand involved."

"That," I said, "could be the reason they killed the guy. He had a fire hand. And if he got caught with it, and we found out he was an Isolationist..."

"We would suspect," said Quetzalli, "that other Isolationists had them too. That's the thread they don't want us pulling on."

"But," said Suguey, "did they want to avoid our thinking it because it's false…or because it's *true*?"

"If other Isolationists have fire hands," said Necalli, "this is bigger than we thought."

"But…why would Isolationists need fire hands?" Izcuin asked. "Nobody bothers them. They pretty much do what they want."

"Nobody *needs* a fire hand," I said. "There's an allure to it. A feeling of power. And Isolationists feel oppressed by the Emperor's laws, or they wouldn't live their lives as far from them as possible. So the power to defy him…"

"…is tantalizing," said Quetzalli.

I nodded. "Exactly."

"Still," said Suguey, "they're called Isolationists for a reason. How do they get their hands on something like a fire hand, that comes from overseas?"

It was a good question. Necalli said so.

"All the more reason," I said, "for me to visit the Western Mountains."

• • •

I remembered Zempoala as a sleepy town with a fast-flowing river, a cozy imperial rail station, and a collection of dignified, old pyramids.

I particularly remembered the charming little plaza in front of the station. Unfortunately, as I emerged from the rail building, I saw the plaza had lost some of its charm.

The chili restaurant opposite the station was still there, still packed with customers. So was the festival shop with its windows full of rainbow-colored candles, ceramic feast plates, and tiny figurines that evoked the gods.

But the flower market, with the statue of Xochiquetzal in the center of it, her pale, slender arms spread in welcome...that was gone. So was the dress vendor where I got Aunt Xoco a shawl for her birth-day, and the antique jewelry merchant, and the creaky hotel my team had slept in before and after a match.

They had all been replaced with second-rate octli houses. A whole row of them, like the one on Mayahuel Street in the Merchant City. It was a sign—and a sad one—that the area had gone downhill.

Not that it came as a surprise. A cycle earlier, the Mirror had shown how Zempoala endured a run of corrupt administrators, greedy rodents who had enriched themselves at the expense of their city.

And the plaza in front of me wasn't the only place that had suffered. Far from it. But to occasional visitors, it was the most visible.

"Maxtla!" came a cry, breaking into my reverie.

I turned and saw my friend Paynal coming for me, a grin on his face that spoke of hard-fought matches and the celebrations that often followed.

We hugged, patting each other on the back as teammates did. Then Paynal gripped me by the shoulders and held me away from him.

"You haven't changed," he decided.

"Neither have you," I said—though he had. There were lines in his face, in his forehead, and around his mouth that hadn't been there when we played in the Arena.

"How was your trip?"

"A little long," I confessed. "I remembered Zempoala being closer."

"That's because you had the rest of us to pass the time. Between Aztlan and here, we were laughing so hard we had no *idea* what hour it was."

I smiled at the memory. "I think you're right."

"Come on," said Paynal, and took my arm. "My sister and her daughter are waiting for us at home. They've conjured up a mountain meal. The kind you can't get in Aztlan."

"Wonderful," I said. "But first, let's pick up some octli. I don't want to show up empty-handed."

● ● ●

Zempoala's city rail system wasn't as efficient as Aztlan's, but it got us where we were going.

Paynal's sister, Mecoatl, looked a lot like him. Ana, his niece, was different—small and wiry, with dancing eyes and dimpled cheeks.

"She favors her father," Paynal told me on his balcony.

Ana and her mother were inside, preparing the meal. I caught glimpses of them as they went back and forth, past the kitchen doorway.

"He was a good guy," Paynal added. "Drove an auto-carriage. A big one, hauling copper to the rail depot at Yautepec. One night he fell asleep at the wheel."

"I'm sorry," I said.

Paynal nodded. "But it didn't keep Ana from wanting to follow in his footsteps. She's taken a training course and is about to take a second one. By winter, she'll be qualified to haul cargo on her own."

"Are you worried?" I asked.

My friend smiled. "A little. But she's a great driver. She'll be the one taking you into the mountains."

I'd thought it would be Paynal himself. I said so.

"Believe me," he said, "Ana's a better choice. Not only can she drive circles around me, she's worked out there. She knows where you can go and where you shouldn't."

I wondered—out loud—why Ana would have worked out West and not in Zempoala.

"Zempoala's not exactly an anthill of well-paying jobs," Paynal told me. "I don't know if you saw it on the Mirror, but our administrators sucked us dry. Even our ball court's in need of repair." He shook his head in disgust. "If it's not the plumbing, it's the heating system. If it's not the heat, it's the electricity."

"Too bad," I said. "I always liked that ball court."

"Of course you did," said Paynal, the smile returning to his face. "You went seven and one here with the Eagles."

"Did I?"

"You did. I liked it here too—until I began playing with Malinalco and Oxtlipa. Then it didn't seem so likable."

"Seven and one?" I repeated.

"Exactly," my friend said. "But who's counting?"

• • •

The meal was wonderful, a well-spiced turkey with maize cakes and sweet potatoes on the sides. The octli I'd brought wasn't the best, but no one complained.

"That was great," I said when the last of the turkey was gone. "Really great."

"Don't tell *us*," said Mecoatl. "Tell your friend Paynal. He's the one who spiced the turkey."

I turned to him. "Is that so?"

Paynal dismissed the idea with a flip of his wrist. "A rub here and a rub there. Mecoatl and Ana did the real work."

"He's lying," Ana told me.

"Careful," Paynal said. "Maxtla makes a living finding out the truth of such mysteries."

I smiled at him, and then at Mecoatl and Ana, and said, "Some mysteries are best left unsolved."

• • •

After dinner, Ana and Mecoatl sat down to watch their favorite program on the Mirror. Paynal took advantage of the time to take a walk with me.

"People will ask you where you're from," he said. "You'll need a story to tell them."

"All right," I said. "So give me one."

"You're my cousin. On my mother's side. You've lived in Aztlan all your life, but now you've decided to come back to us here in Zempoala. Your first step is a pilgrimage to our family's burial grounds in the Mountains."

"And when I reach them?"

"You'll pay your respects, the same as you would in a house

of the dead in Aztlan. Except you'll make a special prayer to Acolnahuacatl."

I hadn't heard of Acolnahuacatl. Paynal must have seen the fact in my face, because he said, "Acolnahuacatl is the god of the Dead. In the Mountains, at least."

"Not Mictlantecuhtli?"

"Not out there."

"I'll remember," I said.

Paynal recited the prayer to Acolnahuacatl for me, and made me say it over and over again.

Not that I'd have to repeat it to the god, because I wasn't really going to visit Paynal's family's burial grounds. But if someone asked me about it, I'd be prepared.

Paynal gave me other details he thought I would need: How the tlacamayeh tecuani greeted each other, when they liked to eat, what they thought about work, and so on.

Then he tested me on them, corrected me when I faltered, and tested me again. After all, my life might depend on my command of them.

"You'll need this," he said, and handed me a bracelet. "It's yours, while you're out here. It belonged to my grandfather."

"Wouldn't he have been buried with it?" I asked.

"He lost it when he was very young. Six or seven, apparently. When you're that young, you can get a replacement. After he was dead, it turned up."

So it wasn't the bracelet Paynal's grandfather had worn most of his life. But I could see by the way my friend looked at it that it was still of great value.

"I'll take care of it," I promised.

Paynal smiled. "I know you will."

• • •

Our plan was for Ana and me to get on the road right after sunrise. That way, we would reach our destination before dark.

Tonatiuh seemed happy to accommodate us. It was a beautiful morning, crisp and clear—perfect for driving, Ana said.

It took less than an hour to pack the auto-carriage with food and blankets. Paynal had filled its fuel tank the day before, so that was taken care of. Everything was going according to plan.

Until my radio buzzed.

I took it out of my pouch, wondering who would be calling at that hour—unable to escape the feeling it wasn't good news they were calling with.

I put my radio to my ear and said, "Colhua."

"It's Necalli," said the gravelly voice on the other end. "You need to get back here."

Aunt Xoco? I thought, my throat constricting. *Calli?* "Is everything all right?"

"No one's hurt," Necalli said. "No one's ben attacked. But you need to get back here."

I didn't get it. "I'm my way to the Mountains."

"Not anymore," he told me.

Had we caught the stalker's killer? Even so, didn't we need to find out where the stalker's fire hand came from? Unless the stalker's killer had already told us what we wanted to know in that regard.

But how likely was that?

Necalli was a great interrogator, the best. But getting some-one to admit to murder took time—and I'd only been gone overnight. "Has something changed?" I asked.

Necalli just repeated what he'd said: "You need to get back here." Then he added, "The quickest way possible. Understand?"

Only that he wanted me to return to Aztlan. But not *why*.

"Whatever you say," I told my boss.

Just before he ended the call.

"What's going on?" Ana asked me.

I looked at my radio. Then I put it back in my pouch. "Looks like I'm going back to Aztlan."

• • •

I apologized to Paynal and Ana and Mecoatl, and thanked them all for their hospitality. Then I took the imperial rail back to Aztlan.

On the way, I tried to call Necalli. He didn't answer.

What's going on? I wondered.

By the time I got back to Aztlan, it was late in the day. I didn't stop at my place to drop off my pack. I went straight to the Interrogation Center, where my first stop was Necalli's office.

I found my boss sitting on the edge of his desk, his eyes downcast, his arms folded across his chest. His expression, or what I could see of it, was that of someone who had eaten some bad gopher meat.

"I tried to call you," I said. "Several times."

Necalli looked up at me, unfolded his arms, and held out his hand. "I need your hand stick, Colhua. And your bracelet."

I looked at him. "What are you talking about?"

He muttered a curse. "Don't make me say it again. You're suspended until further notice."

Suspended? "You're joking, right?"

"I'm sorry," Necalli said, "but I have orders."

I was numb. "To suspend me? For *what*?"

"I have orders," he said again. "And they came from high up. *Very* high up."

"Zayanya?" I said. Why would the First Chief want to put me down?

Necalli bit his lip. "I'm not at liberty to say."

I got the impression he'd already said more than he was supposed to—that whoever had forced him to suspend me had also prohibited him from telling me why.

And nothing I could say was going to change things.

As if in a dream, I took off my bracelet and placed it in Necallli's hand. Then I opened my pouch, took out my hand stick, and turned that over as well.

We stood there for a moment, looking at each other. Neither of us was pleased with what was happening—that much was clear. Then Necalli said, "We'll continue to keep an eye on your aunt and your girlfriend. You don't have to worry about that."

"Someone's still out there with a fire hand. We have no idea who he is or what he's up to. I think I'm going to worry."

"That's the department's concern. You're just a citizen, Colhua."

I shook my head. "I may not have a bracelet but I'm still an Investigator. If I'm back here in Aztlan, I'm going to find the guy."

"Don't," Necalli said. "If you take matters into your own hands, I'm supposed to arrest you."

I felt a spurt of anger and amazement. "That's crazy."

"I know it seems that way. But I will." *I've got no choice.* Necalli didn't say it but I heard it anyway. "You hear me?"

"I hear you," I said.

Then I left.

• • •

All night, over and over again, I replayed the scene in my mind: Necalli standing there with his hand out, asking for my bracelet.

It couldn't have happened. Not in a million cycles. And yet it had.

Eventually, I fell asleep. But not for long. Before I knew it, it was morning.

I rolled over and looked out the window. Tonatiuh was too high in the sky, it seemed to me. I glanced at my chronometer, which I'd left on the table beside my bed. I had slept a half hour longer than usual.

It was an odd feeling. Even as a kid I'd gotten up earlier than my friends to make some beans before school. One cycle, when I was seventeen, I had a job delivering fruits and vegetables that saw me up before the sun god.

In my whole life, I'd slept late only when I was sick. And even then, it bothered me that I'd done so.

Displeased with myself, I swept my covers aside, swung my

legs out of bed, and padded across the floor to the bathroom, where I turned on the cold-water tap. Then I put my head underneath the stream of water and left it there for a while.

It was shockingly cold. But that was all right. I felt like I needed to be shocked a little.

Only after I'd turned off the water and run my fingers through my hair did I pick up my head and confront myself in the mirror. I'd wanted it to be a reassuring, even inspiring sight. I'd wanted to see the same guy I saw every morning, cycle after cycle.

I didn't. I looked weary in the confines of the mirror, despite the cold-water treatment. Downhearted.

Come on, I thought. You're an Investigator for the Empire. *People look up to you.*

But I *wasn't* an Investigator. Not anymore.

I just hoped my aunt wouldn't see what I saw. Her apartment was the first place I meant to visit, after all.

Calli had left Aztlan the day before for a business trip, which—I hoped—had taken her off the bull's eye for the time being. But Aunt Xoco was still very much in the center of it.

Necalli would probably prefer that I stay away from her. At least, as long as she required police protection.

But I meant to see her. Lands of the Dead, did I have to be an Investigator to see my *aunt?*

Holding onto that thought, I got dressed, left my apartment, and headed for the rail station. It was a bright day, the kind I would have enjoyed even if I only saw it through the windows of the Interrogation Center.

Now it seemed hollow. Brittle.

I took the rail line to Aunt Xoco's stop. Then I walked the couple of blocks to her pyramid.

There was a police officer standing outside the place, and probably more in the vicinity working undercover. Plus I would find some at her door.

As I had expected, there were two officers on my aunt's floor. One wore a purple vest—the mark of the police in my aunt's district. The other was Suguey.

"Investi—" she started to say, then caught herself.

She looked like she wanted to tell me how sorry she was about what had happened to me. In the end, she couldn't find the words.

"It's all right," I told her. "Really."

I knocked on Aunt Xoco's door.

"Yes?" my aunt called, and opened it.

"It's just me," I said.

"What's wrong?" she asked.

After all, I wasn't in the habit of showing up during the day. Not when I had a job protecting the citizens of Aztlan.

I didn't want to worry her—and my being stripped of my bracelet would definitely have been a source of worry. So I said, "Nothing," and hoped she didn't ask to see my wrist. "I'm just checking to see if you need anything."

Aunt Xoco smiled. "I don't. My friends out there are taking good care of me. But come in for a moment. I don't get to see you so early in the morning anymore."

Not since I was a boy, I thought.

I entered my aunt's apartment and closed the door. It looked different somehow. But it wasn't the place that had changed. It was *me*.

"Can I make you something to eat?" my aunt asked. "Those two outside—they don't like food the way Takun did."

Despite everything, I smiled. "No one does, Aunt Xoco."

"How is he?" she asked, turning serious. "Healing, still?"

I hadn't heard anything about Takun since I'd left for Zempoala. "I think so. I'll look in on him later today."

"Tell him I miss him," my aunt said.

"I will," I promised.

I wanted to stay longer but I couldn't. Not without raising Aunt Xoco's suspicions. I kissed her on the forehead and told her I'd talk to her later.

"Know the gods' favor," she told me. "And don't forget to tell Takun I asked about him."

"I won't," I said, and left her.

● ● ●

I could have taken a rail carriage to the House of Healing to see Takun. Certainly that's what I would have done the week earlier, when I still had a job.

Instead, I walked.

I didn't have a route in mind because I'd never gone to the House of Healing on foot. I just knew I had to move, to clear my head. To rid myself of the feeling of what I'd lost.

I recalled the conversation I'd had with Ilhica about Tlazolteotl House. I could still hear him talking about despair, and debt, and how they conspired to drive people over the edge.

At the time, the poor souls we were discussing had seemed as far away as Donner's Euros. But they were starting to seem a lot closer.

I hadn't left the Empire the way they had. I hadn't lost my citizenship, or my sanity. And I wasn't destitute.

A favorite of Huitzilopochtli for a long time, I'd barely ended my career in the ball court when the god turned my eyes to the work my father had done. So I had never known a time in my life when I had to worry about my next meal.

But that kind of misery, I was beginning to understand, could come from a lot of places. Like losing your handle on who you are.

I'd been an Investigator. A respected servant of the Emperor. Now what was I?

Something less, I couldn't help thinking.

And as something less, how helpful could I be to the people I loved? To anyone, for that matter?

I walked for a long time thinking such thoughts. Hating them, but thinking them anyway. In the process, I crossed the River. Twice, it seemed to me, though it could have been more.

Then, because I was so deep into myself that I wasn't paying attention, I bumped into something. Not hard, but hard *enough* to bring me out of my daydream.

I saw a woman looking back at me over her shoulder, shooting me a look of irritation. I guessed that she was what I'd bumped into.

"Watch where you're going," she told me.

"Sorry," I said.

Only then did I realize how far I'd walked—because by the gods' favor, I had wound up in a familiar place: On Xipe Totec Street, just past the row of octli shops.

My friend, one-eyed Zolin, was standing across the street with his cart, dispensing his cheerful outlook on life along with the tastiest salamander in the city. As always, there was an impressive line in front of him.

Without thinking, I started calculating how long it would take to get to the head of it. After all, I thought, I had to get back to work.

Then I realized that wasn't a consideration any longer. All I had to do was get to the House of Healing, and it wasn't far.

Tempted by the smell of Zolin's fare, I crossed the street and got on the end of the line. It felt good to be there, to have a goal, even if it was only to fill my belly.

As I moved with the people ahead of me, slowly but steadily, I started wondering if my being there was less the gods' doing than my own. Had I decided, somewhere inside, that I needed a place of pure happiness, devoid of shadows and doubt, to get myself going again?

And what place said pure happiness more than Zolin's street cart?

Regardless of how I'd come to arrive there, I was glad I had. The time went more quickly than I'd expected. More importantly, it went in the company of others who had found their most joyful place—which made it even more pleasant for me.

Strangers talked on that line. People laughed. Despite everything, I found myself laughing with them.

Little by little, I felt the load I was pulling start to fade. The sunlight seemed less brittle. The world began to resemble the one I'd known.

And I recognized a truth: The smell of fried salamander cured a host of ills. I'd known it before, at some level, but it was good to be reminded of it by the people on Zolin's line.

Gradually, I got closer to the end of it. And closer still. And at last, I found myself face to face with my friend Zolin.

He grinned at the sight of me. "Investigator! The gods smile on me."

I didn't mean to say it but I said it anyway: "I'm no longer an Investigator."

But somehow, it didn't hurt to say it anymore. It was just something that had happened.

Zolin looked confused. "How…?"

"It's a long story. And there's a line behind me."

We both looked back. The queue was even longer than when I'd joined it.

"I stop serving around dusk," said Zolin. "Come to see me then and we will talk."

I smiled. "I can't."

Because something I said might reveal some aspect of what I had been working on. Though I was no longer on the force, I was bound by regulations to remain silent about my investigations.

And even if there were no regulations, I owed it to Quetzalli and Suguey and Izcuin to keep what I knew to myself.

"Though," I added, "I'm grateful for the offer."

Zolin placed my order in a couple of pockets of wax paper and handed it to me. Then he said, "If you change your mind, I'll be here. For my friends, I am *always* here."

• • •

As I made my way down Xipe Totec Street, careful to avoid bumping into anyone else, I found myself looking at my situation with fresh eyes. Sure, I'd lost something precious, something I had worked for over the course of many cycles. But I hadn't lost *everything*. Not even close.

I remembered a time when I was little and I'd played badly in the ball court. My father had had to work a case that day, so it was only my mother who had seen the match.

"I was terrible," I told her, a catch in my throat. I'd wanted her to be proud of me and I'd given her no *reason* to be proud.

She'd looked into my eyes and said, "Are you kidding? You're more than the bounce of a ball. By the gods' will, *you're Maxtla Colhua.*"

The way she'd said it was shocking, even more so than the water from my tap that morning. And even then, many cycles before I'd made any kind of name for myself as either a player or an Investigator, I felt what she meant. Felt it in my *bones*.

My mother had been a wise woman. Everyone said so. Who was I to dishonor her memory by questioning what she had seen in me?

I had things to do that day. Important things. And I would do them, even if I wasn't an Investigator anymore.

• • •

If Necalli had prohibited me from going to see Takun, no one in the House of Healing was aware of it.

I was ushered into Takun's room with the same admonition as before: "Five minutes. No more."

"I understand," I said.

My colleague was awake when I walked in. "Colhua," he said.

"Well," I said, "your eyesight's intact."

He looked better too. His head was still bandaged but his face wasn't as swollen. And the light was back in his eyes.

"Five minutes?" he said.

He remembered. It was a good sign.

"Same as last time," I confirmed. "Any chance you've remembered something else?"

"Nothing," he said. "Wish I did." He frowned. "Quetzalli was here this morning. She told me something."

"That I've been suspended," I said, saving Takun the trouble.

"For what?" he asked.

"Necalli didn't say. Probably couldn't."

"What are you going to do?"

"I've cooking up some ideas. But I'll keep them to myself, if it's all right with you."

Takun nodded. "I get pretty chatty on my pain meds. I wouldn't want to get you in trouble."

"Thanks," I said. I looked at my chronometer. I still had a minute left but I didn't want to run into Necalli there in the House of Healing. "Take care of yourself, all right?"

I dug into my pouch, where I'd put Zolin's wares, and took

out a salamander wrapped in wax paper. Its aroma made my mouth water.

"Here," I said to Takun. "Eat it before someone walks in. I've got a feeling it's not on your list of prescribed foods."

Takun grinned and accepted the salamander. "Even *better* than cinnamon gum, Colhua. And that's saying something."

I laughed. Then I left Takun in his medical bed and went home. I had things to do, after all, and people to see.

That is, if I could still see them.

• • •

As soon as I got home, I sat down at my Mirror screen.

I couldn't go into the office to use my Investigator's station. Necalli wouldn't let that happen. But if I hadn't been cut off yet, I might still be able to go through official channels.

I tapped in a number. For a moment, it just sat there on the screen. Then it started pulsing—a sign that the link was still open to me. Which meant Necalli hadn't given the order to shut it down.

Because he'd forgotten? I didn't think so. He wasn't the type to miss something like that. More likely, he was trying to help me without making it obvious.

It was late in the day in Britain, so I didn't know if I'd get a response. For a moment, I was afraid I would have to try again the next day—and hope Necalli hadn't eliminated the link by then.

Suddenly, Donner appeared on the screen. He was no longer wearing the red hat with the white puff.

Good, I thought. I needed his complete attention.

"Investigator," he said, "I'm glad you called. I've been trying to contact you, to no—"

"I've been suspended," I said.

Donner looked at me. "Suspended...?"

For a moment, I thought I'd used a word he didn't understand. Then he said, "Sorry to hear it, mate. Should I ask why?"

"Better if you don't. Listen, I may not have much time before they realize I'm talking to you. Did you find anything?"

"I haven't. You?"

"The guy with the fire hand came from our Western Mountains. I don't know what the connection is yet but I'm going to find out."

"But...if you're suspended..."

"Not a problem. I'd have gone out there undercover anyway."

Donner nodded. "Right. Well, good luck. If I find anything...?"

"I'll get hold of you again—if I can." And I cut the connection.

After all, the longer I stayed on, the more likely it was that someone would notice. Then Necalli would be forced to shut down the link.

It wasn't as if Donner had been so much help to me. But he was a resource—and now more than ever, I needed all the resources I could get.

• • •

Paynal was as happy to meet me at the rail station in Zempoala the second time as he had been the first.

Of course, the last time I was an Investigator claiming to be a regular citizen. This time I was a regular citizen for real.

I'd already resolved not to answer my radio if it buzzed.

Fortunately, it didn't. So, for the time being at least, I didn't have to hear Necalli tell me to go home.

If the gods were looking after me, it would be a while before he knew I was gone. By then, maybe, I would have found what I was looking for.

The blankets I'd packed hadn't been unpacked yet, so we saved some time there. All we had to do was put together a few provisions—and, of course, place Paynal's grandfather's bracelet on my wrist. I would need that, along with the story that went with it.

• • •

Paynal hadn't lied when he said Ana was an accomplished driver.

It was a good thing. There were plenty of turns in the highway that led through the foothills of the Western Mountains, many of them acute and without warning. But Ana took them all at the right speed, neither so slow that we would lose time—which was precious for a number of reasons—nor so fast that we would fishtail off the road.

The further west we went, the steeper the road got for us, and the more the scrub plants around us gave way to stretches of forest. More and more, we drove in the shadows of trees rather than in sunlight.

Ana surveyed the road ahead. She checked our fuel gauge. From time to time, when we were deepest in the embrace of the woods, she activated our headlamps.

What she didn't do was talk. Which was fine with me. I preferred that she concentrate on getting us where we were going.

But I didn't want her to feel uncomfortable. I was an

unfamiliar face, after all, despite my friendship with her uncle, and she might have found the silence oppressive.

So *I* talked. "Your uncle's a good man."

"He is," Ana agreed.

"A good teammate, too. I don't know how much he told you about—"

"I'm not a Sun League fan," she blurted.

The remark caught me by surprise. "Oh?"

"I know," Ana said, "that you and my uncle played for the Eagles, and I know they were a good team. But that's all I know, and really all I care to know."

I had never run into someone so determined to ignore the Sun League. Not that it bothered me. "Fair enough."

Ana frowned. "There's more to life than the ball court."

"I agree," I said.

She glanced at me. "You do?"

"Sure. I became an Investigator, remember?"

"My uncle built a sweat lodge—the best one around—but his heart is still in the ball court."

Where was *my* heart? That was the question she'd left unspoken.

"I loved playing," I said. "I still do—if only in a men's league, once every thirteen days. But my heart is in my *work*."

She didn't say she approved of the idea. But the frown was gone, so she probably didn't hate it.

As we drove, the terrain continued to change. The road got steeper and the forest denser, and I heard birds singing in the branches.

It was a different world out there. Peaceful, I thought. But how could it be otherwise when there were no people around to stir it up?

At least, I added silently, none that we could see.

Hours went by. The trees got closer together and the road narrowed. Our fuel indicator, I noticed, had dipped way to one side.

"We're almost there," Ana said, anticipating my question.

"That's good," I said.

Suddenly, the forest yielded to a clearing, where a couple dozen auto-carriages were parked, their metal skins reflecting a glint or two of dying sunlight. Most of the vehicles looked like ours, down to the dirt their wheels had sprayed along their sides.

A couple were considerably bigger. For hauling cargo, I thought.

Ana turned to me. "Iztactetl."

The largest village in the Western Mountains, and the most populated. If I was going to dig something up, it would be there.

Back in Zempoala, Paynal had asked me where I'd start my investigation. "In the octli houses," I'd said.

"You're in luck," he told me. "There's no shortage of them in Iztactetl."

He wasn't kidding. I could see two octli houses just past the far side of the parking area, illuminated signs advertising them by name.

There were people standing outside them, which suggested there were even more people inside. "Which one do we try first?" Ana asked.

I looked at her. "We?"

"Of course. You think I'm just your driver?"

"Your uncle said you would take me here. I don't need any-thing else."

Ana laughed. "That's a city man talking. You won't last two hours here by yourself. My uncle would tell you the same thing."

I didn't like the idea of Ana's coming with me. She was young. Innocent looking. But then, I thought, she might be safer with me than sitting in the auto-carriage.

"All right," I said. "But stay close."

"I intend to," she told me.

• • •

We started out at an octli house called White Mountain.

It was made of stones. Big ones, mortared together. It looked like it could have withstood the gods' wrath and then some.

As we got close to it, I heard the sounds I associated with the places on Mayahuel Street—a sea of voices punctuated now and then by peals of laughter and vivid curses.

But they were louder here. Wilder. If there was a prohibi-tion against upsetting the peace, or a police force to enforce it, I didn't see evidence of it.

What I did see, once we turned the corner of the building, was a couple of women sitting on wooden crates with their backs against the wall, ceramic cups in their hands. One was slumped against the other, her head lying on the other wom-an's shoulder.

My reaction, which I had to suppress, was that of an Investigator. Public drunkenness was punishable by time in the prison house. It was shocking to see it out in the open there.

In Aztlan—or any of the other towns I'd visited—the police would have been on the women like piranha on a lost crab. In Iztactetl, no one gave them a second look.

I must have been staring at them because the more upright of the women grinned and blew me a kiss. Next to me, Ana chuckled.

"Take it easy, City Man." She said it too low for anyone but me to hear.

"As easy as I can," I said.

At the front door of the White Mountain, there was a line a dozen people deep. The guys on it all wore braids—another thing men didn't do in Aztlan.

A guy with a face like granite stood between the line and the inside of the octli house. As Ana and I approached, someone waddled out of the place, and the guy let the first person on line take his place.

Before I knew it, Ana walked up to Granite Face. "How long's the wait?" she asked.

He looked her over. "How old are you?"

"Old enough," she said without hesitation.

The guy laughed. "Half an hour."

Back in the Merchant City, I had unlimited access to octli houses. But I wasn't wearing an Investigator's bracelet in Iztactetl. And even if I had been, I didn't know if it would have earned me any special privileges.

Ana turned to me. "It won't be less anywhere else."

"All right," I said, and we got on the end of the line.

After a couple of minutes of moving up a step at a time, we

passed a window with a view of what was going on inside. It was a revel, crazier than the last of the Unlucky Days.

"Is it always like this?" I asked Ana.

"All the time," she said.

• • •

It took a while but we got in.

My first step inside was a punch in the face. I'd been in the midst of public drunkenness, but never anything like this.

Men and women were singing, bellowing—staggering from one part of the place to another, spilling half the contents of their cups along the way. Only on the fringes of it was it possible to overhear what was being said, and even then I could catch only a word here and there.

It wasn't going to be easy learning anything about the stalker.

Ana pulled my head down to hers. "We need to get some drinks," she said in my ear. "Unless you want to stand out like a blue macaw."

I didn't.

The bar stood in the middle of the place. It had a ring of patrons around it, some of whom had already gotten a drink, though they didn't seem especially eager to let others do the same.

"Hey!" Ana yelled, knifing her way through the crowd. "I came here to drink octli, not to watch *you*!"

I followed her, as much to look out for her as to make it seem I belonged. Though, to be honest, it was more as if *she* were looking out for *me*.

A moment later, we reached the bar. "Two!" Ana said over the din.

The bartender handed her two cups, each one full to over-flowing. She took them, handed me one, and said, "Pay the guy!"

I reached into my pouch with my free hand and fished out half a dozen coins. Ana plucked four of them out of my hand and laid them on the bar.

"Just four?" I said, thinking she might have miscounted.

"You're not in Aztlan," she told me. "Come on."

Again, I let her take the lead—this time away from the bar, into the recesses of the place where it wasn't as noisy.

As soon as we'd staked out a place for ourselves, she said, "Drink," and took a pull of octli from her cup.

I looked into my own—and saw why the stuff had been so cheap. It was clumpy in places, runny in others. Not the kind of octli I would have brought to my aunt's place.

The taste confirmed it. In Aztlan, people would have spilled the brew into their sinks. But we weren't in Iztactetl because of the quality of the beverages.

"All right," Ana said. "Now what?"

I looked around. People were standing around in knots of three and four, their faces pushed close together. It was going to be hard to strike up a conversation, or even to listen in on someone else's.

Not that I wasn't going to try.

• • •

After an hour or so, we hadn't gotten anywhere. No one wanted to talk to a couple of strangers, it seemed. It was as if we had a disease.

"If we're staying," Ana told me, "we've got to buy another

cup. Otherwise, people will wonder what we're doing here."

"I'll get them," I told her.

I was more lightheaded than I should have been on a single mug of octli. The stuff had been terrible, but strong for all that.

"Wait," Ana said, grabbing my sleeve before I could get going. "Not yet. Someone's pointing at you."

I resisted the urge to look around. "Where?"

"Right behind you. He's coming over."

I waited, hoping I didn't resemble someone the guy had a hate for. I figured Ana would warn me if he looked hostile, and she wasn't doing so.

A moment later, I felt a hand on my shoulder. I turned and looked into the sunken-cheeked face of an old man. He was taller than I was by a head, but so thin I could see every bone in his wrist.

And the bracelet he wore on it. Ozomahtli, like the stalker's.

"New here," he said, "aren't you? Come to see the sights?" He laughed a throaty laugh.

I laughed too, comforted that the idea seemed as absurd to him as it did to me.

"We're on our way," I said, "to our family's burial grounds." I showed him the bracelet Paynal had loaned to me. "To pay our respects to our ancestors."

The guy nodded. "I like that. Staying long?"

I shrugged. "I was originally going to go back to Zempoala. But I kind of like it here."

"You're not from Zempoala," he observed. "Where *are* you from?"

Paynal had told me to be circumspect. "A lot of places."

The guy laughed again. "Good answer." He took a sip of his octli. "Never give anyone a chance to put a hook in you."

I smiled. "That's what my father told me."

The guy nodded to himself for a while. Then he said, "Maybe we'll run into each other again sometime."

"Maybe," I allowed, and watched him walk away.

● ● ●

The old guy was the only nibble I got all night. Finally, I said to Ana, "Let's call it."

"Whatever you say," she told me.

It was cool outside—pleasantly so after the stuffy atmosphere of the octli house. As I was regrouping, trying to think of a different way to get what I needed in Iztactetl, I saw one of the women who'd been sitting on crates before—the one who'd blown me a kiss.

There was a man with her. A rangy guy with his foot on the other crate, leaning over her. As I watched, the woman pointed to me, and the guy turned to follow her gesture.

He didn't look happy.

Ana noticed too. "Come on," she said, pulling on my sleeve and speeding up her pace.

I sped up to match her. But not enough to keep the rangy guy from catching up to us.

"Hey," he snarled, "where are *you* going?"

He put his hand on my shoulder and spun me around. He was that strong.

"I'm not looking for trouble," I said.

"No?" he said, thrusting out his chin. "Then why were you staring at my mate?"

"I wasn't," I told him.

But he wasn't going to accept that answer. He had his heart set on a fight. I could see it in his eyes.

Unfortunately, he didn't look like he'd had anything to drink yet. So he wasn't going to be a pushover.

I knew how to take care of myself, even without my hand stick. Maybe enough to put the guy down. But I didn't want anybody to know that, or to ask how I'd come by that ability.

As it was, people were gathering around, drawn by the prospect of a fight. Some of them looked like they'd been in fights themselves that evening—what often happened when there was too much octli around.

The big guy stripped off his shirt, revealing the kind of muscles you had to work for. Then he advanced a couple of steps in my direction and took a swing at me—which I ducked, though I cut it as close as I dared.

Then I circled to my right to make myself a more difficult target.

"Leave it," Ana told the guy with the muscles, trying to get between us. "He didn't mean anything."

The guy looked like he was going to take a swing at her next. I couldn't let that happen. But I also didn't want to beat him, or even come close. So I took one for the team.

First, I shoved the guy back so Ana wouldn't get hurt. Then I took another step toward him, my hands down where they wouldn't do me any good—essentially inviting him to take another shot at me.

He accepted the invitation.

The next thing I knew I was lying on the ground, my cheek pressed into it. Half my face was numb where the guy had hit me.

But I'd absorbed worse blows, both inside and outside the ball court. If I'd had to, I could have gotten to my feet and continued the fight. But I'd waded into the big guy's punch for a reason.

"Get up!" he barked at me.

I got my palms underneath me and made it look like I was trying to push off the ground. But I didn't.

"Get up!" the guy yelled a little louder, and kicked me in the ribs. It felt like he'd stuck a knife between them, but I didn't do anything about it. I just lay there.

"Leave him," someone called.

"You showed him," said someone else.

The crowd was already dispersing, losing interest. The show was over. Out of the corner of my eye, I saw the big guy move away.

A moment later, I felt Ana's hand on my back. "You all right?" she said into my ear.

"Not as all right," I breathed, "as I was a few minutes ago."

"Can you get up?"

"Sure."

With Ana's help, I got to my feet. But not without a few groans. Those, at least, weren't part of the act.

"You were pretty brave," I told her.

"So were you," she said.

"More stupid than brave," someone said, "if you ask me."

I followed the voice to its source: The old guy I'd met in the octli house. The Ozomahtli.

"You all right?" he asked.

I smiled as best I could. "Never better."

"You're not much of a fighter," the guy said. "That's a good thing." He looked around. "We've got plenty of fighters around here. Guys who waste their time pounding each other. What we need is workers."

"I know what you mean," I said, thought I didn't know what he meant at all.

He spat on the ground, then eyed me again. "You looking for work?"

I shrugged. "What kind?"

"Ever harvest rubber?"

I hadn't. And it hadn't been part of the education Paynal had given me. Was it something a guy from a tlacamayeh tecu- ani family should know?

"He doesn't," Ana said, saving me from having to answer the guy.

"But I'm a quick learner," I added, sensing that the guy might be a bridge to some information.

The guy looked at me narrow-eyed. "A couple of tappers left the other day, and we were undermanned even before that. We can use another hand, if you're game."

"Sure," I said.

He nodded. "Tomorrow morning, the hour of eight. I'll

meet you up the street, in front of the barber shop."

"I'll be there," I told him.

• • •

Using the blankets we brought, Ana and I made our beds in Paynal's auto-carriage.

We weren't alone in that regard. Other vehicles in the lot were occupied the same way. After all, it was a long trip to Iztactetl, even for a lot of tlacamayeh tecuani, and there weren't any hotels in town.

It turned cool at night, good weather for sleeping. But I didn't doze off for a long time. And when I did, my sleep was full of bad dreams.

Not the kind where I could say I was in such and such a place, and I was doing this or that, and here's who was with me. More vague than that. As if I had a sense the world was suffering from some terrible thing I couldn't name, and there was nothing I could do about it.

Finally, I opened my eyes. I couldn't see Tonatiuh—the trees were too thick around us—but I could see the patch of pale blue above us. Ana, I noticed, wasn't in her blankets. I sat up and looked out the window of the auto-carriage, and saw her sitting on the ground cross-legged, pouring herself a cup of tea from one of the canisters we had brought.

I got my sandals on and went outside to join her. It smelled good outside, like cedars—something I hadn't noticed the night before. A hawk was circling overhead. People were beginning to stir, still groggy from their revels.

"How did you sleep?" I asked Ana.

She shrugged. "Well enough." She held out an open jar. "Peanuts?"

I took them and poured myself a handful. We had also brought pickled grasshoppers and dried cactus worms. And of course, the tea.

Not the best breakfast I'd ever had, but not the worst either. I didn't have my mind on it anyway. I was thinking about the old guy.

It was almost eight, after all. Time for me to meet him in front of the barber shop. "I'll see you later," I told Ana.

She got to her feet. "I'll go with you."

"The guy didn't invite you," I said.

She didn't like that answer, but she seemed to see the sense in it. "Fine," she said. "See you later."

• • •

I met the old guy right on schedule.

He made note of the fact. "Good way to start out."

"My mother always told me to be on time," I said.

I thought we'd be walking up the road. We didn't. We headed into the woods, along a meandering path wide enough for only one at a time.

"When we get to the harvesting ground," my guide said, "leave it to me. I know what to say and how to say it." He chuckled to himself. "People in charge like to be in charge, you know what I mean?"

I did. It was no different in Aztlan, though I didn't say so.

"So where did they go?" I asked. "The tappers who left, I mean."

"It's bear season." The old guy said it as if that were explanation enough. "They don't hunt bears where you come from?"

"Not much," I said.

"Too bad. Makes for good eating, bear meat."

"If you say so." I needed to take the conversation in a different direction. "So...what do they hunt with around here?"

My benefactor threw me a lopsided smile. "With bows. What do you think?"

"I don't know," I said—and took my shot. "I've heard some guys hunt with fire hands."

The guy grimaced as if I'd elbowed him in the ribs. "That's not something we talk about."

For my purposes, it wasn't the worst answer he could have given me. "But if we *were* talking about it..."

"We wouldn't be," he told me, in a tone that said I'd be smart not to press him on that subject.

Interesting, I thought.

• • •

Half an hour after the old guy and I set out, we came to a camp. There were twenty or more men and women there, lugging buckets full of milky rubber tree sap in one direction and empty buckets in the other.

The old guy went up to a heavyset woman with a little girl's face. "Forewoman," he said, "my friend here is from out of town. He's looking for work."

The woman sized me up. "What's your name, friend?"

"Yolo Mizquitl," I said, using Paynal's family name.

"What are you doing in Iztactetl, Yolo Mizquitl?"

"I came to pay my respects to my ancestors. But I'm thinking I might stay awhile."

The woman scowled. "Well, you look fit enough. And we need a hand." She told me what the job paid.

"That'll do," I said.

She looked at me a moment longer. Then she turned back to the old guy and said, "The usual fee. But after a week. I've got a feeling this one won't last."

"Whatever you say," the old guy told the woman.

So he was getting finder's beans. That explained why he had been so interested in helping a stranger.

"I'll see you around," the old guy said to me.

I nodded. "No doubt."

The woman pointed a collection of empty buckets at the base of a tree. "Grab one, Yolo Mizquitl. I'm not paying you to look pretty."

I picked up a bucket.

"That way," the woman said, pointing in the direction of those who'd entered the clearing carrying sap. "There'll be tappers there. Watch what they're doing so you can do more someday than lug the stuff around."

"I will," I said.

I headed the way she had indicated, following another path through the woods. It was wider than the one I had taken to get there. I was able to pass workers headed in the opposite direction without moving aside for them.

They all wore rubber bracelets. I didn't get a good look at

the symbols on them. Then again, they didn't seem to get a good look at mine.

To my left, the ground fell away into a slope. Something down there caught my eye—an animal rushing from one clump of underbrush to another, hard to identify thanks to the intervening trees.

A pika? A fox?

Then I realized it wasn't just an animal I'd seen. There was something beyond it. A road. And what looked like an auto-carriage. And people loading it with wooden crates.

A shipment of rubber, I thought, headed for the depot at Yautepec. Then I reached a stretch of path that gave me a better look at the crates.

I'd seen them before, I realized. In the cellar of Acuahe Atotoli's temple. And they hadn't contained rubber. They were full of *fire hands*.

I felt a wave of vindication wash over me. There was a connection between the Isolationists and the fire hands, just as I had suspected—and the proof was down there at the bottom of the slope.

Or was it? What if the tlacamayeh tecuani packed their rubber the same way the smugglers packed their fire hands? All I had seen were some crates. I had to get a glimpse of what was *inside* them.

I looked for a moment when there were no other workers in sight, either ahead of me or below, and I could slip downslope to get a closer look.

The moment never came. And I couldn't linger on the path

too long without arousing someone's suspicion. Eventually I had to move ahead and lose sight of the auto-carriage.

But the fire hands—if that's what they were—had to be coming from somewhere to get loaded on the vehicle. A storage building? An underground bunker?

If I could come back when no one was around, maybe I could find it. Get inside it.

I had come that far. I couldn't leave Iztactetl without knowing for certain what I had found.

• • •

As I expected, Ana gave me a hard time.

"I have to do this alone," I told her.

We were sitting in the auto-carriage so no one could hear us. Still, I thought, people could see we were at odds over something.

"But I can help you," she said. "Two sets of eyes are better than one."

"Not when I can't tell you what we're looking for."

And I couldn't. The fewer people who knew about fire hands in the Empire, the better.

"I can look for...I don't know, guards."

"I promised your uncle I'd bring you back in one piece," I said, "and that's what I'm going to do. You've been a big help. But making our way around octli houses is one thing. Slinking around the woods at night is another."

I could see the disappointment in Ana's eyes. Better that, I thought, than grief in Paynal's.

• • •

In the dark, it wasn't easy finding the trails I'd followed earlier in the day.

I had a palm light, but I used it sparingly. If the place I was looking for was guarded—and it seemed to me it would be—it would be too easy to spot a light in the dark.

So I took my time, picking my way through the woods. After all, I had until morning to get back to Ana.

After what seemed like a long time, I found the clearing. I approached it carefully, thinking someone might still be there. Fortunately, it was unoccupied.

So far, so good, I thought.

The path I had followed with the bucket was wider than the first one, and therefore easier to find and navigate. I tried to remember how long I'd been on it before I caught sight of the tlacamayeh tecuani loading their auto-carriage.

Ten minutes? More?

I passed the ten-minute mark, according to my chronometer, and was starting to think I'd gone too far when I heard voices. *Guards,* I thought. I froze, hoping they weren't asking each other about a sound they'd heard—the scrape and crackle of a suspended Investigator making his clumsy way through the woods.

I called on Tezcatlipoca, Lord of the Night, to keep me hidden—and listened. To my relief, the god answered my prayer. The guards, if that's what they were, were talking about women. Thankfully, not about *me.*

Still, they presented a problem. I needed to get past them to get to whatever they were guarding. It wouldn't be easy. There were two of them and they would be armed—with hand sticks, at least, and maybe with fire hands too.

And if I left even one of them conscious, he would sound the alarm. Then I would have a lot more of them to deal with, in an unfamiliar place. A problem indeed.

But in the next moment, I realized I had a bigger one— because there was a shape moving in the trees behind me. It was too dark for me to make out much about it, but it was *there*.

Then I saw it wasn't just *one* shape. There was a second one moving in the darkness. And a third.

Unfortunately for me, they'd have a better understanding of the woods than I did. And they probably had palm lights, which they could shine without fear of giving themselves away.

I had to get out of there. And I had to do it *quickly*, before they closed in on me. I picked a direction that struck me as the one I'd come from, and took off.

I wasn't on a path, so I got beat in the face by a couple of branches. But then, it seemed, I was running through brush alone, with a chance to get away.

That's when the night came alive with light beams, stabbing me from behind—incidentally giving me a sense of what was ahead, which would have been a good thing if it wasn't another stand of dense forest.

I ducked one branch, plunged ahead despite another. But they slowed me down. I heard voices, urgent shouts to get after me, to take me out.

I spared a look over my shoulder and saw my pursuers had multiplied. There were five of them now, maybe more. And if they had fire hands, they were in range already.

The branches ahead of me cracked as I plowed through them. Suddenly, I felt one of them stick me in the side like a knife, forcing me to twist away and cry out in pain.

And that wasn't the worst of it. It was harder to breathe— *much* harder. *A rib*, I thought. *I cracked a rib.*

I kept going anyway, holding my side against the searing fire inside it. Taking the brunt of everything the forest had to throw at me.

Then something grabbed my ankle. A vine, I thought, cursing it as I tumbled forward head over heels, feeding the flame in my ribs. The next thing I knew, I was surrounded, skewered on a web of light beams.

I couldn't see the faces beyond them, but I could hear the promise of violence in their voices. Clearly, they weren't there to share a cup of octli with me. I was grateful for one thing and one thing only, as I struggled to my feet: That I hadn't let Ana come along.

"Take him!" someone bellowed.

"Put him down like a dog!"

They thought they had me—but they didn't. Not while I was standing. Not while I still had a *chance*.

As they closed their circle around me, I lowered my shoulder and drove it into someone's chest. It felt like I'd been branded in the ribs, but I kept going—ran the guy over and went crashing through the woods again.

I thought my pursuers would take me down from behind. But they didn't.

I didn't see any light beams ahead of me either. I heard cries of surprise and rage, but they weren't as close as before.

For a wild half a heartbeat, I thought had a chance to lose myself in the darkness. Then I saw shadows moving ahead of me, and my heart sank, and I thought: More of them.

There were too many to get away from. Just too many.

The figures ahead of me yelled something—I couldn't make out what. Probably that they had cut off my avenue of escape, and that the others just had to drive me into their arms.

Despite everything, I wasn't going down without a fight. I was an Investigator, after all. But I knew with a certainty what the end of it would be.

As the shadows drew closer, I put my pain aside. Then I swung at one of them and connected—felt the jolt of bone on bone, and heard someone sputter a curse. A moment later, I felt hands on me, grabbing me from behind. I whirled, planted my fist in what felt like someone's mouth.

But that was all I'd get a chance to do. The shadows swarmed over me, shoved me into the ground face first. Then they pulled my hands behind my back, and tied my wrists and ankles with rope manacles—like the ones I'd used before I'd been suspended.

So they could kill me, I thought. *After* they found out what I was doing there.

I rolled the last die I had left: I told them I was an Investigator, that I was there on official business. Neither part was true, but it was worth a try.

They didn't seem impressed because they stuffed a gag in

my mouth. And a moment later, they pulled a blindfold across my eyes.

I heard a voice in my ear: "Don't struggle. We're trying to help you."

As if that wasn't odd enough, it was a voice I *knew*.

"Let's go," the owner of the voice said—but not in my ear anymore.

Someone else gave him an argument. Why was he taking me away when the tlacamayeh tecuani still had business with me?

A strange question, I thought. Weren't they *all* tlacamayeh tecuani?

I didn't hear an answer. I just felt myself lifted by my arms and legs like a piece of luggage, and carried headfirst through the woods.

Despite what I'd been told, I writhed and kicked, hoping whoever was carrying me would drop me. They didn't.

After a good few minutes, I heard a creak. Then I was slid onto something unexpectedly soft and cushiony.

"No," someone said. "On the floor."

The floor was harder and more abrasive. But that's where they put me.

Suddenly I felt a vibration underneath me. The kind I'd feel when Necalli sent me somewhere in an auto-carriage, except more pronounced. Then again, I was used to sitting on a seat, not lying on a floor.

We rode for a while. I didn't know long. Hours, at least.

I began to feel more injuries than the one to my ribs:

Cuts, some of them deep, on my face and my arms from the branches I'd run through.

The cuffs I was wearing, which weren't meant to be used for any length of time, didn't do me any favors either, digging into my wrists and my ankles. But they stayed on. Maybe it would have been different if I hadn't slugged a couple of my captors.

I didn't know where we were going, or—if they really weren't tlacamayeh tecuani—even who had taken me. Or what they were going to do to me when we got there. But I had a feeling I wouldn't have been bound and gagged if the answers were to my liking.

Trying not to attract attention, I tested my manacles, pulling at them and twisting—the same way the guys I'd arrested as an Investigator tested theirs. There was no give in the things. Whoever had put them on me knew what they were doing.

Still, manacles broke from time to time. I had to see if I could get this to be one of those times.

So I kept pulling and twisting. It was painful, the ropes slicing even deeper into the skin of my wrists. But if it meant getting free, I could take a little pain.

Suddenly I felt a tug on my manacles, and heard a voice: "I wouldn't struggle if I were you. It's not going to get you anywhere. Besides, there's no need. Nobody's going to hurt you."

Someone had *already* hurt me. But with a gag in my mouth, I wasn't in a position to say so.

Finally, we came to a stop.

It was a *long* stop. *End of the line?* I wondered, painfully aware of how ominous it sounded.

I heard a door open. A moment later, I was grabbed by two or three pairs of hands, lifted, and slid out of the carriage.

Carefully, I thought. As if my health mattered. So maybe my companion hadn't lied to me about my getting hurt after all.

Or maybe they just had to get me somewhere in one piece— maybe so somebody could see it was *me*—before they started taking me apart in earnest.

In any case, they stood me up and took the bonds off my ankles. It left me free to kick them, to maybe escape their grasp—but where would that get me? I couldn't see and my hands were still tied. If I was going to make a break for it, I had to wait until they untied my hands too.

The blindfold came off next. I saw I was in a hallway—but not like any hallway I had seen before. It looked like it had been cut out of rock, but so precisely that it seemed to bend less than a knuckle.

The people around me—the ones who had carried me to that point—were wearing masks so I couldn't see who they were. But they weren't dressed like Isolationists. They wore better tunics. Better sandals. And they had no bracelets.

Only one of them was bare-faced—a guy with a long, narrow face, about fifty cycles in age. "I'm a doctor," he said. He took out a tube and a handful of bandages. Then he said, "Hold still."

I watched as he opened the tube and squeezed until a white ointment began to come out. Then he applied the ointment to my cuts. It smelled like coconut oil rather than the pineapple extract I'd always used.

He must have noticed me favoring one side, because he felt my ribs there. "Fractured," he said. "We'll have to take care of that later."

There would be a later, it seemed. I took that as encouragement.

The doctor finished put bandages on the wounds that called for them. Then he took a look at me.

"Not my best work," he said, "but it's all I can do for now." He looked at one of my captors as he spoke.

"Thanks," the masked man told him. Then he took hold of my arm and said, "This way."

And we walked the rest of the way down the corridor.

• • •

There was a door at the end of the passage. It was made of a rich, dark orange wood, mahogany or something similar. Odd, I thought, to see a door like that in such a place.

It suggested that what was beyond it was different from the passage. Richer. More civilized.

One of my captors knocked on the door. Then he exchanged looks with the others.

"Go ahead," one of them said.

The guy opened the door.

What was on the other side of it was bright, especially after the relative darkness of the passage. So bright I had to squint to make out the details.

It was a room, six-sided, windowless, maybe forty hands deep. A light fixture made of glass hung from the center of the ceiling. Below it was a six-sided table made of the same kind of glass.

There was a man sitting at the table, his back to me. A guy of medium height and medium build, in a linen tunic not unlike my own, though his was clean and freshly pressed.

He wore a bracelet on his right hand. A thick golden circlet, I could see as my eyes adjusted to the light.

I felt a push—a gentle one—from behind. As I entered the room, I took note of the thick carpet of intricately woven plant fibers underfoot, and the thread-of-gold mixed into the mortar of the walls.

So the guy had beans. So many that he could afford to spend them on a room without windows, that few people would ever see, and a golden bracelet even though he was sitting all by himself.

And, of course, the people who had brought me to him. They had to be expensive as well.

But for all his wealth, he didn't seem happy, if his posture was any indication. His head was hanging in what seemed like sadness, or disappointment, or regret—or maybe all three.

There was something else I noticed about the guy. Something familiar, though I couldn't put my finger on it. Then I realized what it was: His shoulders. They were uneven, the right one higher than the left.

It wasn't a pronounced difference. But it was my job to notice details, especially the kind that helped me identify the people I was dealing with.

And that was a detail I hadn't seen too often. On only one person, in fact. Just *one*.

Can it be? I asked myself, staring at the back of the guy's head.

Suddenly, it all came together for me—the wealth, the secrecy, the shoulders. It was *him*.

As a couple of my captors followed me into the room, I looked past the guy at the tabletop in front of him. There was an arrangement there: A blue plate, an orange bowl, and a puckered-glass cup. The plate held a mound of yellow-green fruit slices—soursop, I thought. The cup contained something clear—cane water, in all likelihood.

The bowl was full of liquid chocolate, for dipping. *Chocolate*, I thought. Only noblemen were supposed to have access to chocolate.

Some noblemen more than others.

"Investigator," the guy said, in the deep, resonant voice I'd heard so many times on the Mirror. "Sorry to bring you here so unceremoniously." He got up from his chair, and turned to look at me.

Like anyone, I had seen him any number of times on my screen: Giving speeches on festival days. Presiding over the funerals of prominent citizens. Making appearances to commemorate great or terrible events in the history of the Empire.

In my experience, when I met people in person, they rarely looked the way they did on the Mirror. His Excellence Yolihuali the First, Emperor of Mexica, was no exception.

On the Mirror, he looked dignified, purposeful. Worthy of every citizen's trust. There in that six-sided room, he didn't look dignified at all. Not especially purposeful either.

"It's all right," I said. "I'm sure you had your reasons."

"Then you have more faith in me," said the Emperor, "than I have in myself."

A funny thing to say, I thought, and an unsettling one. Even to a guy who had lately found out he wasn't the prisoner of the tlacamayeh tecuani after all.

"The least I can do," said my host, "is get you something. Are you hungry? Thirsty?" He stepped to one side, revealing the delicacies assembled on his table. "Chocolate, perhaps? With my permission, you know, you can sample all you like without fear of repercussions."

Aunt Xoco, who had told me on more than one occasion how much she craved chocolate, might have accepted his offer. I felt no such temptation.

"What I'd like," I said plainly, so there would be no chance of my request being seen as disrespect, "are answers, Your Excellence. The first one—"

"What are you doing here?" Yolihuali suggested.

"That," I said, "would be a good start."

He nodded. "I'll do my best to clear everything up. However, I'll require your patience. It's a long story, after all—one that is best told sitting down."

With a gesture he indicated a chair opposite his, on the other side of the glass table. I looked back at my captors, just to make sure I wasn't breeching a protocol.

Positioned along the wall on either side of the open door, they said nothing. So as the Emperor had indicated, I went around the table and sat down.

Yolihuali sighed, as if expelling a spirit of disease. Then he said, "You'll recall the death of my uncle, Aztecatl of honored memory."

I nodded. "Of course."

Aztecatl had been Emperor of Mexica from the time I was little until shortly before I entered the Sun League. My father and mother had loved him for the way he supported the police in Aztlan and other big cities.

"He died young," I noted. It was what people said when Aztecatl's name came up.

"Yes," said the Emperor. "A pity for everyone in the Empire, not least of all for those of us fortunate enough to be his kin. But then, the blood poison—which, as you may know, runs in our family—tends to cut into a man's lifespan. And Aztecatl outlived even his youngest siblings by several cycles, so he never complained.

"However, he left neither a son nor a daughter to rule in his place. Fortunately, rules had been established long ago for determining my uncle's successor—starting with his nieces and nephews.

"There were six of us. It may surprise you to learn that not everyone wanted to become Emperor. In fact, only two of us—I and my cousin Xiuhcoatl—had any desire to ascend to the throne.

"My cousin had the advantage. His father had been the eldest in his generation of the family. If it came down to the two of us, the Council would be asked to choose *him*. But the Council never had to get involved. At the last minute, my cousin gave up his claim.

"There were suspicions that he'd been guilty of impropri-
eties—shameful events, which I find distasteful even to con-
template—which would have cast a shadow over his imperial
leadership. The truth, Investigator, was a good deal less sordid.
My cousin was simply offered something that meant more to
him than being Emperor—and that was *wealth*.

"Not that he wasn't wealthy already—his family had more
beans than some cities, as you can imagine. But a couple of
generations before ours, there had been a problem—an indiscretion I'm not at liberty to discuss. It left scars—the psycho-
logical kind even more than the financial—on my cousin's
branch of the family.

"From that time on, no mountain of beans was high enough
for them. And that was the environment in which my cousin
had been raised. So wealth was of prime importance to him.

"You would think that would make him *more* eager to
become Emperor, not less so. And it would have—were it not
for a group that offered my cousin an alternative. They told
him if he gave up his claim to the throne, they would make
him even richer than he would have been as Emperor. Richer
by *half*. Hard to imagine, I know. But they made good on their
promise. They made my cousin the richest man the Empire has
ever known.

"And he remained such until his death a few cycles ago, at
which time his heirs divided up his estate like a pack of wolves
tearing apart a hobbled elk. Not a happy story, but the pursuit
of beans seldom leads in the direction of happiness.

"And my cousin's tale, I regret to say, isn't the saddest one you'll hear today. Because my own is even sadder. You see, the group that stuffed my cousin's coffers...it wasn't one you would find between the shores of the Empire. It was made up of Euros, one or two from each of Europe's most prominent countries. We tend to think of Europe as a collection of warring nations, with little connection to one another—but the truth is that there are individuals whose power transcends national boundaries. The group that approached my cousin, which calls itself Mercantile, was made up of such individuals.

"Shocking, I know—that a pack of Euros could have a say in who rules the Empire and who does not. But it could not have done so without special access to my cousin. Access provided by someone here in the Empire."

By then, I knew who he was talking about. "Provided by *you*."

Yolihuali nodded. "By *me*."

His words hung in the air.

"You look disgusted," he said. "I don't blame you. I'm disgusted as well. And ashamed, as I've never been ashamed of anything else in my life. To the point that not a day—or a night—goes by without my wishing I'd denied the Euros the chance to speak with Xiuhcoatl.

"But I was young. I could see only the dawn, not the dusk— the possibility of winning the only thing that had ever meant anything to me, and the power that came with it.

"I had earlier in my life received an education in the way things worked in Europe—the way they *really* worked—from my father, a much more honorable man than I, who had never capitalized on his depth of understanding. But I wasn't my father. I contacted Mercantile—reached out to them as secretly as I knew how—and suggested an arrangement.

"If they paid my cousin to give up his claim to the throne, I would grant the group the product of our rubber forests. Rubber, as you know, is at a premium in Europe because they have to import it from parts of Asia where prices are controlled by petty warlords, who constantly have to assert their power or be overthrown. So it's not just beans the Euros spend there. It's also, on occasion, the lives of their traders.

"Any group that could provide Europe with an alternative—especially a cheap one—would make more beans than its members could count. An even bigger mountain, by orders of magnitude, than the mountain given to my cousin. This in mind, Mercantile was quick to accept my promise: If they got Xiuhcoatl out of my way, they would receive a substantial rubber harvest for as long as I lived.

"Of course, they could have made the same deal with my cousin. However, they didn't know how he would feel about it—whether he would embrace it or denounce it in public. I, on the other foot, represented a sure thing.

"There was only one challenge in front of me—I would have to gather a workforce skilled in harvesting rubber, and persuade it to keep what it would be doing a secret. But, of course, that wasn't a challenge at all. There already existed a workforce so remote, so close-mouthed, that no one in the rest of the Empire was likely to discover what it was up to."

"The Isolationists," I said.

"They were working the rubber forest as they had since

they settled Deep in the Mountains, if not quite in the quantities I had in mind. And who kept to themselves better than the tlacamayeh tecuani? Any hint that got out of what they were doing for me would be seen as just another baseless rumor.

"In return for their services, and their discretion, I would pay them well. I would also guarantee them freedom from the government oversight that had always rankled them. Whatever they had gotten away with under Aztecatl, they would get away with that much more under *me*.

"And no one would be hurt except my cousin, I thought. The citizens of the Empire would actually benefit from what I'd done—because, I believed in my hubris, I would do a better job than Xiuhcoatl would have.

"There were times, especially in the beginning, when it seemed to me my plan would fall apart. But it never did. The tlacamayeh tecuani got more jobs and less interference. The Euros who comprised Mercantile got even richer than they were before. And I became Emperor.

"But at what cost, Investigator? A bunch of foreigners had helped me gain the throne. Mexica is supposed to stand on its own, apart from the rest of the world, protecting its way of life, its history…its people. And I had sold it out to make certain I became its Emperor.

"I was young, as I've said. And stupid. I didn't see where my actions might take Mexica in the future. I didn't see that there would be a price to pay for my ascension, and a terrible one. But I see now. I see all too clearly.

"You understand that we had to set up a network to transport

Mercantile's rubber to Europe? From Deep In The Mountains, via auto-carriage, to a tiny and obscure port northwest of Yopitzinco, then across the ocean to an equally tiny and obscure port, and finally by rail to a depot in eastern Europe. Now that network is being leveraged, *in reverse,* for another kind of trade—one I never anticipated."

To my chagrin, I knew what he was talking about. "Fire hands."

"Yes." His mouth twisted. "*Those* things. A plague that, as you know, has taken hold with awful ferocity across Europe—much to the financial advantage of those who profit from it."

The Emperor stopped—looking inward, it seemed to me, and not liking what he saw there.

"It was only a matter of time," he continued, "before Mercantile made a deal with our Isolationists directly—without me in the middle. A deal to import fire hands the same way they were exporting rubber." He pressed his hands together and held them out to me. "And it was my fault, Investigator. Unequivocally. The product of my immature, unthinking hunger for the throne. So I was the one who had to do something about it.

"The Euros speak only one language: Beans. So I spoke to them in that idiom. I offered Mercantile an even more profitable position with regard to our rubber. We wouldn't break even anymore. We wouldn't even come close. We would lose beans on every shipment, and not a few of them.

"But no one in the Empire would notice the shortfall because I would shore it up with my personal fortune. *All* of it. I would lose everything I ever owned. However, it would be worth it to keep the plague of fire hands out of the Empire.

"Mercantile accepted my proposal. They would miss out on the beans they could make on a fire hands trade, yes. But their new rubber deal would give them almost as much business, with a great deal less effort and expense.

"They would take the first shipment of fire hands back and there would never be another one. Our problem, I believed, had been solved."

I believed. The words sent a chill up my spine. "You're saying it wasn't?"

The Emperor sighed. "A second group has emerged in Europe. It calls itself Geneva Conference. Like the first group, it's made up of individuals with the wherewithal to do what they say they will do—and they're a good deal more aggressive than Mercantile. In fact, Geneva Conference would like to *supplant* Mercantile altogether, and have the black market in Europe all to itself.

"Right now, Mercantile has the upper hand. And with the additional revenues from its new rubber deal, its advantage will be even greater. Little by little, it hopes to use that advantage to destroy Geneva Conference. But Geneva Conference has plans as well—to drastically enhance its own revenue stream, and in the quickest way possible."

"By establishing a fire hands market in Mexica."

The Emperor nodded. "Obviously, Mercantile will do anything to prevent this situation from materializing—including going ahead with its own fire hand business. In that case, we would have not one but two suppliers of fire hands in the Empire, each one willing to spill as much blood as it deems necessary in order to win its trade war.

"There will be violence in the streets such as we've never seen, even in our most troubling nightmares. And when it's over, fire hands will be as common an evil here in Mexica as they are in Europe.

"All—*all*—because of me, Investigastor. Since the dawn of the Empire, my bloodline has built an increasingly peaceful and enlightened society. And in a single decade, I have managed to jeopardize everything they created.

"The only way for the Empire to survive is for Geneva Conference to be stopped in its effort to start a fire hands business in Mexica. Then Mercantile will have a chance to eradicate its competition.

"But," said the Emperor, "if Geneva Conference is allowed to go ahead with its plans—"

"Mercantile has to respond."

"You see the problem."

"I do," I said. "But—"

"Why am I telling you this?"

"I work the streets," I said. "I'm not a negotiator. I've spoken with only one Euro in my entire life, and that was over a Mirror link."

Calli would have been a better choice—not that I was going to suggest as much. I wanted her as far from the possibility of a fire hands war as possible.

The Emperor frowned. "I understand your concern. But it's

not a negotiator whose help I need. It's an Investigator—and as far as I can tell, there's no Investigator in Mexica more skilled than you are.

"That's why I had you suspended—hoping it would keep you out of the Western Mountains. It's why I had a man tracking you for the last couple of moons in Aztlan. And it's why I sent a contingent to bring you back from Iztactetl, which—propitiously—arrived in time to rescue you from the tlacamayeh tecuani.

"Because you're the best investigative officer the Empire has at its disposal."

I wasn't so sure about that, but I wasn't going to argue with *the Emperor*. "What is it you want me to do?"

"Mercantile has informed me of a troubling development. Geneva Conference, in its urgent desire to gain a foothold here, has hired someone—an Isolationist who originally worked for Mercantile delivering fire hands to Aztlan—to further its cause.

"To this point we've managed to keep the existence of the fire hands you saw under wraps. This individual has been tasked with tearing the wraps away—making it plain to every last citizen that these weapons exist here in the Empire.

"From there it will be a short journey to a Mexica very different from the one we've known. Which is why it's critical that we keep Geneva Conference's man from carrying out his mission.

"I have spoken with those who run the Mirror, and they have put protocols in place that will prevent this fellow from gaining traction in the Mirror's news accounts. But Mexica is more than the Mirror. It's an Empire of people. And places."

I saw where His Excellence was going. "A public event." In which a fire hand would play a very loud and visible part.

"So public, Investigator, that the citizens of the Empire cannot help but speak of it, spreading the word as surely as if it were indeed a Mirror report."

I'd seen news spread that way, one citizen to the next. Like ripples in a pond. And as big a story as this would be...

"Unfortunately," said the Emperor, "Mercantile—despite all its resources—has been able to learn precious little about this man's plan: Only that his performance will take place somewhere in Aztlan, the heart of the Empire.

"Unfortunately, Mercantile believes he gave them a false name when he worked for them—like a lot of the Isolationists, in case they were caught. So I can't provide you with the man's identity—only his physical description. The other thing Mercantile knows about him is that he is not adverse to murder—because not so long ago, in fact, he killed a fellow Isolationist named Ozomahtli, with whom, I believe, you're somewhat familiar."

Ozomahtli, I thought. The Emperor was talking about *the stalker*.

"This Ozomahtli," said the Emperor, "had worked for Mercantile as well—perhaps right alongside his killer—delivering fire hands to Notoca. When you nipped the fire hands trade in the bud, he became afraid that you would connect it to his people's rubber harvesting—and that without it, the tlaca-mayeh tecuani would see their way of life destroyed."

Something that wouldn't even have been a possibility, I thought, if the stalker hadn't led me down that trail himself.

"He was," the Emperor said, "what the Euros would call 'a loose cannon.' Geneva Conference decided the Ozomahtli's unpredictability was a danger to its plans—"

"And sent their Isolationist assassin to kill him."

"Which he did. So now you know what we're dealing with—a ruthless individual, as well as a resourceful one. If the situation were less complex, I would deploy every police officer in Aztlan to watch every district and street in the city. However, it would raise too many questions. And even if I did deploy the force in its entirety, Geneva Conference's agent would find a way to get around it.

"The only way to stop him," said the Emperor, "is to find out his name—his *real* one—and learn the details of his scheme. And for that work, I don't need a negotiator, Investigator. I need *you*."

I nodded. "I understand."

"To complicate matters, Mercantile views its decision to either accept my offer or launch a full-scale fire hand campaign as a matter of extreme urgency. They believe the next several days are absolutely critical to their efforts—and have scheduled a meeting with me a week from yesterday.

"Of course, Geneva Conference's man may not wait that long. He may decide to move today. Or tomorrow.

"So it won't be enough to apprehend this murderer. We also have to do it quickly—a week at the outside. If we're successful, Mercantile will accept my offer regarding the rubber trade. If not…"

I got it.

I had to find a single man in a city of millions. And do so before the man carried out his mission—which could be at any moment.

Did Yolihuali know what he was asking?

He leaned across the table. "I have faith in you, Investigator. Not everyone can handle a case of this magnitude."

I'd taken down the High Priest, he was saying. He was omitting the fact that I'd almost died in the process.

"Will you do it?" the Emperor asked.

If I was going to have even a sliver of a chance, I had to get moving. I stood. "I'll need my bracelet back."

"It will be waiting for you in your Interrogation Center," the Emperor said. "Along with your radio, your hand stick, and the cooperation of every man and woman in your department."

I would need them—along with as much luck as the gods could provide.

• • •

The Emperor loaned me a radio so I could call Paynal and make sure Ana was all right—which she was.

Apparently, His Excellence had sent a couple of his men to make sure of that, and to send her home—with word that her friend Colhua was alive and well, and in good hands.

Of course, Ana being who she was, she had been reluctant to listen to them. But she could only pretend to leave and then circle back so many times before it became obvious she wasn't going to get anywhere.

"Tell her it's all right," I told Paynal. "I found out what I needed to find out, and I'm taking it from there."

"What else can we do to help?" Paynal asked.

"Nothing," I assured him. "You've done everything I needed, you and Ana. I'm grateful."

I promised myself I would thank them in person one day. Then I returned the Emperor's phone.

Moments later, I was sitting in the back seat of another car-riage—smaller and therefore less conspicuous, I imagined, than the one that had brought me to the Emperor—making my way back to Aztlan.

My driver—the driver of that other conveyance as well, for all I knew—informed me that he had no idea who he worked for, or who I was, or why he was taking me where he was taking me—only that he was paid better than he had been when he was a driver in Yautepec. Therefore, there was no point in my asking him about anything.

It was all right. The Emperor had answered my questions. At least, the ones he could.

I was angry.

Not because the Emperor was flawed. I'd never thought he was perfect, after all. Some people worshiped him as if he were a god but I'd never been one of them.

I was angry because he had done the one thing a leader should never do: He had betrayed the people he was supposed to lead.

It raised a question: How could I follow such a leader?

My answer, in the confines of my own head, was that it wasn't the Emperor I was working for. Not anymore.

It was the Empire.

That was what was left to me as a man and as an Investigator. The Empire was what I would serve with all the resources at my disposal.

I could only hope, as the countryside between cities sped by my window, that my resources would be enough.

• • •

Somewhere on the road to Aztlan, I fell asleep. When I woke, my auto-carriage was standing in front of the Interrogation Center. It was early morning, the sky in the east a fiery spectacle.

I was stiff. I hurt where I'd been hit and cut and gouged during my visit to the Western Mountains, most of all in the rib—or ribs—I'd broken.

I looked at myself. Felt my bandages.

I'll have to explain them, I thought. Then I remembered what the Emperor said: I was in charge. I didn't have to answer to *anyone*.

It was a strange feeling. *But then*, I thought, *these are strange times*.

I thanked the driver, walked as well as I could into the Interrogation Center, and made my way through the building to my Mirror station. It was quiet there. There were Investigators on the premises, as always, but none in sight.

As I sat down in front of my screen, I saw someone walk in. It was Quetzalli. Usually, she was the first one to report for a shift. But not this time.

She looked at me for a moment. Then she said, "You're back? And looking like you stopped in the Lands of the Dead?"

I couldn't help smiling at the sight of her. "Miss me?"

"Like I miss paying taxes," she said. But on her way to her station, she stopped and gave me a little hug.

"Not so hard," I said, wincing at the pain in my side. Then I started doing the Emperor's work.

• • •

I hadn't gotten far before some of the other Investigators showed up. Necalli too.

"Welcome back," he told me.

I looked at him. "It's good to be back."

I knew now why he'd taken my job from me—and that there was nothing he could have done about it. Not when his orders came from the Emperor himself.

"Listen up," said Necalli, drawing everyone's attention. "We're working on something top-secret. Colhua's taking point. Whatever he asks, you do it. You just *do* it. Got it?"

My colleagues looked at each other. No doubt, they had questions. But if Necalli had wanted to entertain them, he would have.

"All right," I said, unaccustomed to being in a position of unquestioned authority. I'd led an action here and there, but nothing like this. "Here's what we're looking for…"

The Emperor had told me how the fire hands got to the Western Mountains. The question was how they got from the mountains into Aztlan.

It had to be through one of the carriers that ran on the city's commercial rail lines. But which one? There were more than fifty of them, each specializing in a different cargo.

However, they didn't all have permits to transport goods

to the Western Mountains and back. We checked to see which ones did.

With a bunch of us working at once, it didn't take long. Six names came up.

I knew the owner of one of them—a straight stick if ever there was one, with more beans than she knew what to do with. I ruled her out. But that still left five.

Notoca wasn't going to be of any help, of course. He had made that clear when I visited him in the Prison House.

But Ximo had known Notoca as well as anyone. He might know what Notoca wouldn't tell me. At some point, after Notoca decided to move up in the world, he'd hidden things from Ximo. But before that, they had been tight. If Notoca had a connection to a carrier, Ximo would be aware of it.

I called Ximo and bounced the list of carriers off him. "Did Notoca ever mention any of them?"

Immediately he said, "Not Notoca. But one of Notoca's friends."

The friend had been a Hawk until he disappeared—right around the time I exposed Notoca—so he was probably in on the fire hands deal. At least Ximo thought so.

The guy's name, Ximo told me, was Pallea Erandi. It was his uncle he'd mentioned—a guy who ran a business supplying Aztlan with wooden furniture made in the Mountains.

Minutes after I spoke with Ximo, Erandi's uncle received a visit from a couple of police officers at his home in District Fourteen—and not long after that, he was on his way to the Interrogation Center.

• • •

As I waited for Erandi's uncle in an interrogation enclosure, Izcuin showed up. It was the first I'd seen of him since I got back. But then, that wasn't a surprise to me.

"How are you feeling?" he asked.

I shrugged. "Not much worse than after a match in the Arena."

It was a lie. I'd never been beaten up so badly in a ball court, professional or otherwise. Not even that time in Yopitzinco when we were up six goals and digging for more.

Izcuin shook his head. "They weren't supposed to go after you like that. But you put up a fight and—"

"I know," I said. I'd been there.

It was easy to stay calm when everything went smoothly. After the guy you were arresting dealt you a couple of licks, it was hard to keep from returning the favor.

"How did you come to work for the Emperor?" I asked.

Izcuin shook his head. "I don't know. When I finished my training, they told me they were assigning me to Necalli's sector. I was excited. It was the big time, you know? The top sector in the city.

"Then they said there was a catch. I'd be working for the Emperor instead of Necalli. In secret, of course. No one was supposed to know.

"It wasn't bad, at first. I did pretty much what I would have done anyway. And the game you invited me to...that was great. Then they told me to step up the surveillance, that you were getting too close to one of the Emperor's secrets. I thought

I'd be reassigned, maybe, when they suspended you—but they kept me on you. I followed you to Zempoala. And then—"

"I know the rest," I said.

Izcuin grimaced. "I feel like a rat."

"But," I said, "you were good at it. I didn't know what you were up to until I heard your voice there in the woods—telling me to relax, that you were trying to help me. And if you hadn't found me when you did, I might not be here. So...thanks."

Izcuin looked skeptical. "Thanks?"

"That's what I said."

"If it were me, I'd be pissed."

"Oh," I said, "I am. But not at you. At myself—for not seeing through you."

"You know, if you want to hit me or something—"

I laughed enough to feel a twinge in my ribs. "Some other time. We've got work to do, and I need all the help I can get."

He looked surprised. "*We...?*"

"You may have been working for the Emperor before," I said. "But you're working for me now."

He smiled. "*Really?*"

"You were serving the Empire. That's what we all do. Some of us above board, honorably...and some of us like a snake slithering in the undergrowth."

He winced. "I guess I deserve that."

I ignored the opening, and said, "But it's still service. Besides...the Scale Beetles are going to be shorthanded for a while, and you did a job for us while you were in there."

Izcuin looked skeptical again. "You're kidding."

"Not when it comes to the ball court. Not *ever*."

He looked as if a weight had been lifted off him. "Thanks. I mean—"

"Don't mention it," I said.

• • •

Mahuizoh Erandi was a tall man with long hair and a cleft lip. I guessed he hadn't been questioned by an Investigator before because he rubbed his hands together—a lot. In my experience, people did that when they were scared.

I hoped that was true of Erandi because I had no time to waste. I told him I knew it was his company that had transported fire hands to Aztlan, that it was colossally bad judgment on his part, and that he'd pay for that decision by spending the rest of his life in the Prison House.

His only hope of getting a reduced sentence, I said, was giving up a man who'd delivered the fire hands to Notoca—a guy who fit the description the Emperor had gotten from Mercantile, though I didn't say that.

I was taking a shot. Notoca could have been involved with some other carrier entirely—someone whose connection with him was less obvious, and therefore unknown to Ximo. But what did I have to lose?

Erandi's face scrunched up as he absorbed what I'd told him. Was he horrified at the mention of fire hands? Or just scared by the prospect of the Prison House? It was hard to tell.

Come on, I thought. I needed a break.

And I got one.

Erandi, it turned out, wasn't a tough guy—not anything

like his nephew's friend, Notoca. He couldn't talk to me fast enough. And by the time he was done, I'd gotten the name I needed from him.

Fortunately, it was an unusual name—Chicle Chi. It wouldn't be hard, I thought, to find the guy in our files.

• • •

I was right. Chicle Chi wasn't a hard name to find.

And in case there was any doubt he was my guy, his description matched the one the Emperor had given me. Matched it *perfectly*.

His birthplace was listed as Zempoala—a common enough notation for those who had grown up in the Western Mountains, far from a town big enough to have its own designation on an imperial map. Only a local would have recognized a more precise location—as if a local would have had any need for it.

Three cycles earlier, Chi had shown up in Aztlan for the first time. His first residence had been the Relocation Center in District Three, a place designed to give newcomers to the city somewhere to get settled while they looked for a job.

Chi had been there less than a week—not because he'd found employment so quickly, but because he'd had an argument with the woman who ran the place. After that, he fell off the map for a while.

He turned up again as a construction worker, employed by a builder who put up bath houses in the less prosperous districts. After a few moons, that job ended as well. The notation in Chi's file mentioned a fight, though it wasn't clear with whom or whether Chi started it.

Chi got a warehouse job a week later. It was the first of several such jobs, each with a different employer. Every time, he left under a cloud—either because he kept showing up late, or because he'd mouthed off to his boss, or because he'd been accused of stealing from another worker.

Except for his last job—at the Mirror, unlikely as it seemed. Somehow he'd left that one in good standing.

Judging by his pictures, he'd been in his share of altercations. Flat nose, puffiness around his eyes, half a dozen thin, white scars across his cheeks and forehead—the kinds of souvenirs you saw in the innermost block of a prison house, where the Empire kept its murderers, rapists, and seditionists.

In the first image of Chi, taken when he arrived in Aztlan, his hair was woven into a braid, like the ones I'd seen hanging down the backs of the Isolationists. In his most recent picture, the braid was gone and his head was shaved. And he wore a couple of earrings with little red stones instead of cardinal feathers in them.

There was no knowing which picture Chi resembled now, or whether he'd ditched both looks for a third one. I made a note of his appearance in both pictures. Then I circulated them to my fellow Investigators.

"Where's his current residence?" Quetzalli asked.

Chi's file said he lived in District Eight, not far from Zolin's salamander cart. But I couldn't send a couple of police officers to bring him in. Not a guy with a fire hand, who was looking to use it before long.

I couldn't even send a couple of Investigators. It would have to be an entire squad of them. A squad I would lead.

It would be tricky. We wouldn't want Chi to know we were closing in on him until it was too late for him to do anything about it. But it wouldn't be the first time we'd been confronted with a delicate situation.

I told Necalli. And I told him which of my colleagues I would take with me.

"Not a chance," he said. "The shape you're in, you'll be a liability to whoever goes in with you."

"It's my case," I said. "Ask the Emperor."

Necalli scowled. "*I'll* pick your team. The Emperor's meddled enough around here."

I was *this* close to telling him off. And I would have—if he wasn't a hundred percent right. The last thing I wanted was to put my fellow Investigators in danger.

"All right," I said. "It'll be Quetzalli's play."

• • •

I didn't like sitting at my Mirror station while Quetzalli was out there doing my job. But I did so. Finally, my radio buzzed.

"Chi's not here," Quetzalli said. "We came in slow and subtle, just in case. But his neighbors say they haven't seen him in months. They thought something happened to him."

Yet that was the most recent listing we had for him.

"More than likely," Quetzalli said, "he kept the place to throw us off."

It made sense. Chi had Geneva Conference behind him, after all. He could maintain as many false addresses as he liked.

"Did any of his neighbors *know* him?" I asked. "Enough to give us a lead?"

"Doesn't seem like it. But I'll keep asking."

Quetzalli was as slick and thorough as any Investigator I knew. In the end, it didn't help. Chi was somewhere in Aztlan, if the Emperor's information was correct. We just didn't know where.

And our chronometer was running.

• • •

I went back to Chi's file and looked it over again, this time more carefully.

What stuck out for me, as before, was Chi's rocky employment history. It was full of conflicts, bad work habits, and petty crimes. Not the sort of record that employers liked to see.

Yet he had gotten a job at the Mirror, of all places. The best place to work in all of Mexica, by most accounts.

I wondered how.

It occurred to me to buzz Chicome for an answer. But I didn't want it to be known I was investigating Chi. Chicome himself was trustworthy, but recent experience had shown me that wasn't true of everyone at the Mirror.

Besides, there was a notation in Chi's employment file—a reference to something called The Emperor's Program. I hadn't heard of it so I looked it up. If it had really been created by the Emperor, everything about it would be public knowledge.

I found the relevant page in no time. The Emperor's Program, which had since been discontinued, was for people who had been in trouble on other jobs—the idea being that if they worked in an exemplary environment like the Mirror, its air of professionalism would rub off on them.

Also, the Emperor had made a pledge long ago that there would a job for any citizen who wanted one. This program had been established in keeping with that pledge.

For me, it was a gold mine.

One of the links on the program's page gave me access to the names of citizens who had gone through the program. Chi was on the list. What I needed was someone who had worked with him, who might be able to help us find him.

The problem was I didn't want Chi to know the authorities were asking about him. And anyone we interviewed might alert him, intentionally or otherwise.

So I had to find someone I could sequester afterward. Someone willing to remain out of circulation for a few days.

It wouldn't be easy, I thought.

Then the gods intervened.

• • •

Culanto Xiomara wasn't happy about getting dragged into the Interrogation Center again. No doubt, he'd believed his friend Ilhica's intervention had ended his problems with the police.

Fortunately, it was easier for me to find him this time. But then, he had gotten a new job—with another banker, apparently—along with an apartment in District Twelve.

Xiomara paused for a moment when he saw the bandages on my face. Under different circumstances, he might have gotten a kick out of them. As it was, he was focused on other things.

"What's this about?" he demanded. "You heard where I was the night Inave was killed."

Like the rest of Aztlan, he didn't know yet that we'd found Inave's killer. And I wasn't at liberty to tell him.

But I *could* say, "This isn't about Inave."

He looked confused. "Then what?"

"You worked for the Mirror."

His eyes widened. "Don't tell me you're going to kill my best job reference for me."

"Not if you give me what I'm looking for."

That focused him a little. "Like what?"

"Like information on Chicle Chi."

"What do you want him for?"

I ignored the question. "So you know him."

"I used to. I worked with him. For...I don't know. Half a cycle, I guess."

"As part of the Mirror's opportunity program."

He seemed surprised that I knew about it. "That's right."

"What can you tell me about him?"

"He was wild. Not at work but afterwards."

"You socialized with him?"

"Once in a while."

"Drank with him?"

"Just once."

"Why not more often?"

"He was out of control even *without* octli. With it..." He shivered. "I was out on good behavior. He was the kind of guy who could wreck it for me."

"Did he tell you where he lived?"

"I went there with him once." He told me the name of the pyramid. "But I doubt he's still there."

"Why do you say that?"

"He was from the Western Mountains. I'm pretty sure he went back there."

"What did he do when he wasn't working? Besides go to octli houses?"

"I don't know. He liked pools. Liked sitting on the edge and putting his feet in. He got this look on his face like he was a kid again. Weird for a guy like him."

"What else?"

"He liked cactus worms. The salted kind. Couldn't get enough of them."

"Cactus worms are expensive."

"I guess they were worth it to him.

"Do you know where he bought them?"

"I don't."

I grilled Xiomara some more, asking everything I could think of to flesh out our picture of Chi. Finally, he ran out of answers.

"Can I go now?" he asked.

"We're going to keep you for a while."

Anger blazed in him. "I told you everything I know."

"If that's so," I said, "you have nothing worry about."

As before, we wouldn't be able to hold him for long. But it might be long enough for us to catch Chi.

• • •

Once again, I sent Quetzalli out with her squad of Investigators. This time, she went to the pyramid Xiomara had mentioned to me.

As before, I sat in the Interrogation Center waiting for my colleague's call. I wasn't optimistic. Time had passed since Xiomara hung out with Chi, after all.

It turned out my pessimism was misplaced.

"Chi's not home," Quetzalli said. "But he lives here. Neighbors saw him as recently as this morning."

"So he's been out all day."

"Looks that way."

I swore to myself. Was he out there somewhere, a loaded fire hand in his pouch, looking for a place and time to use it? Would it be that afternoon? That evening? Early the next morning?

Despite our efforts to stay low, did he suspect we were onto him? Had his Isolationist friends told him about the guy who snuck up on their storage facility at night—a guy important enough for the Emperor's people to rescue?

Had he pieced it together that the Law was after him in Aztlan?

He might if we started asking his neighbors too many questions. But we couldn't set a trap and just wait for him to come home. By that time, it might be late.

"Step it up," I told Quetzalli. "Even if it ends up looking like a bunch of Investigators are doing the asking."

"Acknowledged," she said.

I sat back in my chair, in front of my Mirror station, and wished I could do more.

Lands of the Dead, there was a killer on the loose. Worse than a killer. He wasn't going to end just one life, he was going to tear the heart out of the Empire.

If I were Chi, where would I go? What would I do?

It wouldn't have to be much. He could start a panic pretty much anywhere by firing a fire hand. Anywhere at *all*.

But why settle for a small statement when Chi could make a big one—the news of which would rip from one end of Mexica to the other, making it impossible for the Emperor to make his deal with Mercantile?

And where would that big statement be?

I was still mulling the question when Quetzalli called again. "We found someone," she said. "A woman a floor above him. She says she dated Chi a couple of times. He liked going to the public bath in District Three, on the other side of town. He told her it reminded him of a place where his mother brought him when he was little."

A bath, I thought.

In ancient days, such a place would have a domed roof and be heated with hot stones so bathers could sweat out whatever ailed them. In modern times, baths were open to the sky and as warm or cold as the weather—except for the one in District Three, which still used hot stones in the old manner.

And Chi liked to dangle his feet in pool water. Xiomara had said so.

The bath in District Three…

Was that where Chi would make his statement, knowing it

might be his last as a free man? In a place that reminded him of home? Or, wanting to keep such a place unsullied, would he stay as far away from it as possible?

"Hang on a moment," said Quetzalli. She said something to someone and got a response. "Suguey says there's something going on later at the bath in District Three. Zayanya's giving out awards for valor to a couple of officers—the ones who saved that kid from drowning in the River."

I remembered the story. The boy had had some octli and gone swimming in the middle of the night. The officers had pulled him out just before he went under.

"This could be it," Quetzalli said, an undercurrent of excitement in her voice. "What we're looking for."

I considered it: Zayanya, the First Chief Of Investigators for the city of Aztlan—shot to death in front of a crowd.

There would be a reporter from the Mirror. Cameras to capture the spectacle. Even if they cut the feed once they knew what was happening…it would be too late.

And if that didn't leave an impression on the Empire, what would?

Of course, we could ask Zayanya to call off the event. But Chi would know why. And he would strike at a different place and time, which we couldn't predict.

No—we had to catch him in the crowd gathering to hear Zayanya. I hated the idea of putting the people at the event in jeopardy—but until Chi was taken down, all of *Aztlan* was in jeopardy.

"I'll ask Necalli to call the First Chief," I said, "and let him know what's going on. In the meantime, get over there. Position your team."

"On it," said Quetzalli.

We would be taking a chance. But it might be the only one we got.

• • •

There was one more thing I had to do before Zayanya's speech.

Because I didn't know if we would succeed in stopping Chi. And if we failed, I needed to minimize the impact—so I called Chicome at the Mirror.

It didn't take long to get through to him. No more than it had before his promotion. "Investigator," he said.

I went right at it. "I need a favor."

"What is it?"

"I need you to black out an event. No notice. Keep your cameras there and everything. Just kill the feed as it starts."

"As you know," Chicome said, "we have an obligation to the public. If—"

I interrupted: "The Emperor has already asked you not to run news footage of a certain violent act. I know this *because he told me*. What I'm asking—that you black out the act in advance—is under his authority."

Chicome knew me better than to think I was bluffing. "You've come up in the world, haven't you, Colhua?"

"Not through any desire of my own."

"Right. So...which event?"

I told him.

Chicome sighed. "People have been looking forward to

that one. But if it's that important…"

"It is."

"Then we'll do what's necessary. But…"

I knew what he was going to ask. He might have become a boss but he could still smell a story.

"Not this time," I said.

This was one feature the public would be better off never seeing. And if I did my job, it wouldn't.

Chicome made a sound of disgust. "Too bad."

• • •

First Chief Zayanya, who had spent more than twenty cycles working the streets of Aztlan, took the podium in front of the bath house in District Three exactly at the hour of four.

I watched him look out over the crowd of some two thousand people that had gathered to listen to him. As far as I knew, only one of them wanted to make Zayanya's speech a different kind of spectacle.

The trick, for Quetzalli and her team, was to find him.

It wouldn't be easy for Zayanya to remain composed while he was delivering his remarks. Not when he knew there would be a fire hand discharging at some point, most likely it in his direction. But he hadn't hesitated to go ahead with the event when we described our plan to him.

"Just get the guy," he had said, "before you have to find a *new* First Chief."

Quetzalli's team had begun to try well before Zayanya approached the podium, as the crowd was still gathering. But without any luck.

I didn't like it. It felt to me like we had missed something.

"Maybe Chi's in disguise," I told Quetzalli over our radio link.

"Maybe," she allowed.

Just then, my monitor screen went black. Chicome's done his job, I thought. It was time for us to do ours.

I couldn't see what was going on at the bath house, but I could hear it over Quetzalli's radio. Zayanya's amplified voice sounded strong, sincere, as he celebrated the efforts of the two hero police officers.

I imagined Chi patting his pouch, the fire hand inside it. Making his way through the crowd, closer to Zayanya, as Tonatiuh slid down the sky behind the bath house.

Closer. And closer still, until he was too close to miss his target.

"Anything?" I asked.

"Nothing," Quetzalli told me.

Come on, I thought.

It could happen at any moment. Chi could take out his weapon and fire and make Zayanya an *ex*-First Chief.

Come on…

Zayanya reconstructed the scene the night of his officers' bravery. He spoke of the youth they rescued, of his potential, and what he meant to his family and his community. And he spoke of the perseverance exhibited by his officers when it looked like they had arrived too late to do any good.

I watched the moments go by on my chronometer, one after the other in slow, grinding succession. Quetzalli had to find Chi. She *had* to.

But she didn't. Not the whole time Zayanya was speaking. Which would have been a disaster if Chi took advantage of the fact to get his shot off.

Except it never happened. Ten minutes after Zayanya began his speech, he thanked everyone for coming and left the podium.

"He's done," Quetzalli said, a note of surprise in her voice. "The crowd is starting to disperse."

I swore out loud, my voice ringing through the Interrogation Center. If Chi was going to do something there at the bath house, he would have done it already. So we had gone down the wrong path.

We have to find the right one, I thought. But where could we look? Who else could give us information on Chi?

Then it came to me—and I called Paynal in Zempoala. "There's something I need from you after all," I told my friend.

"Anything, Maxtla."

"There's a bath house in Zempoala. I'm not sure where it is, but—"

"A bath?" Paynal said. "Not in Zempoala, Maxtla. The last of our baths was closed more than fifty cycles ago."

Before Chi was born, I thought. Then the woman he had gone out with must have misremembered. Or lied to us, though that was a stretch.

"You're sure?" I asked Paynal.

"Positive. The closest thing we've got to a bath are our flooded river plazas."

I knew what he was talking about. We had a flooded river

plaza in Aztlan too. A little stone square off the River of Stars—
dammed up except for four weeks a year, when the square was
flooded and prayers were offered to the river god Acuecueyotl.

The water in the plaza was only a few hands deep at such
times, but children had a good time wading through it. And
some, it occurred to me—the littlest ones—sat on the edge of
the plaza and *dipped their feet in the water*.

"I have to go," I told Paynal. "Thanks…"

I could see through the window nearest me that the sun
was starting to approach the horizon. Maybe Chi had decided
to leave his spectacle for another day. But if he was going to do
something *this* day, he would do it *soon*.

The river plaza, I thought.

Unfortunately, it was way across town from my colleagues
at the bath in District Three. It would take Quetzalli an hour to
reach the place on the city rail line, more than half of that even
by auto-carriage.

The Interrogation Center, on the other foot, was a short
walk from the river plaza. I could be there in a matter of minutes.

I made my way to Necalli's office in what felt like a single
heartbeat. He was studying his Mirror screen, just as I was a
few moments earlier.

"Gods," he muttered, disappointment in his tone. "How—"

"Get up!" I told him.

He looked at me with a question on his face.

"Come *on*!" I said, lighting a fire under him. "I'll explain on
the way!"

• • •

I tried to ignore the horror that had seized on me as we double-timed it in the direction of the River.

"What would make for a bigger story than the shooting of First Chief Zayana?" I asked Necalli.

"What?" he asked.

"The deaths of innocent children. Think of all the kids that will have gathered at the plaza for Acuecueyotl."

It was late afternoon, but it was still hot out. All the more reason for a child to want to wade through the cool river water.

"Think what it would be like," I said, "if Chi were to turn his fire hand on them. How many he could kill before the police got there."

We wove our way past gatherings of people on the street, the kind that always showed up on a bright, sunny day.

"What parent," I asked, "wouldn't want to protect their sons and daughters against such unimaginable violence? Who wouldn't do whatever it took to keep their kids safe—even if it meant embracing that violence themselves?"

Necalli didn't say anything. But his face was flushed with more than his exertions.

My ribs felt like there was a leather band pulled too tight around them, keeping me from taking a whole breath. But I didn't slow down. I didn't dare—not even when we came in sight of the river plaza.

There were lots of people there, most of them gathered in clusters around priests in white robes. Through gaps in the crowd I could see the flooded plaza, and the kids wading in it. They were smiling, splashing, laughing. And there were no adults around them except a couple of women.

So Chi hadn't gotten to them. At least not *yet*.

I scanned the crowd and gestured to my left. "I'll go this way," I told Necalli. "You go to the right."

He looked at the way I was holding my ribs. He'd broken a rib once so he knew what I was feeling. Unfortunately, we didn't have an alternative.

"Just *go*," I said.

He went.

And I did too, making my way through the gathering. More slowly and deliberately than I wanted to, to minimize the chances of passing my target without recognizing him.

After all, I was looking for the Chi I had seen in his Mirror file. But he could have changed his appearance since then, or assumed a disguise.

So I made my way from cluster to cluster, checking faces, looking for pouches that dropped heavier than others. Even looking into the eyes of priests because I couldn't rule them out either.

I bit my lip. I had to find him. *Had* to.

I shaded my eyes from the sun—and suddenly I *saw* him.

Maybe two hundred hands away. Standing near one of the priests offering prayers to Acuecueyotl.

I recognized the shaved head. The flat nose. No disguise. Just the guy in the picture. It was him. It was *Chi*.

He looked around, as if sensing that he was being watched. Gradually, he turned in my direction.

I resisted the urge to duck out of sight. After all, he didn't know who I was. If I just stood there, he wouldn't suspect I was after him.

So that's what I did. I stood there and looked past him. And he kept looking around.

I breathed a sigh of relief. But the feeling didn't last. How could it when Chi could take out his fire hand at any moment?

As it was, I was too far away to stop him. I had to get closer. But I couldn't let him see me approaching, so I made an orbit around him. Then another, smaller than the first. And another.

I wanted to go straight for him. But I kept orbiting, each time getting closer to him. And closer...

I was almost there—almost close enough to take him down, ribs or no ribs, and hold him there until Necalli saw us. I moved my hand toward my pouch and the hand stick inside it.

Then, without warning, Chi turned to me.

Maybe he'd realized that I was tracking him. Maybe it was an instinct, or even a coincidence. Whatever the reason, Chi looked me in the eye—and saw, I thought, someone who was there to stop him.

I couldn't wait any longer. Not even long enough to take out my hand stick.

I could only take the last couple of steps and drive my fist into the center of Chi's face—as hard as I could, with all my weight behind the blow. He went down instantly, blood spurting from his nose, and lay there on the ground.

Even better, he hadn't had the chance to draw his fire hand. As far as I could tell, it was still in his pouch. All I had to do was remove the thing from his belt and he'd be unable to carry out his plan.

Bending over the Isolationist, I took out my hand stick and used its blade to start cutting the leather strings of his pouch. I'd been lucky to put him down so easily. *Very* lucky. If he had seen me a half moment earlier, he might have made me miss.

Just as I thought so, I felt something slam me in the side of the head—hard enough to send me lurching into someone, helpless to stop myself. I clutched at the person to keep my feet, my ribs on fire and the taste of blood thickening in my mouth.

Then I got hit again, even harder.

For a moment, I lost track of where I was. Then awareness came rushing back and I found myself on my knees, looking into the face of a man I didn't know. An *angry* man. He grabbed me with a bloody-knuckled hand by the front of my tunic and brought my face close to his.

"You can't go around hitting people!" he snarled. "This is a sacred ceremony. Who do you think you are?"

Other people crowded around me, as angry, it seemed to me, as the guy who'd hit me. "Where are the police when you need them?" a woman demanded. "Hold him until they get here!" another man bellowed. "Help!" someone shouted.

It took me a moment to get out the words: "I'm an *Investigator*!" And to roll up my sleeve as proof.

The people who'd gathered around me stared at my bracelet, and then at each other, as it dawned on them that they'd attacked an officer of the Law.

I didn't stick around to hear their apologies. I couldn't

afford to. Chi wasn't lying on the ground anymore. He was *gone*.

I took out my phone and buzzed Necalli. "He's here!" I said. "I had him but I lost him!"

"Where?" my boss asked.

"I don't know!"

I looked around, desperate to catch a glimpse of my target. He could have taken out his fire hand as soon as I got knocked down and started firing. But he hadn't.

He was holding out for a more prominent stage. Somewhere where everyone could see him, and remember what they had seen.

The plaza, I thought. It was why Chi had come, wasn't it?

I headed straight for it. Shoved people aside. Ran when I saw an opening, teeth grinding against the agony in my ribs.

I had almost reached the plaza when I spotted Chi again. But I was too far away to do anything. He would see me coming in time to draw his fire hand and use it on me, and then on others.

Suddenly, a gravelly voice cut the air: "Hey!"

It was Necalli. He was even farther away than I was, but he was waving his arms like a crazy man. People turned to him, wondered what he was doing.

Chi was one of them.

It was the kind of distraction I needed—and the only one I would get.

I put my head down and pelted across the space between me and Chi. For a moment, Chi was drawn to the spectacle Necalli was making of himself. Then he seemed to notice something out of the corner of his eye—enough to make his head swivel in my direction.

At the same tine, I saw his hand go to his pouch. It would take just a second for him to pull out his fire hand and start shooting. I couldn't let him have that second. *Couldn't...*

With one last, desperate stride, I closed the gap—and reached out despite the fire in my ribs—and grabbed the hand near Chi's pouch with both of mine. Then I drove my shoulder into him as hard as I could.

We sprawled together. Somehow, I wound up on top.

I splayed my legs, trying to keep Chi from getting out from under me. It helped me pin his left hand against him, unable to pull out his weapon.

But his right hand was free, and he used it to hammer me.

I was able to avoid his first blow, but not his second. Or, gods help me, his third.

I moved my face back and forth, trying to avoid the worst of the pounding. But I couldn't avoid it all. And with each blow Chi delivered, I was in a worse position to endure the next one.

Blood seeped into one of my eyes and then the other, until I couldn't see. But I could still hear the curses Chi bellowed at me, the animal sounds of anger and frustration.

At one point I slipped off him, giving Chi more room to pummel me. It didn't matter. I wasn't letting go.

• • •

For a moment, I didn't know where I was. I just knew it hurt to breathe. Then I saw a face hovering over me, and I put up my hands to protect myself.

No, I thought. *I need my hands to keep the fire hand out of sight.*

Then it realized it wasn't Chi's face looming over me. It was *Necalli's.*

"Colhua?" he said, his expression taut with concern.

I was concerned too. About *Chi.* "What happened—?" I started to say.

But it came out funny, through lips too big and puffy to shape the words the way I wanted them to. I tried it again, with the same result.

Necalli shook his head. "Sorry. I can't—"

"Chi!" I groaned.

I saw understanding dawn in his eyes. He leaned down, put his mouth by my ear, and said, "We *got* him." Then he pulled me up into a sitting position, and pointed.

What I saw was Chi lying on the ground face down, a couple of police officers pinning him with their knees. His empty hands were bound behind him.

A third officer was standing off the side of Chi, a pouch in his hand. *Chi's pouch,* I thought. Judging from the shape of it, the fire hand was still inside it.

It had to be, or the officers would still have been searching for it. "Thank the gods," I said. But like the question I'd posed to Necalli, it came out a garbled mess.

Chi rolled his head and cast a hateful look in my direction. It promised all kinds of punishment, even more than what he'd inflicted on me already.

I wasn't worried. He would have a hard time carrying out his threat from the bowels of the Prison House.

. . .

I lost consciousness after that. I must have, because the next thing I knew, I was lying in a bed in what looked like the House of Healing.

Calli was sitting beside me, looking tired and drawn. But still beautiful. "You're awake," she said, as if that was something wonderful. "Are you..." She bit her lip, tears welling in her eyes. Then she tried it again: "Are you all right?"

I attempted a smile. It felt like I was opening a dozen wounds in my face. Still, I got out the words: "Never better."

. . .

Even Takun came to visit me.

He had a nurse on either side of him, ready to support him if it looked like he was going to topple one way or the other. But he didn't topple.

"Son of a coyote," he said, "I think you look worse than I do."

"No one looks worse than *you* do," I told him.

. . .

The day after I left the House of Healing, I sat down at my Mirror station in the Interrogation Center and contacted Donner.

After a few seconds, he appeared on the screen, as cheerful as ever. Then he got a look at me, and grimaced. "You look like you've been through the mill, mate."

I understood the expression. "So I've heard. At least it was for a good cause."

"Oh?"

"There was a guy with a fire hand looking to start a panic here. I stopped him."

"Did you now? Good for you. This was the fellow you were looking for? The one who was stalking your women?"

"No. He's dead. It turned out this other one was the bigger threat."

"Ah. And he's in custody?"

"Yes. That's the important thing."

"Then you never got out to the Mountains you were talking about?"

"Actually, I did. Funny thing. The Isolationists I mentioned… they were ready for me. As if they knew I was coming. But how would they know?"

Donner shrugged. "One of your colleagues, maybe?" He looked around his office, then said in a softer voice, "That's the first place I'd look."

"The possibility occurred to me. But we had an internal Investigation not so long ago. I doubt there's anyone left who would go behind the department's back."

"If you say so. In any case, you stopped the miscreant. As you say, that's the important thing."

"To me, yes. And to the Emperor. But not to everyone. Your superiors, for instance. Their interest in what went on here went well beyond the guy I caught."

Donner smiled an uncertain smile. "I'm not certain I get your drift."

"Only a few people knew I was going out to the Western Mountains, suspension or no suspension: My friend Paynal and his family, who could have betrayed me a lot earlier and lot more easily…and *you*."

Donner chuckled. "Now *there's* an amusing angle."

"I mentioned the fact to my boss," I said, "who mentioned it to *your* boss. And *your* boss shared something interesting with him. Apparently, the authorities in your country had recently identified the guy who created our fire hand problem on the Euro end—the guy who worked hand in hand with a group called Mercantile and the late Farr-Carmody to get fire hands to the Isolationists, and appeared on the verge of working with a second group at the expense of the first one.

"Someone who had regular access to your force's files into fire hands smuggling, not only into Mexica but other places as well. Or he did—until his people uncovered his role in such things. Which, when you think about it, explains why you would want to betray me to the Isolationists running the fire hands trade. With me out of the way, our friend Chi would be that much closer to doing what he'd been hired to do, and the citizens of the Empire would reach for your product with open arms.

"But it didn't work the way you planned. I'd tell you why, but I've been asked not to. After all, we may need a particular resource again sometime."

Donner stared at me. "You're joking."

"I'm not," I said. "But I am impressed. You got away it with it for a long time, after all. Unfortunately, you won't be getting away with it any longer."

"See here," Donner said, "I—"

But he didn't get any further in his defense—because in that moment he was surrounded by a number of his colleagues.

The equivalent of our Ethics people, as I understood it.

I couldn't see their faces, but Donner could. And I could see *his*.

"Thank your friends for me," I said. "They were accommodating enough to arrest you at a time when I could watch."

Donner looked at them, and back at me. His expression was equal parts anger and hurt feelings—the way children looked when they were caught with their hands in a jar of sweets.

In a way, I felt bad for him. He had seemed a likable enough guy in his dealings with me. I couldn't help feeling some of his camaraderie was genuine.

And prisons in Britain, from what I'd heard, were a lot worse than they were in the Empire.

But Donner had earned whatever punishment his government had in store for him. He'd cost people their lives on both sides of the ocean, and would have destroyed the peace the Empire had enjoyed since it beat back Cortes, all without a second thought.

"This is a mistake," he said. "A big mistake. That'll become apparent soon enough. And when it does, you'll—"

"Have a brilliant day," I told him.

Unfortunately, I didn't hear his reply—because someone on his side cut the link.

"You liked that," Quetzalli said from the Mirror station next to mine.

I nodded. "I did."

"So the Euros...they'll put an end to Donner's fire hands operation?"

"They will. But he's not the only source for fire hands across the ocean. There are others, no doubt just as eager. Just as opportunistic."

I wasn't telling Quetzalli anything she didn't know. But I wanted to say it for my own benefit. To remind myself that our job wasn't done. Not until every last fire hand in the Mountains had been eliminated—and even *then*.

As long as the Euros were making the things, and looking for places to sell them, they would be a threat to us.

But we'd bought some time.

● ● ●

I woke in the dark.

My mind raced. Where was I? Not in the House of Healing. Not anymore.

I took a breath, let it out. Calmed myself. A moment later, I recognized the familiar terrain of my apartment.

Home, I thought. *I'm home.*

I reached for my chronometer—and awakened the pain in my ribs. I pulled my hand back, then tried again—gingerly this time. Got the chronometer. Checked the time.

It was afternoon. I had managed to doze off—not unusual for me the last couple of days. I swiveled in bed and sat up, turned on my lamp.

I was still stiff in places. Still sore from what I'd gone through by the river plaza. And going into the office hadn't helped.

I got up and shambled across my apartment, found my cold cabinet, and took out a jug of cane water. Then I made my way to the bathroom to get a change of bandage.

I was just about to remove the old one when I realized some-one was knocking at my door. I hobbled over and opened it.

It was Calli, with a container of pineapple extract in her hand. Her expression, when she saw me, told me I looked worse than the day before.

"Gods of suffering…" she muttered.

"I'm all right," I assured her. "I just probably shouldn't have gone out yet. But, you know…"

"Maxtla," she said, moving forward to hug me.

I held a hand up. "Not the best time for a hug."

She touched my face in one of the few spots that wasn't either cut or bruised. "Can't you do something a little less… demanding for a living?"

She wasn't really asking because she knew I couldn't. Being an Investigator was in my blood, just as it had been in my father's.

"I could become a tax collector," I said. "I hear it pays well."

"You'd be safe, at least."

"And boring."

"*You* could never be boring."

She touched the bandage on my brow. What was under-neath it still hurt. I let out a groan.

"I hope you at *least* saved the Empire."

I didn't say anything. Lands of the dead, what *could* I say? That I'd been on a special assignment for the Emperor?

Calli tilted her head to one side. "Stop it, Maxtla. The *Empire*?"

"Your words," I said, "not mine."

She made a face. "Who *are* you?"

"I'm the guy who took you to the Western Markets and walked with you in the gently lapping surf. Don't you remember?"

Still looking at me funny, she pulled my face down and kissed me, trying to avoid the swollen part of my lip.

I groaned again.

"You can't be that guy," she said. "He wasn't a baby."

Just then, my radio buzzed.

"Don't answer it," Calli said, and kissed me again. "Don't."

But I had to. She knew that. And she knew too that I might want privacy, so she went into the next room to give it to me.

"I'll be just a minute," I said hopefully, and picked up the radio, and said: "Colhua."

It was Aunt Xoco. "I wanted to talk to you," she said, "about your friend Calli."

This was the verdict, and not a trivial one. I was about to hear if the two most important women in my life were going to get along.

I remembered what the restaurant owner on Teteo Street had told me. He'd said my aunt and Calli seemed "uncomfortable" with each other, or something to that effect. So I wasn't all that optimistic.

"All right," I said.

"I *like* her," my aunt told me. "She's a good woman. The kind who would make a good mate. And a good *mother*."

I breathed a sigh of relief. "That's good to hear, Aunt Xoco."

"I thought you would want to know."

"Thanks for telling me."

"I have to go now," my aunt said. "I have things to do."

Normally I wouldn't have asked what they were. But something in her voice roused my curiosity. "What *things*?"

"*Things*," she said.

I wasn't going to press her if she didn't want to tell me. As it turned out, I didn't have to.

"I'm having lunch," she volunteered, "with Nahuatl."

I smiled to myself. "It's good to hear that too."

"If you say so. Know Tonatiuh's blessing, Maxtla."

"You too," I told my aunt.

Nahuatl, I thought. The gods loved to surprise us, didn't they?

I was still smiling when Calli poked her head into the room. "You look happy," she said. "So it couldn't have been Necalli."

"It was Aunt Xoco," I said. "She's having dinner with Nahuatl."

"She called to tell you that?"

"She called to tell me what she thought of you the other night."

"Oh." Calli went to the cold cabinet to put the pineapple extract away, looking anything but curious about my aunt's verdict.

I was surprised. "Aren't you going to ask me what she said?"

"I don't have to." Calli slipped me a sly, sidelong look. "I was there, remember?"

I laughed, despite the cuts and bruises on my face. "So you were."

Everything was going about as well as it could. My aunt and my girlfriend had gotten along. Nahuatl was back in our lives. By the grace of Heaven, the Empire had averted a disaster.

And I wouldn't miss more than a couple of games with the Scale Beetles, as long as I healed as quickly as my doctor believed I would.

"You know," I told Calli, "you still have to have a meal with the *rest* of my family."

"The rest…?" she said, looking like someone who had run a half-day race only to find she had another that afternoon. "But…"

I knew what she was going to say: Outside of Aunt Xoco, Ximo and his brother were my only living relatives. And Calli would know how unlikely it was that I'd be inviting them to dinner.

"Sure," I said. "My family. Necalli. Takun. Quetzalli…"

Calli breathed a sigh of relief and put her arms around me. "For a moment there, you had me going."

"I did," I said, looking into her eyes, "didn't I?"

She caressed my cheek—the good one—with her fingertips. "What am I going to do with you, Maxtla Colhua?"

Despite my injuries, I had a few ideas.

The End

This bonus material is the first chapter of

PHENOMENONS
EVERY HUMAN CREATURE

available from Crazy8Press.com in August 2022.

SALVAGED

BY MICHAEL JAN FRIEDMAN

You know the patch you see on the shoulder of a New York City police officer—a triangle with its sides bulging out a little? It was that shape.

And bigger than most people would think. Thirty-two inches tall and twenty-two across, big enough for a guy to hunker behind to protect himself from a storm of bullets.

Not thick, because that would have made it unwieldy. And not as heavy as it looked, because that would have made it hard to carry for any length of time.

It could have had any color baked into it, any color at all. But the Guardsman, the guy it was designed for, wanted it to be grey like the cowl of his uniform.

He was the *Grey* Guardsman, after all.

No one had seen the shield for years, since it disappeared along with its owner in a monstrous storm over the Andes—a storm created by Charles Casablanca, better known as WeatherCaster, which would have ripped up civilization from Lima to Santiago.

Casablanca was that crazy. And that powerful.

Guardsman was just a man, despite the legend that had grown up around him. A brilliant, freakishly athletic man, but a man nonetheless.

Fortunately, he'd had a chance to study WeatherCaster the first few times he fought him. Guardsman knew the madman's strengths and weaknesses. He knew the kind of targets Casablanca liked, and how he liked to attack them.

So that day in early April, Guardsman could see the earliest hints of WeatherCaster's scheme to destroy the countries in which he'd grown up. He could see the storm taking shape, starting to gather force and fury.

Of course, seeing the threat and stopping it were two different things entirely.

To tame WeatherCaster's storm, Guardsman had to locate his adversary's position in the mountains, penetrate WeatherCaster's defenses, and force the phenomenon's energy back on itself.

Which, miraculously, he *did*.

Instead of cutting a swathe of destruction across the western half of South America, the storm's energy was spent in a feedback loop. Rather than millions of innocents being exposed to its fury, only one human being was placed in jeopardy.

It was a price the Guardsman paid willingly.

As you may recall, it was news when the Guardsman went missing. Big news.

Everyone remembers what they were doing when they heard about his disappearance. They recall the looks on the faces of the people around them: The disbelief, the sadness.

For a long time, people held out hope that he had survived. After all, there was no body, no hard evidence that Guardsman had perished in the face of that storm. Nothing that would have settled the matter for good.

But little by little, they accepted the inevitable. If Guardsman had made it, we would have known it—because he would have been back on the streets fighting for us.

It was sad. Not just because people looked up to the Guardsman, but because his death forced them to confront their own mortality. Hell, if Guardsman could die, so could anyone else.

Not that *everyone* was sad about Guardsman's demise. His adversaries—and there had been plenty of them over the years—were ecstatic to see him go. Some so ecstatic they hosted parties that lasted for days, resulted in some rather colorful casualties, and even, in one case, toppled a government.

Guardsman's teammates in United Front went looking for him, of course. They scoured the Andes, starting with the location of WeatherCaster's facility and expanding outward.

Better Angel searched from the air. Scopes deployed his most sophisticated drones to seek out Guardsman's peculiar heat signature. Luminosity shed her light on the deepest caverns and crevasses in the vicinity.

But even their combined powers couldn't turn up a hint of their comrade. Or, for that matter, a hint of his shield, which had become a symbol of freedom and justice the world over.

Every so often, someone would come up with a new insight into how

Guardsman went down, and soon after an expedition would head south to check it out.

A couple of them were trying to do the right thing by Guardsman. You know, to give him the burial on American soil they felt he deserved. But most expeditions weren't looking for his remains.

They were looking for his shield.

It was indestructible, after all, or close to it. It had protected Guardsman from all kinds of weapons: directed-energy, concussive, projectile, you name it. Even if Guardsman was history, the shield had likely survived.

And there was a market for it. Collectors weren't shy about posting rewards with a lot of zeros in them—the kind that could set up a family for generations.

So there was an incentive to find the thing.

Yet, try as they might, the expeditions in search of it came back empty-handed. And worse.

The last one was the saddest. Of the dozen men and women who'd started out, only half lived to tell the tale. The rest were lost in a river full of piranha. And those who survived lost parts of themselves they wouldn't even talk about.

After that, people figured the shield was in a place where no one could find it—buried so deep in some remote part of the mountains that it would never be seen again.

Then, not so long ago, the rumors started: Someone had found the shield after all.

Katy Lennon, a professor at the University of Pennsylvania, was an expert on the use of game theory in international relations. She was also widely acknowledged as the world's foremost authority on Guardsman.

Lennon's fascination with the hero started when she was a graduate student in Kansas City and Guardsman saved her campus from destruction at the hands of The Light Brigade, a squad of white supremacists. The papers—still the primary source of news in those days—carried a picture of Guardsman helping Lennon up from the rubble of a building.

Since that day, Lennon had published seven papers on Guardsman—more than twice as many as anyone else. So when she walked out on the cherrywood-paneled, otherwise empty stage of New York's premiere auction house, her audience of twenty-two well-dressed men and women listened intently to what she had to say.

"As you know," said Lennon, "I'm here to talk about the authenticity of the shield, not its value in dollars and cents. You can see there's no auctioneer out here with me. His job comes later, after I've done mine."

"And what do you think?" asked a squarish man in a white suit. "Is it authentic?"

Lennon smiled, her eyes crinkling behind her spectacles. "I don't know yet. Like you, I'll be seeing it for the first time since its recovery. If it's in fact the shield of Grey Guardsman, it will display certain telltale characteristics. One will be a set of initials etched into the shield's underside— JA, for James Arrowood, the engineer who forged the shield for Teletron Takahiro Industries."

Teletron Takahiro had been Guardsman's employer, as far as the IRS was concerned. But Guardsman wasn't obliged to do any work for the company, not even when it came to public relations.

"With all due respect," said a blonde woman with her hair pulled into a knot behind her head, "the JA mark is widely known."

Lennon nodded. "That's true. Hence, it would be included in any reasonably detailed replica. However, there are other characteristics that would not be."

Just then a door opened behind the stage, and two armed security guards emerged. They eyed the audience for a moment, then signaled to two other guards standing behind them, who wheeled something out on a hand truck.

A wrought iron stick figure, its legs bent, one arm held in front of it—as if it were the Guardsman, about to launch himself into some deadly fray. And on that wrought iron arm hung the Guardsman's shield. Not a wrought iron copy of it but the shield itself.

I could hear the gasp from the audience. Even though they had known what was coming, even though they were all sophisticated people...to see the shield close up, to know where it had been and what it had done...

I didn't blame them for gasping a little.

Carefully, almost reverently, Lennon slid the shield off the wrought iron arm. Then she turned it around so her audience could get a look at the back of the thing.

"As you can see," she said, "the shield has two enarmes—in everyday parlance, *straps*. The enarme closer to Guardsman's elbow, which is on your left as you face the shield, was torn by the Harpies a few months

before Guardsman's disappearance."

The strap looked damaged, all right. Not so much that it was unusable, but not perfect either.

"Julia Scott at Teletron Takahiro offered to have her people repair it," said Lennon. "It was a simple matter, she said. But Guardsman rejected her offer on the grounds that the shield was a finely balanced instrument—one with which he had become intimately familiar—and that even the slightest alteration to it might throw him off.

"The scientists at Teletron Takahiro assured him that he wouldn't feel the difference. It didn't matter—Guardsman left it as it was. And so it remains."

Lennon gave everyone a chance to absorb the information. Then she turned the shield around again.

"There's also this," she said, pointing to a dent in the artifact's surface. "Made by Bia The Magnificent in his epic battle with Guardsman on the Brooklyn Bridge—immortalized, you'll recall, in the famous photo by Bradon Michael in *The Times*. Bia was in possession of a weapon he'd stolen from the Russians—a force-mace capable of punching a hole in a two-inch-thick layer of titanium.

"Bia's mace couldn't get through Guardsman's shield, but it did leave this mark. As in the case of the enarme, Guardsman had the option of having the damage repaired. Again, he chose not to do so, and for the same reason—a concern that it would affect the shield's performance."

"That dent," said a man with a handlebar mustache, "could have been created with a pile driver."

"Maybe," said Lennon. "However, the impact of Bia's assault embedded particles in the shield that could only have come from a weapon like his force-mace."

"And how do we know it's got those particles?" asked a man with a mane of white hair gathered into a ponytail.

"Three prominent research teams have confirmed it," said Lennon.

"And we have to trust them?" asked a tall woman dressed entirely in black.

Lennon shrugged. "You're welcome to commission an independent analysis." She looked around. "Any other questions?"

No one seemed to have any.

Right on cue, a second figure joined Lennon on the stage. An African-American with light-colored eyes and a big smile. The auctioneer.

Whereas Lennon had been open and unassuming, this fellow was canny, polished. His job was to squeeze every last penny out of the auction, and I didn't expect him to meet with much resistance.

The assembled bidders weren't there to represent Guardsman's admirers, after all. Or even collectors. They were in attendance as proxies for Guardsman's enemies.

The ones he had cheated out of money and power. The ones he had sent to prison. The ones he had humbled over and over again.

With Guardsman out of the picture, a number of them had amassed considerable fortunes, or turned considerable fortunes into even bigger ones. Some had even gone into legitimate businesses. One, the most ruthless of them, by all accounts, had rung the opening bell at the New York Stock Exchange the year before.

"The bidding," said the auctioneer, "starts at a hundred thousand."

No one flinched.

The man in the white suit raised his hand. "A hundred and twenty."

"A hundred and fifty," said the fellow with the handlebar mustache.

"Two hundred," said the blonde woman.

"Two fifty," returned a tall man with a crimson eyepatch.

"Three hundred," said the woman in black.

Inside of five minutes, they had passed half a million. In another five minutes, *two* million.

It was, after all, more than a financial investment for Guardsman's enemies. It was their chance to finally achieve a victory over him.

They couldn't kill him anymore. They couldn't hear him beg for mercy. But they could steal from him the thing he had prized most in the world.

"Do I hear two point *one* million?"

"Two point one," came the response.

"Two point two."

"Two point three."

"Aw, hell," said the man with the ponytail. "Who's kidding who? Three million."

"Three and a half."

"Four."

"Five!"

And so it went, with no sign that anyone had come close to reaching their limit.

Meanwhile, in the penthouse of a building five city blocks from the auction, some of Guardsman's teammates huddled around a sleek, black console, Scopes manipulating its controls, Better Angel and Yoga looking over his shoulders.

"Got it?" Yoga asked.

"Got it," said Scopes.

Before they joined United Front, Yoga was Jill Peters, a personal trainer, and Scopes was Steve Bloom, an eye surgeon. Thanks to Guardsman, they had become crimefighters—and good ones.

Traction, also known as former soccer star Matt Wang, was the only member of United Front standing back from the console. But then, he was known for leaving the strategic work to others.

Abruptly, an image resolved on the screen in front of them. It showed them the room in the auction house in which Guardsman's shield was on display—where one of Scopes's drones had slipped in the night before and affixed a tiny camera to the rear wall.

But that just allowed them to see the auction unfold. It was Scopes's massive digital readout, located on the wall beside them, that showed them the web of electronic communications the bidders were engaged in.

"Hope I'm not too late," called Revek, the last member of the group, as he descended through the room's lone skylight.

Yoga sighed. "I wouldn't know what to do if you showed up on time."

"No problem," said Traction. "You're good, buddy." But then, what would you expect from a guy with the power to eliminate friction?

"Let's focus," said Better Angel.

She was young. Long, blonde hair. The kind of face teenagers swooned over. And bright as hell.

Her real name was Emersen Terhune—but that was all I knew about her. How she got her powers, how she came to join the Guardsman's United Front...that was as much a mystery to me as it was to anyone else. But it was clear that in the Guardsman's absence, she had become the team's de facto leader.

"They've all got someone at the auction house," said Scopes. "Lawyers mostly."

"With one exception," Better Angel observed.

Scopes turned to look at her. "Lars Verdebank."

"You guessed it," said Better Angel.

"Everybody else is represented," said Revek. "Why not *him*?"

A smile spread across Yoga's face. "Because he's there *in person*."

"Which one?" Better Angel asked.

Scopes frowned—and pointed to the man in the white suit. "Him."

Revek nodded. "I think you're right."

"So we take him into custody," said Traction, "as he leaves the building?"

"Not recommended," said Better Angel. "That would alert the others that we've been monitoring their communications."

"And," said Scopes, "send them scurrying to other locations."

"So we wait until *after* he leaves," said Revek. "As long as we can... without, you know, losing him."

"And the shield...?" asked Traction.

While they were going after Verdebank, someone else would be walking out with the evening's prize. And once that happened, it was far from certain they'd be able to get it back.

"Nothing we can do about that," said Better Angel. "Teletron Takahiro could have filed for an injunction, but they're out of business. And none of *us* has a legitimate claim to it."

"Pity," said Revek.

"Right?" said Yoga.

There were two screens in front of us—one that showed us the action in the auction house and one that showed us United Front *watching* the action in the auction house.

"What do you think?" I asked.

My friend Isaiah Anders, who was once my enemy, didn't answer my question. In fact, he didn't say anything for a long time. Then he posed a question of his own: "Why are you showing this to me?"

"You know I like to torture you," I said.

It was a joke between us—a reference to the traps I had set for him back in the day, and his inevitable escapes. "No," Isaiah said, "really."

"I don't know. Maybe because I think the world needs the Guardsman more than ever."

"The Guardsman is gone," said Isaiah.

"Maybe," I said. "And maybe he just wants people to think he is."

My friend shook his head. "He did all he could do. Everything ends, Michael. Even the Guardsman."

"Every rule has an exception," I said. "Didn't you tell me that once?"

"Did I?"

"I'm pretty sure."

The irony was delicious: Me, Michael Niosi, once the Guardsman's greatest enemy, trying to convince him to don his cowl again so he could fight the kind of person I used to be.

"When you see Verdebank and the others salivating over your shield, doesn't that spark something in you? Don't you want to strap it on again and show them the errors of their ways?"

"There are others who can do that. Better Angel, Revek, Scopes...and all the newcomers."

"But there's only one Grey Guardsman. Better Angel and the others would tell you the same thing. No one inspires hope the way *you* can."

Isaiah hung his head. "It's just a shield, Michael."

But we both knew it was more than that.

Sal Velluto's Aztlan Gallery

These are concept drawings Sal provided when he and I were pitching Aztlan as a comic book series. The concepts changed and evolved on their way to a prose narrative, but it's interesting to see how they would have looked way back when.

AZTLAN

SKETCH BY SAL VELLUTO

MAXTLA
COLHUA

AZTLAN

SKETCH BY SAL VELLUTO

CALLI
OLLIN

AZTLAN

SKETCH BY SAL VELLUTO

Tzizoc
Umacatl

AZTLAN
SKETCH BY SAL VELLUTO
POPO
TONATUIH

AZTLAN

SKETCH BY SAL VELLUTO

OXHOCO
MALINAL

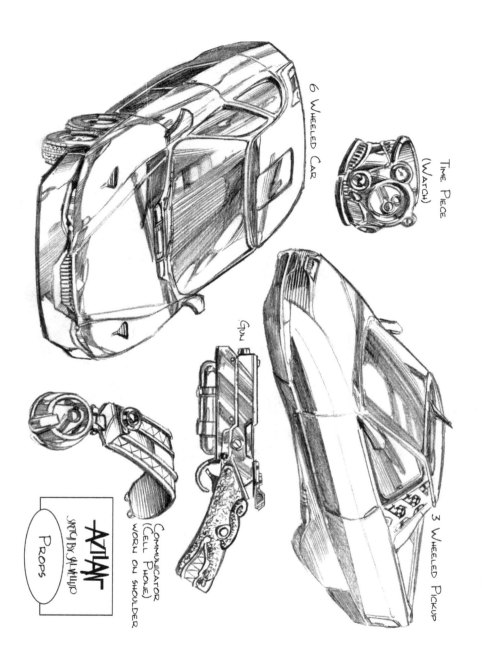

6 Wheeled Car

Time Piece
(Watch)

Gun

3 Wheeled Pickup

Communicator
(Cell Phone)
worn on shoulder

AZTLAN
SKETCH BY AL MELLUP

Props

Acknowledgments

The author would like to recognize the kind support of the following, without whose generosity this book would not have been possible: Jim Arrowood, Stephen Ballentine, Steven Bloom, Hollie Buchanan, Casey Chambers, Richard Deverell, Roscoe Fay, Lynda Foley, Paul Grimard, Brad Jurn, Blair Learn, Marty Lloyd, Michael Niosi, Jennifer L. Pierce, Julia Scott, Curtis Steinhour, Corey Terhune, Edwin Thrower, Ariel Vitali, Shervyn von Hoerl, Judith Waidlich, Matthew Wang, and Steph Wyeth.

About The Author

Michael Jan Friedman is the author of 80 books, nearly half of them set somewhere in the wilds of the *Star Trek* universe.

In 1992 Friedman wrote *Reunion*, the first *Star Trek: The Next Generation* hardcover, which introduced the crew of the Stargazer, Captain Jean-Luc Picard's first command. Over the years, the popularity of *Reunion* has spawned a number of *Stargazer* stories in both prose and comic book formats, including a six-novel original series.

Friedman has also written for the *Aliens, Predator, Wolf Man, Lois and Clark, DC Super Hero, Marvel Super Hero,* and *Wishbone* licensed book universes. Eleven of his titles, including the auto-biography *Hollywood Hulk Hogan* and *Ghost Hunting* (written with SciFi's Ghost Hunters), have appeared on the prestigious *New York Times* primary bestseller list, and his novel adaptation of the *Batman & Robin* movie was for a time the #1 bestselling book in Poland (really).

Friedman has worked at one time or another in network and cable television, radio, business magazines, and the comic book industry, in the process producing scripts for nearly 180 comic stories. Among his comic book credits is the *Darkstars* series from DC Comics, which he created with artist Larry Stroman, the *Outlaws* limited series, which he created with artist Luke McDonnell, and the *Empty Space* limited series, on which he collaborated with Caio Cacau. He also co-wrote the story for the acclaimed second-season *Star Trek: Voyager* TV episode "Resistance," which guest-starred Joel Grey.

In 2011, Friedman spearheaded the establishment of Crazy 8 Press, an imprint through which he and other talented authors publish their purest and most passionate visions. Crazy 8 Press currently features some 65 original titles and is adding more all the time.

As always, Friedman advises readers that no matter how many Friedmans they know, he is probably not related to any of them.

WHEN AZTECS RULE THE EARTH!

It's 2012. Maxtla Colhua is an Investigator for the Empire–an Aztec Empire that successfully repelled Hernan Cortes in 1603 and now stretches from one end of what we call the Americas to the other. But now it is the Last Sun, and someone has decided to punctuate it with a series of grisly murders reminiscent of the pagan sacrifices of ancient times. Can Maxtla find the killer before his city is ripped apart?

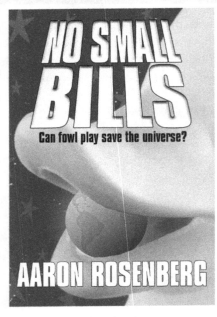

CPSIA information can be obtained
at www.ICGtesting.com
Printed in the USA
LVHW080528130922
728184LV00015B/228/J